THE 11TH INKBLOT

The 11th Inkblot

A novel by J. Herman Kleiger

International Psychoanalytic Books (IPBooks)
New York • IPBooks.net

Published by IPBooks, Queens, NY
Online at: www.IPBooks.net

ISBN: 978-1-949093-51-3

The 11th Inkblot

Prologue

How does one capture, in words, the life he has lived? Though I have spent much of my adult life narrowing my mind and distracting myself from writing this story, I knew the time would come that I would have enough courage to sift through my memories and endure the feelings that would become passengers on this journey. As the years pass with fewer things to command my time and attention, it becomes harder to avoid this moment. Alone in my study, I hear the steady ticking of the clock on the wall. I realize that the time is at hand for my story to begin.

PART I

SPARROW

He who closes his mind to mysteries of beauty and sorrow is but a machine with moveable precision gears cased inside a cold metal hull.
~ Nicolai Keloskovich

CHAPTER I

The Watchmaker and The Dancer

When she entered the room, he turned away. I didn't know why, but children always sense these ripples, even when they don't understand them. I knew her colorful, flowing skirts and draping head scarfs and his dirt-brown tunics and oil-stained aprons. I listened to the strange song of her voice and the familiar gruffness of his commands. I studied her fingers as she moved dark-colored blots of ink around the table when he was not around and his as they maneuvered tiny pins and screws in the meticulous solitude of his workshop. I breathed in all that I knew but did not comprehend. The rhythm of my early years had a constant beat, always with the same inexplicable notes and chords.

Peeking through the crack of the door, I held my breath and watched the hulking figure hunched over a work bench, a tall boy by his side. "Hold the tool this way Chaim and be gentle like the balance wheel is a baby."

My father could sound soft and kind when speaking to my older brother. "You don't want to over tighten the mainspring. Here, see the tiny jewels? Easy, gentle, my *bubelah*." Papa always called Chaim this name, which I thought meant "dearest child" or "favorite son."

I had learned long ago not to intrude. Asking "Papa, can I try?" instantly changed the softness in his voice to a familiar, unwelcome sting.

"Anton, no! Find your mama or go draw your pictures. This is for Chaim to learn, not for you. Now, leave us be!"

Sadly, why are the stinging memories the ones we carry from childhood? When Papa raised his voice and waved me away, I always did as he said. Papa could be so stern. Walking away from his workbench, I would return to draw my pictures at the table. There, I spent long afternoons drawing, sometimes hills, trees, and mountains, but always horses.

All my pictures had horses. I don't remember when I started drawing them. It must have begun with my nightmares, which were always the same jumbled images – moving in terror atop a great beast – darkened shapes in pursuit – furious clomping of hooves – snorting of a terrified animal – shrieks of pain – cries of baby. The fear was so real and gripping that I'd wake up screaming until Nadya or Mama would hold me.

"Shush, *Pidkya*," Aunt Nadya cooed.

"It's safe now, *Kicsi*," Mama would whisper.

It was Nadya who told me that I could become master of my dreams by drawing them. So I began drawing horses.

Papa looked like an important man, always preoccupied with serious matters. His tiny glasses, perched upon his large nose, lay above thin lips. Like his father, my papa, Herman Zellinksy, was a watchmaker. Papa called himself a "horologist." He didn't just make or fix broken watches. Papa studied the measurement of time. He also collected and traded precious old timepieces. He was a master craftsman, the likes of which could not be found even in the larger market towns surrounding our tiny village. In fact, some said he was one of the finest watchmakers in Russia. Passersby would say, "Look, there he is, the great watchmaker! He is so proud but gruff. He does beautiful and important work." The people in our village of Zastavia said Papa could make watches out of dirt.

"Give Zellinksy a scrap of metal, a spring, and a piece of earth, and he will craft a workable timepiece," they would say. One winter, he took Chaim to make watches for the coal miners in Donetz Oblest. All they had there was dirt, but Papa decided that they needed to be able to tell the time.

I was not allowed to enter Papa's workshop unless he and Chaim were there. Yet even when they were working, I felt invisible, an intruder huddled in the corner listening to their whispered tones. His workbench was filled with tiny pieces of metal. The air was thick with the scent of oil and tanned leather. Papa organized screws, springs, coils, and pins in narrow cabinet drawers. He hung tools of different sizes and shapes on the wall. He placed silver and gold casings in a tray in front of him. At the far end of the bench was a collection of watches and clocks, each full of miniature gears, wheels, and pendulums. All were perfectly balanced, engineered with precision. There was no messiness or disorder in Papa's world, no room for doubt or uncertainty in his crafting of such delicate markers of time. On the opposite wall hung a jeweled clock with a perpetual self-winding movement. An original, hand-made by Breguet himself, Papa's favorite clock was over 100 years old. Its ticking echoed loudly in the rooms beyond the workshop. In the shelves above his workbench were rows of catalogs and books written hundreds of years ago by some of the most famous horologists in Europe. Below the workbench, he kept a special case, and inside it, his most precious watches. I'd peeked through the crack in the door enough times to know that was where he kept the finest watches he had made, along with prized timepieces he had acquired through trades.

Mama loved to dance. To our neighbors, she was Marina Vadoma, "the village dancer." When I was little and told people that Mama had performed for the Tzarina, they often looked at me in a peculiar way. Their faces showed surprise, bemusement, and perhaps a trace of contempt. I heard their whispered words, "gypsy witch," as they'd turn their heads and walk away. I was not sure what the words "gypsy witch" meant, but the smirks on their faces made my stomach feel tight and hollow.

What can I tell you about the "village dancer"? I wish I had more memories of her. Mama always looked deeply into my eyes and gripped my hand tightly. She called me "*Kicsi*," her little one. I thought she looked like a princess. Her dark hair and skin matched the color of her eyes. She was younger than Papa and Nadya. Thin and graceful, she always wore brightly colored skirts that flowed to the ground. Mama spoke differently, which is why others could not easily understand her. Nadya said she spoke Hungarian. I learned some of her words but could not say them well. Mama always sang her songs to me in Hungarian. My favorite was called *Idövel Jobban Leszeck*, which meant something like "I will be better with time." It was about how, even when people feel small, scared, or sad, they can grow stronger and braver. Sometimes, she would sing this to me as I was falling asleep or when I woke up from a nightmare.

Mama told me stories of dancing for the Tzarina and her court, always careful to avoid the direct gaze of the mystic Rasputin. She would mimic his look by narrowing her eyes into a frightening stare. Such thoughts about Mama always make me ache. The hole in my heart feels so big. I remember how the "dancing princess" would lift me up, while swaying, singing, and laughing softly in my ear. When she danced, the layers of her colorful skirts flowed and whirled as she moved gracefully across the floor. When Papa entered the room, all singing, laughter, and dancing would stop.

I learned about Papa and his family from my aunt Nadya, Papa's older sister, who lived with us. Kindness radiated from Nadya. When she spoke, my aunt often mixed Ukrainian words with Russian and used unfamiliar expressions or names. That I could not always understand her mattered little for her voice had the softness of a morning song. When she listened, her grayish green eyes radiated warmth and had a penetrating quality that made me feel my words were important. The lines etched around her eyes deepened when she gazed at me and smiled. Slender hands with rivers of blue veins and soft, crooked fingers reached out to stroke my brow or hold my hand when I felt sad or scared by my nightmares. Nadya always braided her hair and pinned it tightly to the back of her head. I never saw her without an apron, which she draped over the few earth-toned dresses she owned. Along the hem of her drab smocks, she always embroidered rows of tiny colorful flowers.

My dear aunt never had a husband or children of her own, but she was devoted to us. Everyone in Zastavia knew Nadya, the kind woman they came to see when not feeling well. They knocked on our door to tell her of a sickness, an ache or pain in their foot or belly. There was old Vychek's gout or Mrs. Chernokov's dyspepsia. She listened and then gave them a potion or a medicinal. People thought she was a healer, always there to comfort the infirmed in our village. I remember most how she cared for animals, not just neighbors' chickens, pigs, or sheep, but the little creatures we'd find in the woods beside our village. If you took a walk with Nadya, she'd always stop and pick up small animals and birds she thought had been abandoned, especially those that looked hungry and needed tending. She'd bring them home and minister to their wounds and broken wings in her little dispensary. Whenever I asked why she cared about animals so much, her answer was always the same.

"This is what I always do, *Pidky*." That's what she called me, *Pidky*, or *Pidkya* and, in her sterner moments, which came very rarely, *Pidkydannya*. "Ever since I was a child your age, *Pidky*, I did this. The world is so full of suffering little creatures, just trying to make their way. Who am I to turn my head from them? Who can really know why I stop for them. It's just what I do." Although she never told me, I thought this must be why Nadya never ate the flesh of animals.

Nadya and Mama took care of the house. They would rise early and build the fire in the stove, while Chaim helped Papa. I watched and drew my pictures.

"Ah, *Pidkya*, that's such a beautiful horse," Nadya would say, as she busied herself with the morning meal. Nadya did most of the cooking and baking. The old stove always had a fire burning and some delicious treat she was preparing. Our small house was filled with the magical aroma of her baking, which was surpassed only by the sweet taste of her honey cakes with poppy seeds, pampushkys, and kalach. Nadya brought her baked goods to others in our village, the old and sick or young mothers at home with their babies. But she always saved extra sweet breads for me. To this day, whenever I smell cinnamon or cardamom, I think of Aunt Nadya.

What I did understand in those early years was that Mama and Nadya loved me. Nadya always told me "Anton, your mama loves you with all the stars in the sky and all the sands on the beach." Later when she would see me sad, she would say, "*Pidky*, a man is rich if he has one person in this world who loves him to the moon and stars. So, *Pidkya*, you are a rich, rich boy. You will always have Mama and Nadya." And I did. All these years later, I can hear Nadya's soothing voice and feel her soft breath whispering in my ear.

My aunt told me stories about her and Papa's father, Israel Zellinksy, who was one of the greatest watchmakers ever. As a young man, my seide Israel apprenticed under legendary horologists like Adrien Philippe and later Jules Audemars. The story was that Seide told Philippe about his idea to make a watch that could be wound by its crown rather than a key. Whether this was true or Seide's way of claiming credit for Philippe's invention was never clear. In any case, Seide knew everything about watch and clock making and had studied with many great teachers to learn about making watches with grand complications. I learned years later that "complications" were all the things a watch could do, beyond measuring hours, minutes, and seconds. More interesting to me than the inner workings of a watch were Nadya's stories about Papa and his handsome older brother, Hyman.

"Your seide wanted both his sons to become watchmakers, but he had special affection for Hyman, his 'jewel,' as he would call him." The story she told was how Seide sent his sons to Le Brassus, Switzerland to apprentice under his old teacher Jules Audemars. After several years working as assistants to old Audemars, Uncle Hyman and Papa returned to Zastavia. Then, something must have happened. When they came home, there were bad feelings between Seide, Papa, and Uncle Hyman that no one would speak about.

"What happened? Why did they not speak?" I asked.

"Who can know such things, *Pidky*. Was it ambition, the rivalry between brothers? Who made more precise chronometers? Whose pieces had more complications? Who stole what from whom? A Swiss girl maybe? Or, who was their papa's favorite son? I cannot know, but when the three entered the room, the air thickened, and all that was left in the awkward silence were tense looks and sad, angry sighs." Nadya said she kept asking what had happened, but no one answered her questions. "To them I was just a silly girl taking care of my sick birds and animals. No one took me seriously. And then one day, your uncle just left. Gone without a word. We were told that he went to America to make watches because he hated the Romanovs who put us in shtetls and treated Jews like animals. But I think there was something more. I will tell you this, *Pidky*, when your uncle left, it crushed your seide's soul."

Nadya said that after Hyman left, Seide spent little time at home and even less time with Papa. When he was not away trading watches and clocks, Seide could be found in his workshop, ignoring Papa, who by that time, had become quite a skilled watchmaker. Papa would try to offer help. He wanted Seide to see what he had learned about engineering tiny complications, but Papa's words fell flat. Seide would hear nothing. Still, Papa would not give up. He stood nearby, silently watching his father hunched over the work bench, driven to perfect these tiny vessels of time. In many ways, my papa became just like his father, making time for strangers but leaving little time for his son.

I met my grandparents, Siede and Bubbe, too few times to remember them clearly. On those rare visits, we loaded up the wagon for Rivne, the village where Siede, Bubbe, and my older cousins lived. When we arrived for our short visits, all my nameless cousins came out and gathered around Chaim, whom they would follow like sheep. Seide and Bubbe remained inside while we unloaded our offerings, which included baskets of vegetables from Nadya's garden, sweet honey cakes, and eggs from her hens. Few words were exchanged. Mostly, there were tense smiles and stories about Hyman in America, punctuated by uncomfortable looks and awkward silences.

Seide was a small man, whose fine white ringlets hung from the sides of his yarmulke. His bulbous nose obscured the other features of his pale face. A pair of tiny spectacles made his gray, watery eyes appear larger than they were. Unlike Nadya's steady gaze, Seide's eyes scanned the room or looked in the distance when others were talking to him. Most of the time, he sat on his throne-like chair in the middle of the room. When helped to his feet, he used a cane to guide his hunched and crooked gait.

Devoutly religious, Seide always wore the same tattered prayer shawl. Not content with the local rabbi, Seide decided to build a shul on his land. Besides making watches, he spent most of his time conducting services in his backyard. Like Papa, my seide was a serious man, who always looked annoyed. When Papa approached him on those visits, Seide usually looked away, busying himself with something more important. But oh, how he adored Chaim. Seide's eyes began to dance when Papa brought Chaim to his special throne. Seide would put his small hands on Chaim's shoulders and say, "Now, this is a jewel, my brilliant boy. One day, I tell you all, he will be a great horologist like his seide. He will craft beautiful pieces, tourbillions, and chronometers, which will mark the time of important noblemen throughout all of Europe."

On cue, Nadya, would then bring me forward to face my grandfather, the master watchmaker. "And here Papa, is young Anton. He, too, will grow into a fine boy. You should see the magnificent horses he draws."

I remember how Seide's smile flattened and eyes stopped dancing at these moments. As if searching for a surface to help himself up from his chair, he would absently put his slender fingers on my head, push down, stand up, and say, "Let's eat now."

None of my other aunts spoke to Mama during these visits. She seemed uncomfortable engaging others because her words and accent sounded strange to those unaccustomed to hearing her speak. Mama looked like no other woman in the room, which made her more of an outsider. They kept their hair in tightly knitted braids, while her long black curls draped down her back. In contrast to their drab dresses and aprons, she always wore bright flowing skirts, often donning vibrant red and orange headscarves with large silver earrings looped underneath. Mama stood next to Nadya and took her meals at a separate table. When I'd glance over to her table, she would smile sweetly. Everyone, except Nadya, acted like Mama was invisible.

After these visits, we'd pack up our wagon and head back to Zastavia. Papa left with some spare crystals, tiny springs, and casings, the ones that Seide no longer wanted. Papa always seemed grateful, like our little dog Spongi when Chaim and I used to sneak him scraps from the table.

Papa sold and traded his watches in the villages and towns nearby. Sometimes he would send pieces to different cities in Europe. Once, I got to travel across the bridge to the big town of Kamenetz Litovsk with Papa and Chaim. Papa sternly told Nadya that I would be in the way, but sometimes she could be forceful. "My dear brother, Herman, you have two sons. Don't leave Anton behind. He needs his Papa." This time, he agreed to let me come along.

It was my first trip to the big town with the magnificent tower that reached into the sky. The streets were full of people pulling their animals past busy street merchants and shopkeepers. The marketplace was teeming with vendors selling everything from vegetables, breads, and spices, to meats butchered according to Hebrew law. People seemed to know my father, the master horologist. He would go into their shops filled with watches and clocks, take a tattered rust-colored pouch with his timepieces inside, and trade with them. Chaim would sit next to him, and I would watch from behind. Such encounters took time. All the watchmakers admired and coveted Papa's hand-crafted pieces, especially the ones he kept in his old pouch. Despite their cajoling, Papa refused to trade or sell his most prized possessions. Once, he was bargaining with the wily old jeweler, Chazanovich, and I had to pee. When I was no longer able to hold it, I approached Papa, who gave a "Shush" and brushed me away. I wandered into the street looking for a place to relieve myself. After finding a spot, I tried to retrace my steps back to the shop but got lost. It was growing dark when Chaim came to find me. He warned that Papa was not happy.

"Sparrow" – that is what my brother called me – "Papa is not happy that you wandered off. You know how he can be, little brother. But follow me; I will take you back."

After my trip with Chaim and Papa to Kamenetz Litovsk, I thought I would be invited to accompany them on other important journeys. When Papa decided to go make watches for the coal miners in Donetz Oblest, all the villagers thought he was very important. I wanted to go with him; but this time, he insisted only on taking Chaim. Even Mama and Nadya agreed I was too small and would be a burden. Papa and Chaim must have been gone for two months. To me, it was like two years. It was after they returned from the mines that Mama changed. I didn't know why. Something happened, and she was never the same.

Memories now tumble through my mind as I think back on those early days. Mama had her secrets. She loved her few books she kept hidden. No one knew what was in those books, but I can still picture her reading. She read early in the morning or late at night by candlelight, long after everyone had gone to sleep. I would awaken from my dreams, and she would comfort me, sing softly, and return to her books. I watched her dark eyes move across the pages until I fell back asleep.

Mostly, I recall her secret blots of ink and how some of the village women would come by our house to talk with her about what her ink pictures meant about their lives. Mama kept her blots hidden in a special satchel under her bed. To me, these pictures looked like messy smudges, like when I dropped a sauce that Nadya had prepared onto the floor. Just splats or smudges that looked like nothing. But for Mama, her blotted pictures were something special. During the day, when Papa was gone, neighbor women would come to see Mama. She would sit with these women, bring out her pictures, and move the dark blots around on the table. Then, one of the women would come forward and sit before her. I can still see Mama and hear her muffled tones, as she moved her pictures back and forth and said, "Tell me my dear, what do you see?"

Transfixed, the woman would say something like, "It looks like pretty flowers; but in the center they look dried and….Oh, and I see a face, or a mask behind it."

Mama's eyes would darken, as she answered, "I tell you what this means. I see you hide behind smiles but with such great sorrow. You yearn for life, a baby perhaps, but are sad because…maybe you barren." When she sensed her pronouncements touched too deeply and created undue distress or worry, she resorted to more mundane answers. With a trace of boredom in her voice, she would tell them that the ink smudges meant their cows would birth calves or their crops would be bountiful.

The women's faces changed as they listened and watched. Then, they left our house, placing a coin, a bow, or some fresh eggs on the table. Mama put these offering in her apron pocket and then gathered her smudged ink pictures back in her satchel and hid them under the bed. I didn't understand the whispering and thought it was silly, but I never said this to Mama.

Once, I asked Nadya about Mama's ink spots. Nadya said, "Shhh, *Pidkya*, such a question." Instead of stopping, I pressed her in the pesky ways of a child. When I repeated my question, Nadya always looked away and said something like, "Who can be sure? They could be this or they could be that. They could be nothing or they could be something very special. They could be smudges, or they might be magical. But if you ask me, I think your mama can see into the eye of God; and her inkblots let her see into the future of people's lives." Nadya made me promise to never tell Papa because he would not understand. This was to be our secret. Then, as always, she gave me a sweet.

Nadya's words still haunt my dreams. They fill in some of the empty spaces, but not all. I remember most how Nadya smelled. How those rosy, sweet cardamom memories stay with me. When she held me close, I would be filled with the scent of those magical fragrances. Sometimes, when Papa ignored or pushed me away to teach Chaim, she whispered that everything would be fine. She told me that Papa loved me but was a busy and important man, yet sad in his own ways.

"Your papa is a man who makes exquisite timepieces for all the villagers, and some have rumored, even the Tzar!" When Papa turned his back to me, Nadya always saw the hurt on my face and quickly moved toward me with soft reassurances. "*Pidky*, you know that your papa is a good man. He is busy with his work, and he wants your brother to become a watchmaker just like him. That's why he spends so much time with Chaim. You will find other important things to do because you are such a smart and wonderful boy, my *Pidkya*. Why look at these magnificent pictures! You will be just like Kandinsky one day." Nadya's words, mixed with the scent of her skin, was a balm which helped ease some of the sting of Papa's harsh words.

I knew about Papa's family, my seide and bubbe, my missing uncle Hyman, the nameless bunch of cousins, aunts, and uncles, of course, Aunt Nadya. But Mama's family remained a mystery. Who were they and where did they come from? Why did she speak differently than Papa and Nadya? There was much confusion for a small boy. Whenever I'd ask Mama, she would start to sing or say, "*Kicsi*, draw a nice picture for me." When no one else was around, I'd ask Nadya. Her answers were always the same riddles,

"Who can know? It could be this or it could be that. It could be something or nothing at all. What do you think? You are such a curious boy, *Pidky*."

And that's how it was left whenever I asked. Nadya's riddles were like Mama's dark smudges. No answers, just more questions about what is and what might be. Sometimes, Nadya flashed a cryptic smile as she got up and busied herself peeling potatoes or feeding her small animals, leaving me wondering what this all meant. Then, with wistful a sigh, I'd return to drawing horses.

CHAPTER 2

My Golden Brother

If Mama and Nadya were my moon and stars, Chaim was my sword and shield. He was my protector, my "golden brother." Mama and Nadya saw me as a helpless boy with bad dreams. They had their little names for me, "*Kicsi*" or "*Pidkya*," but Chaim called me "Anton." Yes, it's true, sometimes, he called me "Sparrow;" but I didn't mind that because it came from him. There was no one stronger, smarter, faster, or happier than Chaim. Even though he was clearly Papa's favorite, his "precious gem," Chaim treated me as an equal. He always knew I was there. When he was with Papa at the workbench, Papa never turned around to acknowledge my presence; but my golden brother did. No words, but always a sweet smile, as if to say, "I see you, little brother." It was Chaim, you may recall, who came to find me when I had gotten lost in Kamenetz Litovsk. He saw that I was frightened, scared to be lost in the big town, but even more afraid that Papa would be angry. Chaim tried to comfort me, saying that he would tell Papa that he had found me and that we had gotten lost together trying to find our way back to Chazanovich's shop. That was not the only time that Chaim took the blame for something I had done.

More than once, my curiosity lured me into Papa's workshop, while he was out with Chaim. I wanted to touch Papa's beautiful watches. I secretly longed to be a great watchmaker like my papa, the important man who made beautiful timepieces. One day, I picked up a watch on his workbench. As I held the golden orb, my small hand slipped; and the watch crashed to the floor. I thought my heart would stop from fear. I didn't know what to do, except hide the broken watch and swear to myself to tell no one, ever, ever. Except that night I told Chaim.

At first, he looked worried, but then the crooked smile appeared on his face. "Don't worry, Sparrow. Papa will be less angry with me, especially if I tell him I was in his workshop trying to fix the balance wheel and over-tightened it by mistake. I will tell Papa it was me."

That night I heard grumbling from Papa's workshop. First, there was Chaim's voice, explaining how he accidentally broke the balance wheel. Then, came Papa's roaring response.

"OYE, CHAIM! How could be so careless, CHAIM?!" Then quiet. Later, I watched as Papa and Chaim came from the workshop with Papa's hand on Chaim's shoulder. As they walked out the front door, Chaim turned his head and flashed a smile.

In those days, the top of my head reached Chaim's broad golden shoulders. Four years older and 18 inches taller, my brother seemed to be everything that I was not. He had flowing brown hair that he could push back from his face with the stroke of a hand. My hair, like Mama's, was bristly, black, and curly. My brother's eyes were robin's egg blue with flecks of gray that shimmered when he laughed. Mama's and my eyes were dark, admitting no lightness or contrast. Even our skin coloring was different. Chaim's smooth white skin glistened in the sunlight. My skin had the same dark tone as Mama's. Chaim's features were sharp, his square jaw the opposite of the round and indistinct landscape of my face. With an ever-present dimple carved into one side of his mouth, Chaim had a crooked smile as if he'd just learned a secret he couldn't wait to tell. His shoulders were broad and his legs strong and straight. My legs were short and bent. He was fearless and as strong as a grown man. I was often scared and weaker than most boys my age. Chaim could run like the wind. The sight of me hobbling behind to keep up made others laugh. But the laughter would cease when he glared at those who made fun of his little brother.

Once, Ber Choetz and his cousins found me by the house drawing my horses. They laughed, pushed me down, and tore my picture. I remember Ber taunting, "Here, look at these ugly pictures he's made. Hahaha! He scribbles like my baby sister, Helma."

When my brother found out what had happened, his eyes flashed angrily. That night, Chaim went to their house and pounded the door. When Ber peaked out, Chaim pushed his way in, grabbed Ber with one hand and his cousin Max with the other. Those boys never laughed at me again. You see, everyone in Zastavia seemed to know my brother. Everyone liked him but learned that no one should ever threaten him or his little brother.

Papa may have wanted Chaim to become a watchmaker like himself, but he expected both of his sons to learn to read and write. Our small village had a cheder, a one room school for the children who lived in our village. There, we learned the alphabet and began studying the Torah. Chaim was smart. When we sat with the rabbi, a short, sour-looking man, my brother could answer most of the questions before the other children. The rabbi, like most adults in our village, favored Chaim. He finished his work quickly, and with a smile, won the approval of our teacher, who dismissed him from class. I always took longer. The words were harder for me to read, the verses took more time to commit to memory. My hand did not shake when I drew, but it was less steady when I tried to write letters.

When I finally finished my lessons and was allowed to leave, Chaim was always waiting outside for me. He'd run up from where he had been with the older boys and tussle my hair. "Come, little sparrow. Flap those wings of yours brother, there're things we must do."

He would run off with me limping behind, doing all I could to keep him in sight. But I knew that he would always come back looking for me, playfully teasing me to keep up. Chaim made up endless games, which I eagerly followed. We played until we both knew it was time to go home.

With the light growing dim, I would sit at the table drawing. Sometimes Nadya rubbed my legs, which were sore from running and chasing after Chaim. Mama sang softly while lighting a fire in stove. Chaim usually disappear into Papa's workshop. Such was the rhythm of our lives, day after day.

Two events from those early years marked my childhood memories of my brother more than anything. Each came as a surprise that shook the ground under my crooked legs. The first arose unexpectedly one day when Chaim and I were lying in a field watching the white clouds drift by. I can't recall what else we might have done that day or what happened after. But I remember Chaim suddenly talking about Papa and his watchmaking. Up to that point no one ever questioned whether Chaim would follow Papa and Seide and become a great horologist. It was as clear as spring following winter or day growing from nighttime. One day Chaim would take over for Papa. But on that sleepy summer day in the field with only the birds and butterflies as our witnesses, Chaim confessed that he had no desire to become a watchmaker. He quickly swore me to secrecy and explained that he had always known how much Papa wanted to have a son who would become like him. Chaim told me that he didn't like tinkering with tiny springs, housings, and crystals. But he was a smart and sensitive boy who saw how much Papa needed him to follow in his footsteps. So, Chaim dutifully stood by Papa's side, showing interest when it was expected, partly out of sadness and partly out of fear that if he told Papa what he really wanted, it would crush our father's soul. Then, Chaim looked me in the eyes and said he wanted to become a soldier. It was his dream that one day he would fight in the Imperial Army for the glory of the Tsar.

"Sparrow, to fight for the glory of our homeland, to stand with my brothers in battle, now that is my dream! Not making these tiny time machines that people hide in their pockets. No, Sparrow, I seek the path of triumphant warrior. I will lead men with proud sounds of trumpets announcing the charge. This is what *I* want!"

Chaim's words made little sense to me. My understanding of such matters was that of a boy who spent his time drawing horses and watching others from the corners. But something seemed both exciting and strange about Chaim's secret dream. How could a boy, a Jewish boy, become a soldier? I knew about the mean soldiers that Nadya called *khappers* and how they came into villages, snatching boys to serve in the Tsar's army. Not too many Jews in Zastavia wanted to become soldiers and serve the Tsar. I was too small to understand such things, but I knew that the soldiers who came to our village did not look kindly at or say nice things to Mama and me. They came to the village wearing long coats and riding big horses. They were rough men who scared me with their boots and harsh voices. "Get this swine boy out of my way," one podgy soldier once said when I tripped and got dirt on his boot. Nadya quickly stepped in and offered an apology.

How was it that my golden brother wanted to become a soldier like them? Though this didn't make sense, you must realize that I always took what Chaim said as wisdom, never to be questioned. I adored my golden brother and never doubted what he told me. But this dream to become a warrior and fight for the Tsar did not make sense. Still, I never told anyone.

Little did I know that all this and more would someday become a painful reality, eventually altering our lives forever.

If the first secret about Chaim fell like a thundering oak, the second felt like a crack in the earth. It began one day when I asked Nadya a question I had asked many times before.

"Why, Nanya" – which was my name for her – "Why is Chaim so tall and I'm so short?" "Why is his hair so light and smooth, and mine so dark and rough like old Kruehke's goat?"

Nadya typically ignored such questions or answered with one of her riddles. "Why, what do you think it could be, *Pidkya*?"

But when I asked her why Chaim never seemed to talk to Mama, Nadya stopped and looked away. No singsong riddle or pat on my head. Just unsettling silence. Why didn't Chaim and I look anything alike? Why did he seem distant from Mama and act as if she were a ghost? The answer did not come that day but would come later, after Mama disappeared.

I don't remember why Nadya finally told me. Maybe I was crying as I drew my horses, wondering why Chaim didn't seem to share my grief that Mama was gone. It might have been then that Nadya sat down beside me and whispered that Chaim and I had different mamas. She said that I was old enough to know that Mama had not given birth to Chaim.

"You see, my *Pidky*, Chaim had a different mama. When he was so little, his mama became sick and died. You were not even born yet."

Nadya never told me how Chaim's mama died. I was afraid that my questions would be met with her annoying riddles, but she told me enough for me to figure out that there had been a sickness and fever that had taken his mother's life, leaving Papa and Chaim alone. Nadya said that's when she came from Rivne to take care of them. My aunt told me a great deal that day. Yet, as the years went by, she never answered the questions most important to me – why did Mama leave and where did she go?

CHAPTER 3

When Mama Disappeared

I was ten that cold winter when Papa and Chaim went to Donesk to make watches for the miners. Winters were always cold; but that year, the winds blew through the cracks in our walls and forced us often to huddle by the stove. They were gone until the spring thaw began. Mama, Nadya, and I managed to warm ourselves by the fire in the stove and also by singing and dancing in the evening. Although I missed Chaim terribly, we never sang and danced when Papa was home. Life was simpler. Though I supposed that I loved my papa, my stomach felt tight when he was in the room. Whenever he walked through the door, I stiffened, stopped drawing, and stood up. When he saw me drawing at the table, he sometimes nodded but more often just walked through the room into his workshop. More than once, when I was smaller and more foolish, I would say, "Look Papa, I drew you a special horse. It is a big and important one, just for you." If he took my offering, he did so only with a nudge from Nadya and responded with a "Hrumph…yes, a horse."

Food was scarce that winter and our pantry quite barren. Though we lacked cabbages, beets, and potatoes, we filled ourselves with singing and dancing. That winter, even the scraps of parchment I drew on grew scarcer. I had always scavenged paper from discarded boxes and wrappings that carried Papa's watchmaking supplies or books and would fetch those before they were burned in our stove. Now, with fewer scraps to use, I began sketching on the backs of the drawings I kept in my special hiding place. If I haven't told you, I had a little place where I kept my treasures. Behind the stove, there was a small opening in the wall, which I kept covered with pieces of wood or a few stones. There, I had my private vault that no one, not even my golden brother, knew about.

With Papa away, Mama felt freer to read her books during the daytime and to have people come to the house for her inkblot gatherings. With no timepieces to sell, it was left to Mama to support us with the offerings that neighbors brought her for "seeing into the eye of God." Familiar faces crowded into our tiny rooms, watched, and listened as Mama began her practice of moving the pictures around and peering into a hidden world that I did not understand. Mostly women visited Mama seeking a glimpse into the unknown, but a few men came by asking for messages from the spirit world advising them about their futures.

Her ritual always began with a shuffling of her blots and then asking, "What does this look like to you?" Once, I remember old Kruehke came with his daughters Esther and Danute, who were regular visitors at Mama's meetings. Why they'd brought their old father, the goat tender, I do not know.

Kruehke was not nice to anyone. He did not like children, except for Chaim, and he treated me like a nudnik bug to be shooed away. A bent and sagging man, with large ears and little tufts of hair on his broad dome, Kruehke came to resemble the old goats he kept by his house. He walked with a large stick that he was said to have used on some of the boys who tried to pet the few kids in his small herd of aging goats.

That day, I spied Kruehke watching Mama move her blots around as she began to whisper in a tone that seemed strange to me. His face had a dismissive, stench-encountering look, like when the corners of the nose are pulled back in disgust. After Mama made her pronouncement that Mrs. Kortz's daughter Belle would leave Zastavia with a Russian soldier, old Kruehke's loud cackles pierced the silence in the room.

"*Oye-yoy, mishegoss*! This *shiska* is *fercockt*. It looks like *shmutzik*! And you, my friends, are nothing but fools with no more sense than my goats! To listen to such *bubkes*."

With that and an even sharper look of repulsion, he grabbed both Esther and Danute by their hair and pulled them out the door. I did not understand some of his words but could not mistake his harsh tone and nasty expression as he pushed his cowering daughters into the snow.

That night, after Nadya had gone to sleep, I asked Mama why old Kruehke had made such an ugly scene. She said there are many who are afraid of what they cannot understand. Mama called Kruehke a "lonely old man, who smelled like a goat and did not believe what he could not see before his own eyes." Drawing me near, she said, "And dear *Kicsi*, that old fool not believe anything that come from mouth of woman. He believe anything man like Papa say, but will always mock what women tell him. Many men will not believe that women, like Mama, have brains and can think, *Kicsi*."

Emboldened by her openness in this quiet moment, I asked Mama to tell me more about her books and ink pictures. Without Nadya to whisk me away or answer with a riddle, Mama revealed that her inkblot pictures were called "*Klecksograpia*." She told of her travels to Germany and how she and her brother learned about these blots from a man named Wolfgang Kerner. His uncle Justinius, a doctor and poet, had made the blots and used them to see into the spirit world. Mama said that she was more interested in seeing into people's minds and hearts to make them know themselves better.

Her inkblots and books taught her many important things. She said that someday she would teach them to me. I asked if she was a healer like Nadya.

"Your Nanya is a healer, *Kicsi*. She make potions to take sicknesses away. But Mama a different healer. My *klecks* blots are for all people. You see they can be everything and nothing. They can be anything at all; and when people look, they tell me things they cannot know. I help them know what they cannot."

Mama then told me about her family in Hungary and how she had grown up with her brothers and mother in a village called Felsögalla. She told me about all the amazing books she would find for me to read. What I regret most about that night was that I drifted off while Mama was talking about her family. I recalled little, except for the name of her inkblots, something like "klecksogia," the town where she was born, and the name of her older brother, "Andras."

Most people, I think, can count on a few fingers the moments from childhood that changed their lives forever. Learning Chaim's secret wish to fight for the Tsar and about him having a different mama were such moments. But those times did not compare to the day that Papa returned from Donesk. That day plays like an endless loop of pictures in my head. I still see it unwind in front of me as if it is happening again.

The morning begins like many others. Nadya prepares the morning meal of tea, bread cakes, and berries. Mama has three or four visitors fixed upon the movement of her kecksogia blot pictures. I am in the corner drawing, while watching with one eye and listening with one ear to her familiar whispery sounds; when suddenly, the door bursts open, and there stands Papa! His beard is longer and more tattered, and the scowling lines around his eyes are growing even deeper than usual. Behind him, I see Chaim standing motionless. To the other side of Papa, I glimpse the figure of old Kruehke, scornfully leering into the room. Papa then moves quickly, knocking over the few pieces of furniture we had, raging with disapproval. The few visitors scatter, dodging Papa and rushing out the door. If there was any good in such an awful moment, one of the fleeing visitors, a large neighbor woman, named Mrs. Ovinshkia, plowed straight into old Kruehke, sending him flying into a puddle of mud and cow dung.

Papa's words are ruthless and unforgiving. He calls Mama that awful name I had heard villagers whisper – "gypsy witch!" Papa then grabs all of Mama's *klecks* blots, opens the stove, and hurls them into the fire. Next, he finds her books and angrily throws them into the flames. Mama and Nadya are huddling in the corner while Papa stands menacingly over both bellowing, with clenched fists, something about their evil doings while he was away.

"THESE ARE NOT REAL! THEY MEAN NOTHING! THEY ARE NOTHING BUT THE *SHMUTZIK* THAT PIGS WALK ON!"

He storms out and slams the door to his workshop. Mama is sobbing while Nadya strokes her hair. Chaim, still frozen, stands motionless and looks my way; but I turn my attention to something I've glimpsed from the corner of my eye. The flames in the stove are turning Mama's inkblots into charred curls of paper dancing fiendishly in the fire; but something more interesting stands out.

In my quiet way, I had always watched and noticed things that fell through the cracks of our lives – little bits and shreds, whether words, looks, or sometimes, discarded trinkets that others had left behind. There, beneath the woodpile, next to the stove, I see the edge of a piece of parchment. I fix my gaze, hoping that others have not seen it. After Chaim goes to the wagon to unload supplies and Nadya takes Mama outside, I move closer to inspect the edge of the parchment. Pulling it gently, I discover a single *klecks* blot. In Papa's fury, he had thrown all of Mama's pictures into the blaze. All are destroyed, except one - a single inkblot has survived! I do what I have always done when I found discarded or forgotten treasures. I hide it in my secret place.

That spring, Chaim became more interested in the older boys who liked playing soldiers, like he did. We still spent time together, but it felt different. Papa spent most of his time in his shop, crafting complicated pocket watches that kept track of seconds, minutes, days, months, and cycles of the moon. No one in the house spoke about what happened that awful morning. Mama grew quiet and sad. No heartwarming singing or dancing; no more laughter. She stopped trying to speak Russian, spoke only brief sentences in Hungarian, and used words I had never heard. Before my eyes, Mama began to fade away, long before she suddenly disappeared from my life.

I stopped drawing horses for a while. Instead, I turned my attention to making *klecks* blots for Mama. It would seem a simple task to make smudges that looked like *shmutzik*. I tried mixing oil with dirt, while sneaking drops of ink, a precious commodity in those days. I rubbed them all together and used my chalk to make them look like Mama's pictures. When I was finished, I had made 10 inkblots. Though they did not really look like Mama's pictures, maybe they would make her happy again. Maybe they would bring singing and dancing back into our lives.

One afternoon, when Mama and I were alone, I pulled my 10 pictures from their secret hiding place and set them, one by one, in front of her. Her sad and dark eyes looked empty, as the corners of her mouth struggled to imitate a smile. She mouthed the words, "Thank you *Kicsi*."

When I showed her the 11th inkblot, the one that had survived the fire, her eyes widened and began to glimmer. She raised up and said,

"Anton! Where? How?"

I told her I'd found her last card under the woodpile and kept it hidden for her. She hugged me and said that it would remain our secret. "Tell no one, my *Kicsi*, not even your brother."

I felt happy. In that moment, I believed I had brought life back to Mama's eyes. Maybe our lives could return to how they had been. But, Mama would never come back to how she had been before. She began to sing again, but it was not the same. There were the times when she would wake me in the dark of night, take me by the embers of the fire, and dance with me while singing loudly.

"Shush, *Kicsi*, don't tell Papa. Don't even tell Nadya. This is our dance, *Kicsi*. You will be a great man one day. You can become an artist! I will teach you *kleckographia* so, like Mama and your Uncle Andras, you will be able to see into people's hearts and help them learn the mysteries of their lives so you can offer them comfort during dark and uncertain times."

Although her words were soothing, there was something about them that sometimes scared me. When she looked at me, it was not like before. She looked, but I didn't think she really saw me. It was as if she were looking at something far away.

Over time, the secret delight of our forbidden nighttime dances became more unsettling than soothing. Mama's singing grew louder, and her movements quickened like a spinning top. These nighttime dances haunted my memories for years to come.

Mama acted as if she were listening to someone, responding to an invisible presence that only she could hear and see. Her eyes would dart around the room, and she sometimes spoke to unseen visitors who now inhabited her world. Suddenly, she would open the door and dance, singing into the night, knocking on neighbors' doors, inviting them to dance with us in the darkness. Nadya always came running and pried me from Mama's arms. Papa then emerged with an angry but exhausted expression. I cannot recall how often our night-time dances were interrupted by the rescuing interference of Papa and Nadya. Looking back, I wish these sad and painful memories were nothing more than bad dreams.

The worst part of these scenes was not their abrupt stoppage or the staring neighbors and their whispers, but the change in Mama the next day. She slept long hours. Worse, she didn't speak or look me in the eye. Even when I showed her the 11th inkblot I had hidden away for her, she looked but was not really present.

Papa, Nadya, and Chaim never spoke of these this nighttime mania. Once, I asked Nadya what was wrong with Mama. I never received a reply, only a far-away look as she hugged me tightly.

Then, one morning, Mama was gone….I can't remember exactly when. The nighttime voices had been like a dream – the shuffle of boots, doors opening, hushed tones, and then silence. I thought I heard Mama's voice cry out for me, but I can't be sure. The next morning, she was gone. Papa said very little. Chaim put his arm around me and said that one day she might come back. I looked to Nadya who hugged me and said, "Who can know why or where she has gone, *Pidkya*, but it might be for the best." I could tell from Nadya's face that Mama would not be coming back.

The day Mama disappeared was my worst. No one would tell me why she left or where she went. I searched for her throughout the village and in the surrounding countryside but couldn't find her. Nothing left, only the smudged picture I had hidden for her. So many decades later, that is still all I have – a single blot of ink and distant memories of my Mama -- the village dancer.

CHAPTER 4

From Mudhuts to Mainsprings

learned about the concept of grief, with its many faces, movements, and monuments, long after I first lived inside it. Though in the years ahead, death would often darken my path, there is nothing so painful as the first loss. Mama's disappearance felt like a withering ache that would not relent — days of crying without speaking, weeks of staring without seeing, months of eating without tasting. Walking through my life, feeling half alive. Confusion soaked in tears. No songs of comfort or solace. Nadya often tried to reach out. Sometimes, her soothing words touched me momentarily but then faded, as I remained encased in stone, unreachable and inconsolable. Papa was always busy, sheltered in his workshop, surrounded by books and the endless supply of sharp tiny pins and cold metal screws. Chaim still spent time with Papa but was often away playing soldier games with the older boys. He checked in on me daily.

I stopped drawing horses after Mama disappeared. My mind no longer worked that way. No more hiding from the world, immersed in my pictures. At first, I tried. With a shred of paper and charcoal in hand, I'd begin to draw the body, head, and mane, only to be overcome with dark, muddy images, which would morph into scribbles that covered the page. Murky smudges would suddenly appear, beginning in one corner and then bleeding over the unfinished form of a horse until the entire page became a darkened swirl. Soon, I began seeing Mama's inkblots everywhere.

Inkblots crowded my mind as I moved from darkened charcoal pictures to making my drawings with mud and grease. I wandered the rain-soaked fields looking for puddles of mud. Not content with smearing in two dimensions, I began rubbing mud on my face and then making structures with mud, some so large that I could sit in them. Sometimes, I'd stay there for hours until Nadya or Chaim would come looking for me. After fetching me from my mudhuts and cleaning the darkened smudges from my hands, arms, and face, they would urge me to speak and eat. This daily ritual of mud and water, exhortation and silence continued for months. No amount of cajoling and threatening was enough to keep me clean or make me speak. I walked through the village covered in mud and became known as "mud boy." Other children taunted me with cries of "*schmutzie.*"

In my mud-covered, ink-stained ways, I also became indifferent, not just to the jeering whispers and taunts, but to the many things that used to scare me. I didn't feel I needed Chaim to fight my battles. Something in me became hardened. I could stand up for myself now and no longer needed him to be my sword or my shield. When two nameless boys pushed me down, I got up, pushed back, and then hit. Blood mixed with mud brought color and texture to my ink-smeared arms.

One moment in time lives endlessly in my mind. Walking home that day, I happened upon old Kruehke, cane in hand, as he threatened two smaller boys peering into his pen at the piglets suckling at their mother's teat. In a flash, it comes alive again, as I see myself moving in quickly. Like one of Papa's tiny springs, tightly wound and then snapping forth with teeth catching hold of a gear, I grasp the old man's stick as he raises it overhead.

Pulling it away from him, I catch sight of the shock and fear in his eyes, as I bring the stick down forcefully on his head. First a "thwack" then a "thud" are the sounds of the cane as it hits its mark. I remember striking him once, maybe twice. Old Kruehke falls to his knees, as the trickle of blood darkens the dirt on the ground beneath him. I hear grunting sounds, which could have either been from that battered old man or from the startled sow in her sty. I run home and say nothing. When word came that the old goat Kruehke had been attacked, no one suspected me, except Nadya, who innocently asked why I had his cane.

Though she did not deserve my sassy reply, I responded, "Well, Nanya, what do you think it might mean? It could be something and then again, it might mean nothing at all. How can one know such things?" I regret such impertinence to someone who was always kind to me, but, in those months, I spared no one from feeling my venomous pain.

Though I protested, Papa and Nadya insisted that I continue with my studies. I'd sit through my lessons with the rabbi and other children, drifting off to the sounds of his voice. Without explanation, I began bringing some of my mud and ink drawings with me. I felt I needed to see and touch them every waking hour. Once, a boy named Noam asked me what these were and I answered, "What do you think? What might they be to you? They could be nothing or something very special."

The rabbi, unsettled by my withdrawal, queer behavior, odd ramblings, and preoccupation with mud, promptly took me home. Interrupting Papa in his important work, the old rabbi said, "Mr. Zellinsky, we need to talk about your Anton. He is not right."

That night as we sat around the table, Chaim was silent and Nadya wept quietly. Those who ate Nadya's stew and hard bread did so without speaking. I had no interest or appetite for food, even Nadya's honey cakes. I saw little that took place around me because my head was buried in my arms, in my pit of anger and grief. This is how it often was those days during mealtime.

But that night, after sitting in a dreamlike haze, I felt a heavy hand upon my shoulder. I looked up and saw Papa say the words,

"Anton, come with me."

Without saying more, he guided me through the door into his workshop. He sat on his stool and motioned for me to sit next to him. He worked as I sat with my head down. The faint clinking and snapping sounds made me curious. I lifted my head to watch him work, up close this time, instead of from the corner of the room. His long slender fingers worked quickly, moving from piece to piece. With his round eyepiece fixed to his whiskered chubby cheek, Papa became lost in the wordless inner workings of the timepiece he was crafting. Using first the smallest tweezer and then a larger one, Papa chose his screws and pins carefully, knowingly, fitting each in its proper place. Finding the correct screwdriver with his left hand, he began gently turning each miniature screw while searching for pins and springs with his right. That night, as I watched him, transfixed on the symphonic movement of his hands and fingers, my world of mud, ink, emptiness, and swirling confusion shifted from mudhuts to making watches.

I rose early the next morning and breathed cold air into my lungs as I walked toward the well. Pumping vigorously, I took off my nightshirt and held my arms under icy water, which cleansed deep muddy smears from my skin. Ruddy and pale flesh tones emerged as the dark smudges were washed away and replaced by goosebumps. I felt alive. I felt reborn!

In the weeks ahead when I entered Papa's workshop, I often caught Nadya looking my way, perhaps wondering about my sudden transformation. The abrupt shift in movements and rhythms in the home had not escaped her notice.

"*Pidkya*," she began. "You spend long hours in Papa's shop, No? How different for you…. And you've stopped drawing your pictures, *Pidky*. Here, I have a parchment I saved for you to draw a nice picture of a horse for me."

I shook my head and looked away.

"Why *Pidkya*? Why have you stopped drawing your lovely pictures? Why *Pidky*, why do you not eat? What is it that you want?"

Without a pause, my words poured out with a louder and sharper tone than I had ever used with my dear aunt. "MY NAME IS ANTON, ANTON ZELLINSKY! MY PICTURES WERE NOT REAL! THERE ARE NO HORSES HERE! WHAT I WANT IS TO KNOW WHAT HAPPENED TO MAMA! NO MORE OF YOUR SILLY RIDDLES!"

The seconds between our words stretched into minutes, marked only by the loud ticking from Papa's Breguet. Finally, Nadya spoke. "I see….Alright. Anton, it is. Yes, Anton now. But your pictures *were* real. I know. I've kept them. As for your Mama, I can't say, I'm so sorry my dear. I'm sorry."

I interrupted her as my words grew louder. "THIS IS WHAT YOU'VE ALWAYS TOLD ME! YOU WERE THERE THAT NIGHT. YOU SHOULD KNOW!"

More silence.

Then, Nadya went to the window and said, "My whole life, I have lived here on the ground. Like the mouse and small creatures in the woods, I see what is in front of me. I don't ask or search afar. I see what is in front of me. I gather things up and care for what needs fixing. *Pidky*, er Anton, I am not of the sky, a bird who sees in all directions, gazing into the past or wondering what might be."

She continued, "Mama came into our lives. One day, long ago, I found her in the woods. She was just there – a young peasant girl from Hungary with a tiny baby in her arms. She seemed wounded, in need of food, warmth, and a home. But sadly, like Chaim's mama, one day, your mama became sick and had to leave. That's all, Anton. That's all I can tell you. The rest, to me, is like the clouds or Mama's dark pictures. I'm sorry."

Not satisfied with what she told me, I stood up abruptly, the chair falling behind me with a thud. I turned my back on Nadya, walked into Papa's workshop, and quietly shut the door. That was the last time I asked her, or anyone, about Mama. This marked the sad change in my relationship with my loving aunt.

Over time, my Nanya receded from my life. Though she was always present, the joy seemed to have drained from her face. She spent her days gathering vegetables from her garden, but most of the time she seemed lost. Villagers sometimes found her wandering in the woods and gently guided her home. There, she would sit, tending to one or two small birds or mice in the corner of the room.

Days became months, which stretched into years, as time crept forward in unexamined and mechanical intervals. The oscillating pendulum of time moved me to my fifteenth year as new routines replaced the old. My legs grew longer and shoulders broadened. My chrysalis self gave birth to new forms and complications. Everything changed. Not only had I grown taller and stronger, but I now had a sense of purpose. I was no longer the sad and angry, strange and muddy boy, waiting to be noticed but afraid to be seen. I no longer had room for despair or rage. I allowed no space for blots of ink shrouded in mystery, which, like Papa had said, made no sense. I closed the doors to those old rooms and opened my mind to new fascinations. Now, I was learning to make watches.

Satisfied with gaining admission to his sanctified workshop, I took my place next to Papa. First, I silently watched him work, while memorizing the names of the tools and mechanisms. Then, I turned my attention to his vast row of books on horology. I proudly sat next to Papa but always knew my place. Rule one: pay attention but remain silent. No idle chatter, and questions had to be brief and clear. When Chaim arrived, I took my place in the corner, as the two of them worked in concert. I unpacked the boxes of watchmaking materials and tools, catalogs and books, and packed up the timepieces he was ready to sell and trade. Graduating from my role of packer, sweeper, and loader, I learned to clean the watches, and assemble some of the pieces. My clumsy fingers moved more slowly than Chaim's and certainly Papa's; but in time, my hands grew stronger and more adroit. Over time, the tiny brains in each finger developed, and I could use each hand independently of the other. This is how I became the watchmaker's apprentice.

One day, Papa looked at the watches I had cleaned and grunted, "Good." The next day, he allowed me to accompany him and Chaim on their journey to Kamenetz-Litovsk. With Papa driving the wagon and Chaim by his side, I was content to sit with the chickens that Nadya had Papa bring to sell at the market. Though at times, I felt like our old dog Spongi, who was satisfied with a scrap here and a scrap there, I was content. The Zellinsky boys were making watches with their important father, the greatest horologist in Russia.

I watched and listened to Papa bargaining with the watchmakers and jewelers. Some tried to get him to sell his finest pieces, the ones he'd crafted with his own hands, as well as the few treasures he'd collected over his lifetime. They'd known about those pieces because Papa often brought them along to show off the fine craftsmanship and the intricacy of his vintage timepieces. They had seen in his collection, precious pieces like the vintage Vacheron & Constantin and the first edition Patek-Philippe, famous for its 16 complications, crafted by none other than Philippe himself. But it also became clear to everyone who did business with Papa that these precious pieces were *not* for sale. Still, Papa's friend, Beringer, a Swiss jeweler with silver teeth, urged him to sell them to the grand houses in Zurich.

"Herman," the silver-mouthed Beringer would begin, "you could profit handsomely from Vacheron & Constantin. They would pay you well and you would never have to make another watch."

But Papa showed little interest in such deals or promises of wealth. He waved off Beringer's offers with simple words, "That's not what I do, Beringer. Selling to the highest bidder. By now, you should know this."

Among his most treasured watches was an old one, encased in silver with gold inlays. This piece had no trade markings, symbols, or house names on its white patina face. On the back was engraved, "*IZ to HZ*" and the words, "*for all time.*" Chaim told me Seide had given this watch to Papa. Of all the timepieces Papa had built and owned, this was the only one he kept in his breast pocket. It was not until much later that I wondered if the watch had actually been made for Papa's preferred older brother, *Hyman* Zellinsky, another "*HZ.*"

I pressed Chaim to tell me everything he knew about making watches. One day, as we walked home from our lessons, I must have asked him fifteen questions in the span of a minute. "How does the escapement work? Are the tiny beads Papa inserted into watches really jewels? Did he know that Papa and Uncle Hyman learned watchmaking from famous Swiss horologists?"

Yawning and looking into the distance, Chaim finally interrupted. "Sparrow, Sparrow, what happened with all that mud and your pictures of horses? What is it that you want?"

Why did they keep asking me these questions? My blood began to boil. The angry rants at Nadya from years before suddenly surged again in my words, "MY NAME IS ANTON….The mud dried up. The horses were not real and I WANT TO MAKE WATCHES LIKE PAPA!"

At this, I ran ahead. There were no words between us for some time afterward.

❖ ❖ ❖

When I first asked to see his books, Papa said, "Yes, but you won't be able to understand them." They were written in French or German, languages that he had learned when apprenticing in Le Brassus. Who could teach me these languages? Not wanting to bother Papa and risk his annoyance, I approached the rabbi for his help. No longer the mudhut boy, behaving in strange ways, I had become studious and obedient. The rabbi's beady eyes widened when I made my request, one that he was unaccustomed to hearing from a fifteen-year-old student. His beard moved from side to side when he smiled and agreed that he would teach me French and then German, if I remained interested.

With rudimentary understanding, I began reading Berthoud's *Histoire de la Mesure du Temps par les Horloges*, a history of the measurement of time, and then Allexandre's general horological text, *Triate' General des Horloges*, both written over 100 years ago. Under the rabbi's tutelage, I worked my way through the histories. From there, I struggled through some of the more obscure and impenetrable volumes on the discrepancies between true and measured time. I pondered the relationship between time and the earth's axis of rotation and studied the mechanical concepts of timekeeping and the microengineering of the caliber. I asked Chaim to explain the role of the chronograph on the battlefield, thinking I'd pique his interest in precision timekeeping as it related to military matters. I struggled to comprehend the function of a tourbillon, one of Breguet's inventions that compensated for irregularities of gravitational force, and then tried to build a crude model of one. I became fascinated with the myriad complications, *le grandes complications*, as the Swiss called them, and the infinite functions that could be engineered into such tiny casings. Beyond the simple movement and more common functions of the timepiece, the geniuses of *haute horologerie* competed with one another to craft ulta-complicated watches with close to 20 complications.

I learned about the German Frederic Japy, who brought watchmaking into the industrial age, transforming the way watches were made. Supplanting the role of the individual craftsman, Japy and his sons after him began mass-producing watches in factories. I felt a deep respect for proud independent watchmakers like Papa, who resisted the onslaught of mechanized watchmaking factories, with their rows of soul-killing machine tools, favoring, instead, the painstaking craftsmanship that could only come from the hands of a master horologist. I learned more about luminaries like Audemars and Piguet, Patek and Philippe, LeCoultre, and of course, the early pioneers in Swiss horology, Vacheron and Constantin. I was in awe when I remembered Seide's claim that he, and not Adrien Philippe, had perfected the crown winding system, which made keys cumbersome vestiges of the past.

By my eighteenth year, my knowledge of horological principles and microengineering was expanding, but my skills and manual dexterity in making watches remained rudimentary. Papa began showing me the more intricate details of orchestrating tiny pieces into a ticking watch. Like a parent hearing for the first time the beating heart of his baby, I was mesmerized when the escapement brought a soft pulsing life to the watch.

Among his other tasks, Papa was immersed in crafting a chronometer that he hoped to sell to the army officers who came to Kamenetz. This piece was to have 10 complications, one of which Papa said had never been attempted. His design included a small device for encoding messages that could be transmitted securely during battle. With this unique cipher complication, officers could feel confident that even if intercepted by the enemy, their encrypted messages could not be decoded. Papa relied on an old text of Bazeries called *Les Chiffres Secrets Dévoilés*. When not trying to read his tomes on watchmaking, I tried to understand Brazeries' theories about ciphers and the steps involved in encryption.

In what little spare time he seemed to have, Papa had also begun building a special pocket watch. I thought this must have been an important piece because Papa only worked on this late at night when alone in the workshop. Because I had a knack for seeing, while not appearing to be looking, I noticed that Papa seemed intent on crafting this piece privately. When I entered the workshop, he quickly put the pieces into a box and moved about uncomfortably, as if caught in the midst of an unacceptable act. I also knew this watch was special because Papa did not usually engrave his watches. On more than one occasion, I caught a glimpse of him painstakingly engraving a message on the back of this piece. Learning long ago that questions were unwelcome unless they pertained to a mechanical detail, I silenced my curiosity but could not help wondering privately who this special watch was for. Chaim? Possibly…me?

If you had asked me years ago who Papa would be crafting a special pocket watch for, I would have unhesitatingly answered, "Oh, his jewel Chaim, of course." But things had changed with Chaim. Now, *I* was becoming immersed in the inner workings of the watch and the arcane developments of horologists from the past. Chaim was spending more time away from home, immersed in the outer-workings of the world. He became friends with Alexi and Drogan Valeski, sons of a gentile farmer, who all lived outside of Zastavia. Alexi was close in size to Chaim but not nearly as strong. Drogan, the younger brother, was known for his breathtakingly large ears. The Valeski brothers, like golden Chaim, had dreams of glorious battles. With Chaim, they practiced being soldiers, playing war games along the ravine that bordered our village. Like my brother, they romanticized wars of the past and fantasized becoming soldiers who would fight for the glory of the Tsar.

Chaim had other interests too. He couldn't walk through the village without girls and young women staring at him. My radiant brother had become a grown man, whom the women in Zastavia and Kamenetz-Litovsk noticed. He surveyed them as well, and, when not drawing up battle plans with the Valeski brothers, Chaim could be found flirting with groups of admiring young women.

Papa noticed the shift in Chaim's comings and goings. No longer the predictable movement from one place to another, from studies with the rabbi to helping Papa in the workshop, how and where Chaim spent his time became erratic. This bothered Papa and often soured his already dyspeptic disposition. "Where is your brother?" he asked without looking up from his work.

When my "I don't knows" did not satisfy him, I would try to make some vague excuse, followed by, "But I'm sure he'll be here soon, Papa."

I secretly decided to try my hand at making a watch without Papa's help. I had slowly moved from being his clean-up boy to his apprentice, from fetching his tools to assisting in crafting timepieces. I decided it was time to apply all that I had learned to make my first watch. And who better to present it to than Papa! After all, Papa may have been making a special pocket watch for me, as well, just like Seide had made one for him.

My plan set, I decided to get up even earlier each morning to tiptoe into the workshop before the sun rose. By candlelight, I quietly began constructing my first timepiece, a smaller one that could be worn on the wrist. Conscious of my limits, I knew that adding too many complications would slow my work, so I settled on a simple piece with two additional functions – days and months in addition to two hands for minutes and hours. Working in the dim light was difficult, especially while trying to use Papa's ill-fitting eyepiece to place the tiny screws and pinions. I selected several jewels that were difficult to pick up with the fine prongs due to their miniature size. When I'd hear rustling in the other room, I would blow out the candle, wrap my watch and loose pieces in a cloth and tuck them inside my shirt. I moved quietly through the door leading outside and then came inside through the front door, so whoever was up would think I had gone out to wash. Later, when I was alone again, I would place the cloth in my special hiding place.

Over the years, I had emptied almost everything from my dark niche. I even considered not using it, feeling I had outgrown this leftover piece of my boyhood, when, like a mouse, I had collected scraps and shreds that others had left behind, stowing them in my little nest. Now, the space was mostly empty, leaving substantial room for my cloth bundle. A folded piece of paper, encased in cobwebs, blocked the way as I tried to shove the cloth into my hideaway. I pulled it out, ready to discard yet another useless relic from my past. Unfolding the tattered edges, I was suddenly gripped by a disquieting feeling. With pins and needles hesitation, I unfolded the parchment, knowing what I would find. Staring at Mama's inkblot, I was keenly aware of the ticking of the Breguet, my shallow breaths, and my rapid heartbeats. Refolding it, I quickly shoved it back into its hiding place, behind my watch project.

I worked steadily on my timepiece, completing it in about six months. Not content to stop after assembling the basic structure of the watch, I decided to ink a monogram on the face before trying my hand at engraving. If Papa was engraving a watch for me, then I should make an inscription on mine as well. But first, I wanted to draw a small insignia on the face. I had in mind a simple "*AZ*." Removing the crystal from the watch, I carefully dipped a pinhead brush into the ink and slowly painted the small letters above the center point. While focusing on the letters, I neglected to notice a pooling bubble of ink on the back of the brush. Before I could wipe it with a cloth, a small spot of ink dripped onto the face of the watch. Sickened by this disaster, I quickly tried to blot the ink, only to see it seep into the surface, leaving a tiny, but noticeable, smudge. I had no replacement face. If I took another one, Papa would notice. Dismayed that my gift to Papa was ruined, I tried to comfort myself by wishfully imagining that he would understand that errors, such as this, were permissible in one's first effort at building a timepiece. In my mind, I heard Nadya's reassuring voice telling me that Papa had surely made such mistakes when he was an apprentice.

Realizing the hour was growing short, I wanted to complete the inscription on the back of the watch. From the corner of the room, I'd watched Papa take his sharp stylus and slowly etch tiny letters and characters onto the back of the golden pocket watch he was creating. My inscription would be similar to the one Seide had given to him so long ago. After practicing on pieces of scrap metal, I slowly traced the letter *A* followed by *Z* and then sketched the word *to* and an *H*. Before I could finish with another *Z,* I was startled by the sound of the front door opening then slamming, followed by the loud and angry voices of Papa and Chaim. Quickly, I wrapped my watch in its cloth and stuffed it back in my shirt. I huddled in the corner of the workshop and listened as their voices grow louder.

"I told you, Papa, I was with Alexi and Drogan, down by the ravine. You have Anton to work with you. YOU DON'T NEED ME NOW!"

Then Papa, "Of course I do, foolish boy. Anton cannot do the work that you can. HE HAS HANDS LIKE ROCKS! He can go back to drawing his horses or playing in his mudhuts, but he will never become a watchmaker like you. Chaim, I know you, my son. Ever since you were a small boy, you always wanted to make fine watches just like your papa and Seide. This is what all the Zellinsky's have ever done. I just need you here at my side so we can be together like we have always been. I can't teach you to become a skilled watchman unless you are here, Chaim."

Papa's words stung deeply. In the numbness of the moment, I froze, not knowing whether to die or scream louder than I ever had before. Then, I heard Papa begin to plead with my brother.

"Chaim…Chaim…LOOK AT ME. See…Chaim, I've made this for you my son."

At this Papa, pulled the golden watch from his pocket and placed it in Chaim's hand. "I made this for you. It is for all time, my son, my Chaim."

Then, silence; the Breguet ticking a warning for what was to follow.

"Papa… I DON'T WANT TO BE A WATCHMAKER. I NEVER HAVE! NEVER HAVE!" It was so long since I had heard my brother weep. "Papa, YOU wanted me to become a watchmaker, not me. YOU saw this and only this! YOU wanted me by your side, EVERY DAY, sitting quietly on that stool until my back ached and my legs grew numb. YOU made me go into those stale shops in Kamenetz and the dusty mines, where the tips of my fingers froze. Old man, it was YOU who wanted this, not ME!"

Time collapsed in that moment. The suffocating silence engulfed the corner where I crouched. The sweat running down my back.

When Papa finally spoke, he simply asked in a barely audible voice, "Why?" and then "What is it you want then?"

My brother calmly answered that he wanted to be a soldier, that he and the Valeski's were going to join the Imperial Army. Next week, they planned to meet up with the 10th regiment from the 2nd Army in Kamenetz, which was sending personnel officers to recruit those needed to defend the country.

"Papa, there is a war coming! All of Russia is mobilizing. The Prussian army and Uhlans will not stop until they take our homes. They are coming, Papa! Only we can protect our homeland against the Kaiser and Archduke."

At this, Papa erupted and told Chaim that the Tsar cared nothing for Jews, so why would he want them in his army!? He angrily lamented that he had sold many of his precious watches over the years so he would have money to pay off the captain of the regiment who came to conscript boys from our village.

"I WAS PROTECTING YOU, CHAIM! FROM WHAT!? YOUR OWN FOOLISH IDEAS OF BECOMING A SOLDIER FOR THE TSAR?! THIS IS WHAT YOU'RE TELLING ME YOU WANT?!"

Chaim's final answer to Papa, as he walked out the door, was, "Yes, to become a soldier is all I ever wanted."

When I was finally able to stand and emerge from my dark corner, I moved mechanically through the door and found Papa slumped in his chair. He barely looked up to acknowledge my presence and only muttered a soft, "Anton?"

I didn't stop to respond. I knew I must leave. Papa's stabbing words pierced my heart. His special watch had been for Chaim, all along, not for me, his son with hands made out of rocks. What a fool I had been to imagine that Papa would grace me with a token of his respect and most of all, his love. I knew I must leave for there was no place for me in this home. The foolish boy who drew horses and made huts of mud had grown into an even more foolish young man who thought he could make watches and believed that his Papa truly saw him. I knew I must leave. Though I didn't know where I would go, I knew I must leave.

I exchanged few words with Papa, Chaim, or Nadya in the days before I left. Our small home was heavy with anticipation that my brother would be leaving. Looking back, I am saddened that I was not able to take a last walk through the woods with Nadya. Papa spent his time in the workshop. We avoided looking at each other. When I saw him from afar, I thought for a moment that his stern face had softened with sadness, and possibly regret. However, the thought that Papa would feel regret over the words he used to describe me might have been more a wish, on my part, than a reality, on his.

Early one morning, I took my rucksack and packed it with my two shirts, some of Nadya's bread and began to leave. I stopped before reaching the door and returned to my hiding place to retrieve my watch. I didn't know why I decided to take the cloth bundle with me. Reaching into the cramped space, I felt the dusty folded parchment paper. Without giving it a thought, I grabbed that as well and stuffed both into the bottom of my rucksack. As I approached the door, I paused in front of Papa's workshop. In a moment of quiet rage and bitterness, I stepped into the shop, bent under the workbench and opened Papa's watch case. There, I grabbed three of Papa's most precious pieces, his prized Caliber 34 Patek Philippe, a 100-year-old Vacheron Constantin chronograph, and an original LeCoultre wristwatch with a chain-linked strap. I wrapped them separately in soft cloths and put them in his old leather pouch, which I placed in the bottom pocket of my rucksack. If I had had room for the jeweled Breguet, I would have taken it too, if for nothing more than to smother the incessant ticking of that old clock. Then, I left my home and my life in Zastavia forever.

My plan was to make it to Kamenetz Litvosk, where I would catch a train for Brest and eventually find my way to Zurich. I would sell one of the precious "old ladies" in my rucksack for train fare and provisions. Once in Zurich, I would seek work, hoping that someone would recognize my skills and take me in. I rode to Kamenetz with the village cooper and his family, who were traveling to town to sell barrels and baskets. Once in Kamenetz, I made my way to old Chazanovich's shop and pounded on his door. The old man didn't recognize me, but let me in when I told him I was Herman Zellinsky's son and that Papa had instructed me to sell one of his vintage watches. If Chazanovich was suspicious, this could not compete with his greed, for he had long coveted some of Papa's vintage timepieces. The old jeweler said he would give me half of what I knew the LeCoultre was worth; and when I told him I would go to the silver-toothed Beringer instead, Chazanovich doubled his offer.

After finding something to eat, I walked to the train station. The plaza was crowded with soldiers waiting for trains. I overheard people talking about the Tsar's declaration of war and his call for mobilization across Russia to meet the German and Austrian threat. I recalled Chaim's rantings about war coming and his plan to travel to Kamenetz to join the 10th Regiment. Chaim had always talked about his heroic dreams of fighting for the glory of the Tsar. That never made sense to me as a boy, and it still didn't.

I made my way to the train platform to buy a ticket for Brest, but the crowd thickened and no one could move. There were soldiers all around. In the corner of the plaza, I caught sight of the familiar face of Alexi Valeski and then, his big-eared brother Dragon, as both men quickened their pace to catch up with a tall man in front of them. It was my brother Chaim. I watched as the three fell in line, rucksacks flung over their shoulders as the Lieutenant made his way toward them. As I stared at my golden brother, I thought that Chaim should follow his dream and become a soldier.

They say that when you are thinking about or looking at someone, that person is often aware. This must be true because, at that moment, Chaim looked across the plaza and found my face in the crowd. Our eyes locked onto one another for a lingering moment, only to be broken by a loud shuffling behind me. A group of beefy infantry sergeants was moving through the crowd grabbing young men and boys, some barely in their teens, and shouting brusquely, "General Samenov needs conscripts and you are chosen to serve the Tsar."

Mothers screamed as they tried to hold on to their son's being ripped from their arms. "No!" their voices wailed loudly. "He is too young!" "He is our only son and we have our farm!" Unmoved by the plaintiff cries, the gruff sergeants were suddenly approaching me.

I ducked down, hoping they had not seen me and backed away in the other direction, only to be met by another crew of soldiers grabbing men and boys of all ages out of the crowd. As I turned to get away, a towering figure in a gray uniform grabbed me firmly and in a mocking tone said, "You will come with us, conscript."

My heart pounding and throat almost too dry to speak, I managed to protest, "No, I'm not here to join the army. My brother is here. He is the soldier." As I was dragged further through the crowd, I stuttered, "I…I'm a watchmaker, not a soldier." I got no response from the hulking figure as he pulled me like a toy through the crowd. Finally, I shouted hoarsely,

"YOU CAN'T TAKE ME, I'M A JEW!. The Tsar doesn't want Jews in his army!"

To this final retort, the large soldier stopped, gripped me tighter and uttered a foul-breathed reply,

"The Tsar will take pigs now, and you will do! May your god have mercy."

In the fog of the moment, the last thing I saw as I was whisked through the line and shoved onto the train was the image of Nadya and Papa standing in the crowd; Nadya weeping as Papa fell to the ground. As I think back on this moment, as I have so often over the years, I cannot be sure if this is what I really saw or if it was something I imagined. Real or unreal? One can never know. But one thing was true on that day, two, not one, Zellinsky boys became soldiers, one a golden warrior and the other, a frightened sparrow.

PART II

MAYHEM TO MADNESS

It takes only but a handful of madmen to unleash madness in all men
~ Nicolai Keloskovich

CHAPTER 5

Into the Trenches

In the sweltering summer heat, we were hustled onto train cars; and amidst a mind-numbing drone of voices and the stench of young men crowded too closely together, I said goodbye to my past, or so I thought. The short trip from Kamenetz to Brest Litovsk remains a blur. I have a vague recollection of faces, some laughing, others boasting, but many with blank, frightened stares. A few boys sobbed that day, like children. Some were little more than children.

Large bodied men with wide stances took up the space for two men, but no one was about to ask that they make more room. Thin, gaunt-looking boys wearing baggy trousers and yarmulkes huddled together, trying to avert their eyes from scary-looking brutes, seeking to mask their uneasiness with bravado and shows of force.

There was little room to move about, much less sit down; but some stooped and hunched in corners. Loud laughing voices bragged of their plans to kill Germans and Austrians, while sobbing voices protested to any who would listen that they shouldn't have been included among the conscripts; mistakes were made!

Through it all, I remained quiet, still too stunned by all that had happened in the past week, the preceding day, the last hour: Papa's betrayal of me; Chaim's betrayal of Papa; my thieving betrayal; leaving Zastavia, as I sought a new life; the sudden grip of the hulking sergeant; the glimpse of Chaim; and the final, mirage-like image of Nadya and Papa collapsing on the crowded train platform. I watched these pictures replay themselves as if they were part of the same event – these fragmentary memories stitched together, frozen in a capsule of time.

My jumble of images gave way to the reality of boarding another train from Brest to the Warsaw Military District. There, I heard rumors that we would join the Second Army under the command of General Alexander Samenov and march west to glory. Thousands of new recruits and conscripts filled each car to capacity. There were young men of every age, shape, and size. Some were peasant boys, no doubt, plucked from their mothers' arms; others looked like farm boys, hayseed still in their hair. Then, there were the eager recruits, like Chaim and the Valeski's, who, with patriotic verve, flexed muscles and spoke loudly about their march to glory. As my numbness wore off, I realized what had happened and what unimaginable fate awaited me. Somewhere, faceless, uniformed strangers, speaking undecipherable languages, marched toward me. Taking up arms, they would try to take my life, as I would try to take theirs. What did I know of war? Nothing! And this war, even less. I never had an uncle or cousin who'd gone off to fight and come back to tell battle-worthy tales of glory and horror. There were only Chaim's stories of great victories for mother Russia at the Siege of Izmail or battles of the war in Crimea. Yet such tales of military conquest had never captured my interest as they had his.

My morose attention was suddenly captured by raucous laughter behind me. I turned and watched an older, rotund man with green eyes and straggly red-haired holding court with several younger men standing around him. His voice had a resonant quality, loud enough for the crowd around him to hear.

"Seems a Hussar named Rheshevsky is putting on his pants and riding boots and about to take leave of a charming whore he had serviced the previous evening:

'My dear man', she purrs teasingly, 'aren't you forgetting about the money?'

Rheshevsky turns to her and sez proudly: 'Oh no, dear madam but Hussars never take money!'"

His audience moaned in laughter, which was muted by the hissing screech of the train careening toward Warszawa Wschodnia Station. The corpulent redhead caught my eye as I watched, surprised me with a wink, and then went about howling with his pals.

Then, I caught the softer banter of a group to my right, engaged in a heated discussion about the decay of the Imperial Court. A slightly built and thickly bespectacled fellow, barely out of his teens held a copy of *War and Peace* and labored to argue that the "t...t-tangle of blindness, wickedness, and i...i-gnorance" of Imperial Russian would soon come to an end. He added that "m...m-onk" Rasputin had cast his poisonous spell and should be removed. Despite his pronounced stammer, this young fellow sounded quite sure of himself. Still, I noticed red splotches forming on his neck as he struggled to mouth words stuck in his throat. As he labored to speak, he often began or ended sentences with fluent expressions like "I would like you to know" or "So that's what it is," which gave his tortured speech an even more unusual quality. Another man, politely trying to ignore the speaker's obvious stutter, questioned why we should have to sacrifice our lives for the Romanovs, noting with bitter irony, that the cousins Tsar Nicky and Wilhelm II were equally corrupt scoundrels.

When the bright-eyed boy-man stammered the names of Lenin and Trotsky, who "should return t...t-o mother Russia to set things right," a loutish man and his comrades moved in quickly with taunts.

"I'm t-t-tired of listening to such a m-m-moron, t-t-talk r-r-rubbish," mocked a tall man, who was missing his front teeth.

Others laughed and jeered Their derisive words turned quickly into shoving and swinging fists. The ensuing melee ended as abruptly as it had begun when the train slowed, and brakes hissed and shrieked sharply. When the train reached the station and made a rough stop, a mass of young bodies slowly detrained onto the dusty platform and into the sweltering heat. All that remained in the crowded car were shattered spectacles and torn book pages.

Throngs of men lined up as directed by smirking NCO's and junior officers. Large signs told us that we had reached Warsaw Military District, a vast assembly of huts, tents, and colorless buildings. All around, soldiers were marching. The sky was gray, the air heavy with humidity, and the ground wet from last night's rain. I looked for my brother, but all I could see through the fog was a sea of young faces awaiting direction. Thousands of men were shuttled into sections like goats, then regrouped into lines, according to where we were from. We shuffled in single-file, stepping carefully to avoid the mud and muck around us. To no avail, our boots became heavy with sludge. As we trudged forward, I heard a sonorous voice in line behind me.

"Seems a royal princess attends her first formal ball and dances with a young count."

And here, the corpulent storyteller raised the pitch of his voice, "Sez she,

'Why Sir, isn't that grease on your collar?'

'Oh my,' sez the count, 'How could I miss such a terrible flaw in my costume, I'm totally destroyed!'

Then, she dances with a dandy young officer and sez 'Oh Captain, isn't there a smudge of ink on your tunic?' To which, he faints. Finally, she's dancing with our friend Rheshevsky: 'My dear sir, your boots are all covered in mud!'

And the Husser replies, 'Oh dear madam, it's not mud, it's shit. Don't worry, it'll fall off once it dries up.'"

I was not surprised that is was none other than the winking ginger-haired raconteur from the train, whom I dubbed, "Rheshevsky," later, "Shev" for short, because I never learned his proper name. At the end of his story, I turned my head, as his audience groaned, laughed, and pushed each other. Like before, the jokester caught my glance and rolled his eyes.

A corporal approached and directed us to a large hut where it was our turn to be outfitted as soldiers in the Imperial Army. We entered the dry, musty-smelling building, a welcome relief after spending hours in the humidity and mud. The interior was vast. It was divided into many sections, each serving a different function in the process of outfitting, assigning, and indoctrinating raw recruits and conscripts into something resembling a solider.

Against a hum of voices and waddle of boots, we were moved through one processing line after another. First, we were ordered to take an oath, swearing allegiance to the Tsar. Those who could sign their names did so. The illiterate made their marks. We lined up for uniforms. Sizes were irrelevant. The bored-looking supply clerks handed out trousers, black leather belts, foot wrappings, green-gray blouses, coats, *sapogin* boots, and *furazhkas*. The *furazhkas* were caps made of wool, and the visors were greenish-black with an imperial rosette. Although the mid-August temperatures were scorching the earth, we were issued winter *papakhas* to keep our heads warm in the freezing weather. Protests about sizes were met with glares from behind the counters or more often, simply ignored. The uniforms smelled like they had been worn in the last war. The material was scratchy. My trousers were baggy and long for my legs. The boots were new but had a wooden stiffness that would rub ankles and calves raw in the weeks ahead.

Next, they issued knapsacks. I quickly folded and padded my smaller rucksack, with its precious cargo, into a bottom compartment. We were all given mess kits, shovels, canteens, and bread bags. In the adjacent room were the armaments. The rumor – fostered by the excited, war-thrilled among us that we would all be issued a *Mosin-Nagant* rifle, with its razor-sharp 18-inch bayonet – was quickly met with disappointment when we were informed there were not enough for each man. Those who looked like fighting men would be issued a rifle; those who did not would become carriers of supplies. I was less surprised than others when it was quickly determined that I would be a carrier and not a rifleman. I was given two heavy pouches containing ammunition. Because I was a designated carrier, I was also not given a helmet or gas mask. Pity because the emblem on the underside of the standard gas mask was stamped "Zelinsky," a close spelling. At the last station, we received our assignments to our divisions and regiments. For reasons that I didn't care to understand, I was assigned to the XV Corps and the 36th Infantry Division, commanded by Lt. General Martos.

Exiting the supply building, I felt the weight of the ammunition bags digging into my shoulders and the stiffness of the boots carving into my caves. It suddenly struck me that I had skills that were not being utilized. True, I was not a warrior like my brother, who had long prepared for this day; but I had valuable skills too. As they marched us over to the barracks, I saw a grizzled old drill sergeant enter an adjacent tent. Where my boldness at that moment came from, I cannot say; but I promptly broke rank, entered the tent, and limped up to the desk. The old sergeant barely looked up as I approached him.

"Excuse me sir, but I just arrived and was assigned to the 36th Division. I believe that there has been a mistake for you see my father was a great watchmaker, and I've acquired some of those skills myself. As a result, sir, I believe that there is a more fitting place for me where my talents could be better utilized in some technical capacity."

In the minute before the sergeant spoke, beads of sweat formed on my brow and my blouse suddenly grew hot and itchy. He finally looked up and eyed me carefully,

"Hmmm… I'll see what we have. But of course. Follow me, lad. Here, this way." Relieved by his kind response, I followed him to the far end of the tent. There, he stopped, abruptly turned, and grabbed me by the collar, wherein his large fist made crackling contact with my nose. Then, I felt the heel of his boot against my backside as he kicked me out the door and into the mud. "There is a fitting place for you!" He called to his corporal and said, "I believe this man has the technical skills to dig our latrines and burn our shit. That is an important job that should serve his talents well!"

I don't know what was worse – the mud and bloody streaks on my new uniform, the pain of what I was sure was a broken nose, or the howling of the others who were still in line, waiting for their bunk assignments in our barracks. In time, my uniform would become caked with even more mud and blood, and the other soldiers too preoccupied with their own misery and fear to remember my humiliating treatment by the old sergeant. What mattered most from that moment was that my nose never healed properly and continued to bleed and ache for years.

My hazy memories of the next week include marching and more marching, learning basics of military survival, and wiping blood and seepage from my aching nose. Those with rifles spent time at the shooting range, while those without watched enviously from afar. We were ordered to lift, cart, load, and unload heavy crates of supplies and munitions, while drill sergeants barked orders, looking for the weaker among us to single out and humiliate. Later in the week, we were instructed on techniques of hand-to-hand combat, including how to skewer the enemy with bayonets. Those of us without rifles or bayonets had to drill with old broom handles until our hands were swollen with splinters and raw with blisters.

When the first train carrying Cossack cavalry arrived, we lined up to gawk at the pageantry. Gallant horses carrying fierce-looking soldiers streamed by. Those beautiful horses stirred distant memories, which were quickly dulled by choking dust and burning pain in my nose. All boys growing up in Russia learn about the legendary military and equestrian exploits of the Cossack warrior. With their fur hats, swords, and long beards, Cossacks were the Templar Knights of the Imperial Empire. Though many were educated landowners, schooled in military arts, Cossacks were widely feared as an unstoppable horde. Rumors were that panic had begun to spread among Austrian villagers who ran amok with screams of, "The Cossacks are coming!"

Several days passed before Chaim found me digging a latrine. I glanced up shielding my eyes from the golden glint of the sun and I saw him standing above me in his tailored officer's uniform, holstered *Prilutsky* semi-automatic pistol on one side of his belt and a sword on the other. Chaim helped me up from my trench, slowly looked me over, and then gave me a bear hug, asking, "Sparrow, what happened to your beak?"

I wiped my nose and told the story about my encounter with the old sergeant's fist and how my technical skills were rewarded with a promotion to latrine digger. His look of concern softened as he suddenly broke into laughter. I could never resist Chaim's laughter, not as a boy and not at this ridiculous moment. I can't remember when we had last laughed together. I gazed at my side and motioned to my shit trench and shrugged. "I guess big brother, that the absurd became all the more absurd. Didn't Nadya used to say something like that?"

Chaim's smile faded, and his eyes welled with tears. "Anton…I'm so sorry. You shouldn't be here. This was all my fault. You're not a soldier, never wanted to be. I'm sorry about Papa. I know you heard what he said. I'm so sorry."

It was easy to accept his apology. Chaim wore his sorrow and guilt all over his face, yet I knew that I had awakened to a more complicated set of feelings about my brother. The love that I had always felt was now darkened. Golden Chaim, always the jewel in our family, who had never wanted what I coveted most, was now an officer, while the "sparrow" – my god, that he kept calling me that – was a private, digging latrines and burning *schmutz!* In an attempt to silence my thoughts from this wave of gloom, I asked about his commissioning as an officer and where he had been assigned.

Chaim eagerly volunteered, "They made me a *Podporuchik*, a low-level officer, because of my knowledge of the Imperial Army and my skill at shooting targets. Really, they didn't take much convincing. I was put in charge of a company in the 1st Rifle Brigade, Anton." I heard excitement and pride in my brother's voice.

Just then, we were interrupted by the now-familiar falsetto coming from another trench, "And she asks the old gentleman," 'Sir, where are you going to put that?….'"

Momentarily distracted by the commotion coming from the other trench, Chaim continued, "Perhaps I could request that you be transferred to my company. That way I could keep my eye on you Sparrow, maybe even get a *Nagant* into your hands. We could practice. I will teach you to shoot!" Something about this felt old and worn.

Then, laughter from the nearby trench, "Madam, I'll put it wherever I want, once the shit is returned to your bed!"

Chaim shot an irritated glance toward the scatologist in the other trench; and just before he made his move to discipline the red-headed jester, I responded to his offer, "Thank you for looking out for your little sparrow, sir, but I think I'd rather employ my technical skills digging latrines."

His quizzical look told me that he was confused, yet cognizant of the irritation behind my sarcastic response. My brother, the under-lieutenant, paused then responded, "I see, Anton. But if you should change your mind, I am here. I will be looking out for you."

I watched with a sickening swell in my gut, as he pulled out his pocket watch, which I immediately recognized as the one Papa made for him. He glanced casually at the time, placed the piece back in his pocket, and said that he needed to return to the officer's barracks. As he strutted away, I lit a torch to the trench of putrid excrement. At that moment, I felt a spark of contempt for my brother, the officer, whose golden sheen had been tarnished. In my irritation, I felt I didn't *need* him to look after me. As I watched him disappear behind a black cloud of burning shit, I quietly mouthed the words, "good riddance."

We began our movement in the early morning. The ponderous pace of our sizable caravan yielded at most 30 kilometers by day's end. *Ryadovoi*, or privates, like me, occupied the lowest rank. We were told little; but if you ignored the buzz in front of you and listened to the voices in the background, you could learn a lot. News from up north apparently spoke of a great victory for the 1st Army at Gumbinnen on the border of East Prussia. A distinguished-looking colonel and his lieutenants passed word to the sergeants that we were to continue northwest. In time, the two Imperial Armies would coalesce to push the Germans across the Vistula River and then make our way straight to Berlin! A gruff sergeant gathered us around and announced,

"Mother Russia sent her finest sons, but you goats and mice must rise to fulfill her promise. We march at dawn. We march, with our Cossack brothers, until we skewer the Kaiser and roast his Landwehr swine!"

Yes, the Cossacks were coming, but we faced a problem. Our destination was nearly 170 kilometers away. To make matters worse, our journey was slowed by sandy roads and rut-filled tracks, intentionally left in this sorry state to guard against invasion from the east. The sand slowing our advance was a lesser problem than the disorganized, and in some cases, nonexistent supply lines.

After two weeks, we were running out of stale black bread. Water was scarce. My mouth was parched, and each breath of hot, dry air burned my still swollen nose. The little bread I had left tasted like dung I'd inhaled from the trenches.

There was little left to feed our overworked horses that hauled heavy wagons over the dusty and pock-marked trails. The wide-eyed beasts struggled to lug overloaded carts up narrow rocky paths. Those that were unable to continue were left to die by the side of the road. The stench of these once noble creatures fouled the air, as bony carcasses lay rotting in the heat.

My backpack grew heavier with each step. Bags of ammunition were lead weights that rubbed my shoulders raw. The unbearable heat rose into the 90s and forced many to fall out of formation. When a soldier dropped to his knees, the NCO's used threats and brute force to coerce him back on his feet. I struggled constantly to maintain my footing and resisted the temptation to seek momentary relief in the shade by the side of the road.

Worst of all was the condition of our feet. Not a man among us was spared from broken blisters and skin rubbed raw by our stiff, ill-fitting boots that tore into our heels, toes, and calves. My feet bled with the blisters. Sweat, blood, and sand formed a toxic brew that stung from my calves to my toes and felt like a swarm of wasps set loose inside each boot.

When we finally broke for rest, we collapsed in a wordless stupor, only to be roused long before our exhausted bodies were rested. It took all my will to pull my legs beneath my frame to stand up and continue. Through all of this, my swollen, packed nose continued to ache and seep, while the dry, dusty air made breathing more painful.

That evening we encamped; and while others rested, I tended to my collateral duties of setting fire to the trenches of excrement. Someone said that it was Napoleon himself who discovered that the position of his advancing armies could be betrayed by the stench from human waste his soldiers left behind. So, they burned their shit, and we burned ours. The smoky smell of excreta permeated my clothes, while the ash darkened my skin. I was reminded of my mudhut days when villagers referred to me as "*Schmutzie.*"

I learned early on that protesting my duties made matters worse, and that the best I could do was dig, torch, walk away and find something to wash the stink from my skin and hair. On the third day, before setting the dung heap afire, I found a coarse brush and a small pan of water. Water was carefully rationed, so I had to be careful that I wasn't caught pilfering the supplies. I aggressively rubbed and scoured the grime and foul smell from my arms and neck until I noticed streaks of blood on the brush and in the water. I wiped the oozing sores and put my coat back on. I realized it was time to go back and set the trenches on fire.

As I finished igniting my latrine, a group of soldiers sauntered to a nearby trench and began to relieve themselves, only to be startled by a voice coming from the dark end of the trough.

"You swine, filthy swine with the sense of a cow. In the name of the Tsar and all that is decent, hold your dirty business til we're finished!"

I looked over to see my fellow shit burner, "Shev," digging an adjacent trench with another man. By now, it was clear that Shev, too, must have had the "technical" skills to be assigned this important work. Then, Shev looked over and saw me. He smiled and continued,

"Seems in biology class, the teacher draws a cucumber on the blackboard and sez, 'Children, could someone tell me what is this?'

Young Rheshevsky raises his hand and sez 'Why it's a schmeckel, teacher.'

The teacher bursts into tears and runs out and the headmaster rushes in and sez, 'All right, which one of you brought your instructor to tears? And who in God's name drew that schlong on the blackboard?'"

My fatigue had reached a peak. My shattered nose throbbed and burned. My feet and calves stung; and now, I had to contend with these self-inflicted brush scrapes on my arms. But, this ridiculous story told by this ridiculous-looking man made me double over in laughter. Shev seemed pleased to see that his ribald humor amused me so much. I don't know if it was his story or the absurdity of our situation. I have no idea what he might have done before he ended up digging latrines for the Tsar. He had the air of a peasant, the demeanor of a buffoon, the body of a oaf, but the sharp wit of a jester at the Imperial court. I realized that I liked this fellow, whom most regarded as a fool. I sensed that he liked me too.

A small circumstance the next day was to change the course of my brief military career. At our first stop, whilst my exhausted comrades were unshouldering their loads and reclining in the grass, I saw my company commander, Captain Volkov, shaking his wrist and cursing under his breath. When his NCO asked him what bothered him so, the good captain, said, "I paid a hefty sum of rubles for this watch, Swiss-made, and now it's stopped!" The nonplussed noncom shrugged and offered the captain a canteen, which Volkov batted away.

I had no energy to spring to my feet, but I managed to rise and cautiously approach my commander. "May I interrupt Sir and forgive me, but I overheard your frustration with your timepiece. In my life before now,

I knew something about such matters, Sir. If you would allow me, I would be happy to look at your watch to see if I may be able to help."

The surprised look on his face shifted to annoyance, followed by interest that I might be of some use. Pausing in uncertainty, the captain said that he would send for me this evening and see if what I was telling him was true. Before walking away, he warned, "Mind you private, if you further damage my watch, then you will regret that you ever opened your foolish mouth!"

A quick look at the piece on his wrist, a Breitling Transocean Chronograph, made me confident in my assertion that I could be of value. "Yes sir, yes, I believe I can put this fine timepiece in working order by nightfall, sir."

He did not look reassured but reluctantly handed me his watch and left without saying a word. The final comment came from the NCO who overheard our conversation. As Captain Volkov walked away, this sergeant put his gnarled face close to mine and spit the words,

"I will be watching you, boy. After you've done more harm than good to this piece of shit watch, I'll have the pleasure of tossing you headfirst into the shit pit where you belong."

Papa had several of these in his workshop and had allowed me to take them apart. His laconic words came back to me. "Yes, a well-crafted piece but for the looseness of the bezel, which allows moisture to cloud the crystal. You see, Anton, the moisture smuggles dust, which is the enemy of the escapement. A good cleaning, oiling, and resealing will conquer these intruders."

As the captain had promised, I was summoned later that evening and brought to his tent. I mentioned that I was expected to be digging a latrine and burning the deposits of our soldiers this evening. Volkov waved off my words and said my services were required here. But he warned me again,

"If you damage this piece any further, you can be assured, private, that you'll be digging latrines and bunking in them for the remainder of the war!"

I took out the small set of tools I'd taken from Papa's workshop when I made off with his watches. I had a vial of lubricant and thin strips of soft cloth. Carefully twisting the bezel, I immediately found the problem. Just as Papa had described, the seal had come loose allowing bits of sand and moisture to cloud the crystal. Trying to sound sure of myself, I parroted Papa's words,

"You see, Captain, the moisture smuggles dust, which is the enemy of the of the escapement."

Captain Volkov watched as I worked carefully, holding his precious piece as if it "were a baby," hearing Papa's words in my mind. When the job was completed, I polished the watch, cleaned the strap, and presented to my commander what looked like a new timepiece. The skeptic in Volkov suddenly became a convert as he thanked me, patting my aching shoulders and asking me more about how it was that I knew so much about watches. He listened as I recited my years of apprenticeship, which I admittedly embellished here and there.

After an hour, Volkov turned to his sergeant and said, "Our advance requires precise timing and the weather has made many of our timing devices inoperable. A man with the private's technical skills should be assigned elsewhere, perhaps to the signal corps where he can serve the Tsar by repairing timing devices."

The granite-jawed sergeant, who had threatened me earlier, seemed disappointed by my success. He nodded and took me to my crowded tent to gather my gear. After he assigned me a different crowded tent, he said that I was relieved of latrine duty. Not content with simply turning and leaving, he faced me, and, with his stubby finger, poked my chest and bristled,

"A lucky day for you vermin, but I am not as easily fooled as your commanding officer is with this pretty jewelry he wears on his wrist. Don't think I've forgotten you. We both know your place will never be far from the shit that you burn."

Maybe it was the force of habit or maybe I'd hoped to see Shev, but I wandered over to the edge of our encampment and heard the sound of his voice, muddled with digging and laughing. I approached the edge of his trench as he looked up and winked.

"Ah, we have the young squire, who comes late to our festivities tonight. Pray tell your colleagues what brings you to us so late?"

I explained that I had a new assignment; how in my previous life, I had repaired and made watches and that now it was time for me to use that skill. To this, Shev paused and said, "*Quia revera pertinet Omnia Tempus est nobis; et qui non habet etiam quod habet aliud.*"

After a moment of stunned silence, I blabbered, "W…w-hat… huh… did you?"

Shev smiled and said that these words were from a 17th century Spanish Jesuit named Baltasar Gracian. "It means, 'All that really belongs to us is time; even he who has nothing else has that.' In your past you were a watchmaker; in mine, I was a monk."

More sputtering on my part, "But… how… did you….?"

Shev, smiled and said, "Well, young watchmaker, that is a story that has too many complications, no? But, one more question for you, my friend, before you go off to your new post. Who was that fine-looking blonde-haired officer standing above your shit trench the other day?"

In a few sentences, I told him about Chaim. Shev bowed and shook his head, softly saying, "*Les grande complications de la vie.*" He went back digging, his voice trailing off as I walked away. "Sez, the young lad to the bawdy mistress…."

CHAPTER 6
Imperial Slaughter Fields

During war, you can learn most everything about a man in 24 hours. That's how it was with Vasily Steponovich – the boyish man from the train that dreadful day; the one who stammered about the decadence of the Empire and a yearning for the return of Lenin and his Bolsheviks; the bespectacled fellow, pummeled for stuttering his beliefs – that was Vasily.

I saw him again on my first day in the signals tent, where he was sitting by himself. It was immediately clear that he was *persona non gratis*. Others in the tent either ignored him completely or mocked his stutter when they passed. When our eyes met, I smiled faintly before setting up my small watch repair bench in the corner of the tent. He sidled up to me and began talking. Regardless of his difficulty completing sentences, he was hungry for connection.

In those initial 1,440 minutes of shared time, Vasily spluttered out the details of his life as I tried to listen intently. Like the rusted gears of a mainspring that prevented the smooth movement of a second hand, something blocked Vasily's words from moving with a natural cadence. Realizing that speaking was a struggle for him, I assumed the role of listener, restraining myself from impatiently trying to finish his sentences. Vasily's awareness of his labored speech was fixed upon his face, set in eyes, and marked by red blotches on his neck. He began sentences sometimes with ease and fluency, only to reach a word that became stuck in his mouth. These pained moments of verbal paralysis registered in his eyes as he fought to find a lubricant for his rusted words, so he could complete his thoughts. After our first several hours together, I queried his frequent use of expressions like, "So that's what it is," or "I would like you to know," which he always seemed to say smoothly without clutter or blockage.

"A…ah, I would like to tell you that you noticed those – my t…t-ricks. W…w-hen I can't g…g-et my m-outh around a word, I use my t…t-ricks, so that's what is, to distract and stall for time."

Of my wartime comrades, two touched me so deeply they remain with me to this day. Shev captured my heart and imagination with his comforting wit and cryptic wisdom. Vasily was my true friend and companion, his sharp mind and gentle soul reminding me of my humanity during the madness and mayhem of war.

The third son of an economics professor at the University of Vilnius, Vasily lived in the shadows of his older brothers who worked for the Vilnius Land Bank. Vasily's professor papa expected his sons to become financiers, but didn't know what to do with his youngest who showed no interest in acquiring wealth. With his interest in theoretical, rather than applied mathematics and other impractical things of little interest to the professor, Vasily was easily dismissed as an embarrassment – an accident of genetics. His father and brothers ridiculed his cluttering and stuttering speech, paying far more attention to the halting formation of his words than to the incisive content of his mind. Sadly, his mother, unable to do more than look forlorn, would leave the room when his father railed impatiently against Vasily for the way he spoke.

His father successfully bought his oldest sons way out of military service to the Tsar. And much like my own golden brother, the professor's middle son dreamed of glorious service in the Imperial Guard. Shortly before the mobilization, he was commissioned as an officer. This left Vasily a likely target for conscription. Papa Steponovich felt it an appropriate compromise that he should have one son protected from service, one a vaunted member of the officer corps, while his bumbling third, an offering to the Tsar. Unlike my own accidental conscription, Vasily's had been the product of a plan, a plot everyone in the family, save Vasily, seemed to have known about. While I was grabbed at the train station in bright daylight, Vasily was seized in his sleep, the front door to their sizable estate having been left unlocked to facilitate the soldiers' nighttime procurement.

Like me, Vasily was a Jew. But some of us could hide our Jewishness when it proved convenient or even necessary, while others, like Vasily Steponovich, could not. When Shev first learned I was a Jew, he told the story about the old Jewish woman who approaches a young man on the train. Think of Shev's high-pitched voice here,

"'Excuse me, young man, are you Jewish?'"

The young traveler, both startled and mildly annoyed, responds with, 'I beg your pardon madam, but no, I am not Jewish!'

The old woman persists, pestering the fellow with the same question, 'Young man, are you *sure* you're not Jewish?'

Growing both irritated and weary of her nagging questions, he finally relents, 'Yes, madam, Yes, I am Jewish!'

To which the old biddy responds, 'Funny, you don't look Jewish.'"

Although others had their suspicions about my Jewishness, no one doubted that Vasily was a Jew. His appearance, his countenance, and his demeanor announced all the tired and ugly racial stereotypes. He, more than I, suffered from mistreatment because of this. He always wore his yarmulke; I never had. His nose was larger than mine, which was broad and flat. His hair was frizzy, while mine was coarse and curled at the ends. Unlike me, Vasily could not easily blend in or disappear in a crowd. Even more than his appearance, it was his peculiar manner of speech that was hard to miss. Cruel whispers and mocking taunts frequently followed his attempts to make a point or share an idea, of which he had many.

However, during his indoctrination the day we arrived by train, it was quickly apparent that my stuttering friend had impressive knowledge and "technical skills." Because he was a mathematician, Vasily was assigned to the Signal Corps where he was expected to help with message encryption. This is where I met him on the first day of my reassignment as division watch repairman. What I knew about cryptography was dwarfed by Vasily's mathematical understanding of ciphers and codes. Sadly for my friend, and more tragically for mother Russia, as history would one day show, Vasily was met with the worst kind of anti-Semitism and savage harassment by officers and NCOs in the Signal Corps. The junior officer in charge quickly made it known to his noncoms, that "Jews, especially sputtering ones, are no better than spies for the Kaiser;" and that Vasily would not be allowed near the wireless dispatches. As a consequence, he had no official role and was made to sit in the far corner of the tent, scribbling notes to himself idly while he watched lazy and incompetent signal corps officers ridicule him, under their breath.

When I first saw him – actually saw him again after the melee on the train – I was struck by his comic appearance. Beyond his unique manner of speaking, even a silent Vasily drew unwanted attention. His spectacles had been smashed on the train, leaving him almost blind. Necessity and ingenuity had forced him to fashion crude lenses from discarded ink bottles and thin cable wire into a pince-nez, which hugged his nose and magnified the size of his brown eyes. If he had wanted to draw more scorn and ridicule to himself, there was little more he could have done. But Vasily was not content to disappear into the background. He incessantly piped up about the dangers of sending messages "in the c...c-lear, so that's what it is" without encryption. The fat, baby-faced lieutenant, growing weary of

Vasily's corrective counsel, dispatched one of his underlings to place a piece of tape over his mouth. This crude gag masked the bruising from other beatings that became a constant feature on his face. Each day, when the gag was removed, he was eager to talk.

When it was time to move forward, we marched together, trudging slowly along the sandy trails. To the sides were rocky fields with scrubby plants that grew low to the ground. The temperatures rose, and our muscles ached; but Vasily never stopped talking, stammering, and using his speech tricks. During our time together, my attention to his halting and rusted speech receded as I took note of his brilliant mind and rich, creative ideas. He spoke in a fragmented way about the measurement of time, a subject that, of course, captured my interest. An even more unlikely soldier than I, Vasily had a deep knowledge of shadow clocks and the Arabian development of timekeeping. He spoke about ancient time-measuring devices, called "clepsydras," and other arcane contraptions used to track trajectories of stars and the passage of hours, nights, and days.

Beyond his vast knowledge of mathematics, philosophy, and politics, I learned about his fascination with the Persian mathematician, Omar Khayyam, and the mysterious numbers and symbols of the Kabbalah. I knew little about Jewish mysticism. In those dark and frightening nights before she disappeared from my life, Mama had spoken that some believed numbers and symbols could unlock all that we did not understand. Inkblots were her way of interpreting the unknown, but she had told me about other keys, as well. Vasily's facts and stories always provided a welcome distraction from my hunger, my badly blistered feet, and my constantly burning nose.

"The earliest system for d…d-ivining the mystical properties of numbers, I would like you to know, was none other than P…P-ythagoras. Did you k…k-now that Anton? Pythagoras knew about the heavenly b…b-odies and speculated about numbers, time, and their p…p-lace in the natural order, so that's what it is."

The final night before shots were fired, we were seated in the corner of the signals tent. The lieutenant had moved Vasily to my small table, where I was working on a few watches. While I cleaned and oiled a colonel's pocket watch, Vasily's face softened, as he spoke quietly about his hopes and dreams. He wanted to discover something important but was uncertain of what that might be.

Peering through the magnifying lenses of his pince-nez, Vasily looked up and asked, "W…w-hat, d…d-o you want for yourself, Anton?"

Caught off guard, I had never given much thought to the future, much less what I wanted for myself. I responded, "This," pointing to the pocket watch in my hands, "Make and clean watches, I suppose."

Then, to my surprise, my young comrade, with his mind so often preoccupied with numbers and recondite philosophers surprised me by saying, "I would like you to know that what I would most like in life is to some s…s-omeday become a p…p-apa, but one who will listen to his children, and so that's what it truly is." I had nothing to offer in response, but his words long echoed in my mind.

I had seen less of Shev because of my new job and the rear placement of the Signal Corps. Yet, I always knew where he was by the laughter that would follow him. Today was no exception, as his voice rang out,

"A dim-witted Irishman was determined to attend the parish bazar for the serving of free lamb stew and dumplings, but because he was a dullard, he had brought along his prize hen.

At the door, Father Murphy sez, 'Stop right there, Thomas O'Leary. Ye shall not bring yer filthy poultry into the vestibule.'

O'Leary's stomach was rumbling, so he quickly tucked the chicken into his trousers and entered right away. The thing was, he'd forgotten to button up his fly. With stew and dumplings in hand, he found a seat between two old biddies. Immediately, he lost himself in his plate of dumplings and stew and didn't notice his curious hen poking its head out from the fly of his trousers.

Suddenly one of the biddies nudges the other in shock and sez, 'Mother o' God, Mary Agnes d'ya see what O'Leary's got comin out of his trousers?!'

To this, the other old biddy replies, "Oh dear, Margaret Rose, but surely you've seen one before now.'

And with a slight pause, the first sez, 'Aye, Mary Agnes, but this one's nibblin at me dumplins.'" When the howling and groans died down, I spent the next few minutes explaining Shev's story to Vasily, who always needed help in understanding the off-colored humor.

Suddenly, the air erupted with a deafening blast, followed by shots fired from ahead, and explosions on all sides. Panicked, we dove into the ditch at the side of the road. Almost instantly, the sound of shells exploding and dirt flying was replaced by the sounds of terrified horses and men moaning in agony. This sequence of sounds – burst and crackle of gunfire followed by cries of terror and suffering – was to be a gruesome chorus in the days to come.

I always had an ear tuned to the message-senders. Identified by their distinct shoulder badges, they spoke quietly about our mission and where our tormenting marches were leading. I learned we were heading northwest toward the village of Neidenburg.

The Germans greeted our arrival in their lands by opening artillery fire on our convoy. Snipers were positioned as well, and skillfully picked off some among our group. As we advanced, the soul-crushing realities of war violently bombarded us. A young officer lay by the side of the road, face down, the back of his head a bloody pulp. At the sight of this, Vasily heaved on his boots. As horrible as the sight of this officer was, more disturbing was the image of the horse that had been shot through the neck but wouldn't die,making gut-wrenching, tortuous sounds as it tried to stand. Though the moans were impossible to ignore, we tried to do just that. We looked the other way and continued moving like cold, unfeeling machines.

Smoke stung our eyes and singed our nostrils as we entered the first small village on the outskirts of Neidenburg. More bodies and homes smoldered with dying embers. Cottages had been looted with the contents strewn on the roads, as dazed and starving villagers wandered the fields. Two small children stood over the body of a man, presumably their dead papa, who was laid out at their feet. The younger of the children wept; the older stared our way in silence.

Unexpectedly, Vasily ran toward them. Our sergeant screamed, but Vasily kept running toward the children. He opened his knapsack and handed them the remainder of his ration of black bread. The younger child hungrily accepted Vasily's offering, while the older boy eyed this Russian intruder warily. Finally, hunger won out and he, too, took a piece of Vasily's stale bread.

Sudden commotion and screaming ahead diverted the sergeant's attention, and he left us behind. When Vasily returned, I shouted in disbelief, "WHAT IN GOD'S NAME ARE YOU DOING!" Didn't he know that this could have gotten him killed!?

My friend simply shrugged, fixed his pince-nez on his nose, and said, "B…b-ut they looked hungry t…t-oo."

A half a day later, we marched into Neidenburg, which had been overrun by the forward advance of our Cossack cavalry. There we remained for the next several days. A larger village, Neidenburg was filled with an incongruous mixture of the living and the dead. Corpses had been left in the streets, some in German uniforms and others, civilians who had given their lives resisting our occupation. Signs of looting were everywhere and so were the vile sights of soldiers forcing themselves on village women. General Martos surprised us by issuing an order that any man caught stealing, looting, or violating women would be shot. In the next three days, four soldiers were executed for thievery, killing villagers, and raping women.

The afternoon that Shev, Vasily, and I got drunk at a small café in the town square was a farcical contrast to the death surrounding us. It was a perfect day, with a clear blue sky and a gentle breeze that broke the oppressive August heat. We found a table in the shade of a giant oak. Shev had procured several bottles of vodka, and I found enough sausages and potatoes for us to feast on. I made sure that this was not looting. The frightened old woman at the café nervously offered us bread, potatoes, and smoked kielbasas. The sausages were flavorful, filled with onion and garlic, and doused in marjoram. There, we sat in the pristine afternoon, stuffing ourselves, while drinking into oblivion. The unspoiled setting was marred only by the remaining corpses that littered the streets. Neither Vasily nor I had much experience drinking alcohol. I had tasted vodka once, years ago with Chaim. But clearly, Shev was well acquainted with liquid fermentation, as he greeted our first flagon of vodka like an old friend.

"D'ya hear the one about the Christian, the Jew, and the Russian, who were about to get sozzled?" We waited….Shev laughed, "No? Well drink up my young friends, and we'll soon find out!"

Listening to the banter between Shev and Vasily was like nothing I'd ever heard. They couldn't have been more different or more alike. Though Shev, the paunchy, educated monk, liked playing the role of a shit-burning buffoon, his knowledge of languages, poetry, and history complimented the innumerable facts about mathematics, philosophy, and politics espoused by the frail and timid Vasily. But where Shev's vast erudition came from his travels, Vasily's fund of knowledge came from his books. While Shev found beauty and humor in the absurdity that surrounded us, Vasily was challenged to find humor in much at all. Yet the strangest thing I noticed was that the more vodka Vasily consumed, the less he stuttered. With the aid of alcohol, he spoke smoothly with the fluency of an orator.

As we drank, Vasily and Shev argued about the old and new testament, the mysteries of numbers and symbols, the power of geometry versus algebra, and whether Oman Khayyam should be remembered as a poet or a mathematician.

"The Persians gave us algebra. It will outlast poetry!" argued Vasily, with uncharacteristic passion and increasing fluency in his voice.

Shev, who never uttered a word about Vasily's stuttering, responded, "True, my mathematical friend, algebra is of great value, but only poetry can heal the soul. Now drink up and toast the man who makes vodka as fine as this!"

Their sparring continued over the implications of the Fibonacci sequence, the corruption of the imperial order, the splendor of the female form, whether the heart or the brain is the seat of the soul, and the coming of a great revolution that would liberate minds and spirits. Vasily would lunge with his argued point, quoting a great philosopher or mathematician about how the essence of reality lay in the precision and predictability of numbers. Shev's riposte provided innumerable quotations, in their original languages, about how beauty lay in the impenetrable mysteries of the natural order. As we emptied a third flagon, their repartee devolved into the physics of eructation versus the poetry of flatulence. Though the banter was comical and riveting, their friendly parries and stories faded into the background, as I succumbed to the inebriating command of the fermented potato.

My last words before passing out were, "And my friend Vasily seems to have found the oil for his words in the vodka he drinks, so that's what it is!" I must have lost consciousness midway through our shared laughter.

My short slumber on this unforgetable day was rudely interrupted by coarse voices around our table. There before us were two noncoms from the signals tent. I immediately recognized one as the goon who delighted in taping Vasily's mouth shut. Looking at both Vasily and me, he taunted, "So, they serve Jews here, eh?" Then he took his paw and began stroking Vasily's hair, adding, "And sputtering little Jew girls too."

Their laughter was suddenly stilled, as the anti-Semite was silenced midsentence when the monk's meaty fist found the center of his nose. The schmuck fell silently to his knees, and his stunned pasty-faced accomplice was even more shocked when a flagon of vodka came crashing down on his thick skull, felling him like a mid-sized oak. Shev drew back, slapping his hands on his rotund midsection and simply said, "I think we are done here. May the good Lord have mercy on their wretched souls." He stood up and helped a speechless Vasily to his feet, while I once again heard gibberish spewing from my lips, "what in the…where did you learn…*THAT*!?"

Shev looked over his shoulder and replied, "Before I was a monk, I served a wealthy lord in Japan; but that was many complications ago."

I woke early the next morning, still feeling queasy. The night had been interrupted by several trips to the latrine where I retched violently. As I wandered back to the tent a misty fog enveloped the streets. I found my way to the tent and saw Chaim standing there, looking my way. He embraced me firmly as I stepped forward. I put my arms around his broad shoulders and was reminded that my brother was still much taller.

"You don't look well little sparrow, err Anton." Catching a whiff of the vodka, he continued, "Oh, I see! You've loosened up some, Brother. Good. Good for you. But I came to tell you that tomorrow we are moving north toward Allenstein. The German Landwehr is in retreat! We are beating them back, Anton; and soon General Rennenkampf will bring his army down from the north to join us in victory. I came back to warn you to stay to the rear. Our Cossack patrols say there are still some German divisions in the villages ahead. The fighting will be heavy. You need to be strong, Brother, and stay to the back, as far from the artillery fire as you can. I will come and find you. I can't stay; have to go now. Be safe Anton." Before I had much chance to say anything, he gave me another hug and disappeared into the fog. Later, when the fog lifted both in the village and in my head, I wondered if this had all been a dream.

At first light, the NCOs noisily roused us from our sleep. Captain Volkov's lead sergeant took particular pleasure in kicking me firmly in my rump and spewing the words,

"UP, SHIT BURNER! Up, you worthless maggot! We'll see if you can be a soldier today and do more than make jewelry or burn shit. We leave in one hour. Now get your arse moving!"

The fog had cleared and the morning sun was intense, even at the early hour of our decampment. Our departure from Neidenburg marked an ending, which gave way to a darker beginning. The course of my life had been bent and would be twisted further. The journey from Neidenburg to Frankenau was a day's march. Under normal circumstances, the 15 kilometers might have taken a third of the time, but these impossible conditions slowed our pace to a crawl. The heat cooked us inside our heavy blouses.

Those who weren't carrying weapons were loaded with double the number of ammunition pouches. The weight was unbearable in this heat. My knapsack bulged with gear. Inside was my canteen, mess tin, first aid kit, gas mask, knife, and entrenching shovel. All were packed atop my securely wrapped bundle of Papa's watches and Mama's tattered inkblot. Around my shoulders, I lugged two satchels of ammunition, each weighing over 25 kilos. Vasily tried to carry a similar load but stumbled to his knees several times in the thick sand and rut-filled roads.

Severely underfed horses lowered their heads to the ground, foraging for anything they could find. Mostly, they ate dirt. They snorted and the veins popped from their necks as they labored to pull overloaded wagons of supplies up rocky slopes. In the hot, dry air, dust kicked up by thousands of marching boots, made breathing an arduous task. With each breath, my nose burned as if someone had cruelly poured hot embers into my nasal passages.

These physical conditions alone might have caused our march from Neidenburg to be insufferable, but a great uneasiness had descended that made this unlike any march we'd had so far. A somber apprehensiveness thickened the air. Though it was rumored that we were chasing a retreating German army, as Chaim had told me the night before, everyone knew that retreating soldiers were like cornered animals. Many would eventually surrender; but others, knowing of their imminent deaths, would fight savagely.

Throughout our march, our brooding silence was punctuated by distant sounds of artillery. The booming, blasting, and thundering percussion kept time with our ponderous pace. Animals sense when great danger is at hand. The guttural groans and grunting sounds that beasts of burden make when their instincts flash internal warnings echoed around us. An ominous hush had fallen over my comrades. No longer was there the patter of cynical complaints about empty bellies and blistered feet, or the jingoistic songs of patriotism and glory. I, too, felt apprehensiveness in the air.

Behind me I caught Shev's eye as he quickened his pace. "Ya look a bit green, good Squire. Too much of the fermentation, no doubt."

I looked him in the eye. Fighting back angry tears, I grumbled, "I guess the time is at hand, but I don't know what all this *means*. Everything…all of this is such a tragic waste. And what about these pathetic beasts!? Marching, digging trenches, burning shit, starving and terrified villagers having their homes plundered. I…and all these bloated bodies on the side of the road – Germans, Austrians, Russians, Serbs? I don't hate these people. I don't wanna kill anyone. It's all a cruel and sickening waste. All of this suffering; all this wasted and lost time, for what?"

I'm not sure what I expected from Shev at that moment – reassurance, some words of comfort? I felt afraid; yet he seemed fearless. I felt lost, and he acted like the world was his home. From the estate of a Japanese warlord to the monasteries of eastern Europe and now, to the suffocating stench of trenches filled with shit, Shev accepted that home was where he stood.

The monk warrior paused, and with a sober expression, placed his heavy hand on my shoulder. He smiled wistfully and said, "But Squire, lost time can *never* be found again. I believe it was Khayyam who told us, 'Be happy for this moment, for this is your life.'"

When others heard his resonant voice, one man spoke up. "Hey, old shit burner, tell us one more bout Rheshevsky."

"Yea, give us another story," goaded another.

Never one to disappoint, our Friar Tuck, took his cue and began, "Our dear Rheshevsky spies a fellow drinking his toddy at the inn and approaches him gingerly. He sez, 'Ahem, good sir. I happen to live in the establishment across from yer apartment, and last night you left yer shades up, and I watched you ravish yer misses til the early hours, sir. Good God man, pull down yer shades.' To this the startled man grew offended and tartly replied, 'Oh, ya think yer such a smartie, but I wasn't even home last nigh – '"

CRRRAAACCK! BOOM!! The sharp, whistling sound of incoming fire, no longer the distant drumming, but the immediate POPPING and SNAPPING bursts surrounded us as we instantly came under fire. Trees split, and dirt rained down heavily. I turned to face Shev, once again catching his eye and enigmatic smile, just at the moment his head suddenly exploded like a soft squash in slow motion. Blood and bits of brain and skull sprayed in my face, as I watched a body, which had once belonged to my beloved friend, fall lifelessly to its knees and then to the ground....

In that horrific moment, time slowed...then stopped. The ticking of the ancient Breguet suddenly ceased, and I have never heard its echo again.

Frozen and unable to move in my silent scream, I was suddenly grabbed by a large man, who dragged me to the side of the road and into the surrounding woods. With his face pressed up against mine, the corporal screamed for me to keep down. His loud voice sounded muffled like he was shouting at me underwater. He pulled one of my ammunition satchels from my shoulder and dragged me behind a large rock. Against the thundering sounds of mortars and gunfire, I huddled and shook, wetting myself like a terrified mutt. Time lost all meaning. Seconds in real time stretched into minutes and then hours. My ears rang and blood began to dry on my face. My hands shook, and I could not speak.

When the deafening sounds subsided, there was movement on both sides of the road. Figures began to move in the smoky air. NCO's and officers tried to restore a semblance of order. Then came the sounds of men in pain, some begging for help, others imploring anyone who would listen to end their suffering. Men in battle who lie waiting to die often call out for their mothers. I saw a dazed Vasily kneeling on the other side of the road. Crouching behind him was a short, sharp-eyed man in a dark uniform gripping a long gun.

Some men were getting to their feet, making sure that their bodies were intact. The silent corporal who'd pulled me from the road stood nearby. The name on his badge read "Glagolev." He helped me to my feet and pushed me forward, as our ragged convoy began to move again. Vasily and the dark man fell in step behind us. The heat had begun to break, and a late afternoon fog rolled in.

After slogging for several hours, we established a makeshift bivouac to regroup, rest, and reload. That night, there was little left to eat. From the beginning, our supply lines had been badly punctured; and except for our brief feasting in Neidenburg, we were hungry most of the time. Except that evening, I had forgotten about my empty belly.

I approached Vasily who sat silently with his knees pulled to his chest. He was still shaking. One lens of his improvised pince-nez was shattered. Our eyes met in wordless recognition of what we had both witnessed but would never speak of. I pointed to Vasily's companion, the man in the dark uniform cleaning his long rifle and asked, "Who's that?"

Vasily shivered and struggled to speak. "A S…S-erbian s…s-ergeant, K…K-restovic, so you see. I t…t-hink, but I've h…h-eard p…p-eople call him Luka. D…d-on't know w…w-here he c…c-ame from. C…c-an't understand much of what he says. He j…j-ust grabbed me when the fire c…c-ame. I would like you to know I remembered hearing s…s-omething about Serbian snipers joining our c…c-ompany."

There was no rest that night. The distant staccato of artillery, mixed with gruesome images of Shev's last moments and the sounds of suffering all around us made sleep impossible. Corporal Glagolev approached and crouched by my side. He took off his badly scratched and dented helmet to reveal a shortly cropped head of hair that had begun to gray at the temples.

He offered me water from his canteen. His eyes were light in color. For a moment, I thought of Chaim and the pale hue of his blue eyes. Glagolev's brow was deeply furrowed, and his eyelids sagged under the weight of his massive forehead. The corporal also had huge hands that made his rifle appear like a toy as he gripped it firmly. Perhaps for no other reason than the bonding that comes from saving another man's life, Glagolev seemed to have taken an interest in keeping me alive, as if he had made some unspoken commitment and was protecting his investment.

"You should sleep, now. Hell will visit us tomorrow."

Vasily had already dozed off; and before I shut my eyes, I saw the weathered-looking Serb kneeling behind him, still ritualistically tending to his long rifle.

We roused ourselves at dawn's light and moved forward even more slowly than the day before. The road toward Frankenau was pock-marked with war's wreckage. The waste, devastation, and suffering made me numb.

Soon, we came upon a clearing where the meadow was ripe with primrose in full bloom. A field of dazzling yellows, reds, and oranges stretched for as far as one could see. Among the glorious blossoms lay a scattering of dead soldiers. Some were curled and looked as if they were sleeping, while others were twisted and wore masks of horror, reflecting the last moment before their lives were violently snatched from them. The sweet fragrance of primrose blossoms fought with the sickening smell of blood and guts that coated the leaves and seeped into the earth.

Ahead, on the side of the road, was a burned-out wagon of smoldering embers. Men lay lifeless on the ground near the surrounding grove of trees. Several voices rang out that among the dead lay Captain Volkov, face down in the dirt, a large part of his midsection torn away. As I passed, I caught sight of the glistening crystal of Breitling around his wrist.

Several times, we came under fire. Though not as terrifyingly intense as the day before, we lost men with each incoming volley. Glagolev remained behind me motioning for more ammunition as he returned fire into the thick woods to our right.

When the last skirmish ended, we approached a trench filled with bodies of Germans and Cossacks, who had fought with their bayonets and hands to claim the trench that was now their grave. Next to the trench, there were medics tending to a seriously wounded man, his *Mosin-Nagant* laying by his side. Lacking usual hesitation, I asked the medics if I could have his rifle. Without looking up, one shrugged and uttered, "He'll soon be another corpse. He won't be needing it."

I knelt to pick it up and saw that it was covered with sand. Lifting it with both hands, I immediately felt its weight and heaviness. I felt a mixture of confidence and fear, which I imagined many had felt when their trembling fingers first gripped a killing machine. The *Mosin* weighed close to 10 lbs and measured over 4 feet in length. Affixed to the top was a sharp, four-edged bayonet that lengthened the weapon by another 3 feet.

"That won't fire," said the Glagolev. "Will take some work to clean the bolt and carriage before it can be of any good." I ignored his words, as my eyes were drawn to the sharp end of the bayonet. I slung it over my shoulder, not minding the added weight to my aching back.

The instinct to seize a dead man's weapon was apparently not mine alone. From the corner of my eye, I watched Vasily scamper to the trench, jump in, and emerge with a saber that had been left by one of the dead officers. This sight, of my fragile-looking friend with a crudely fashioned eyepiece on his nose, running with a long Cossack saber, added a new element to what some would call our theater of the absurd. He skittered back to the road and stammered a response to the men jeering from behind. Their taunts were silenced when Luka stepped forward and glared at them. His stare caused them to look away, stop what they were doing, and shift uncomfortably. And so, we resumed our march, now with two new armed soldiers, both comical sparrows, one totting a sand-logged gun and the other dragging a Cossack sword.

Frankenau was another carnage-filled village with the skeletal remains of buildings left smoldering in a thick blanket of smoke and fog. Surrounded by shrouds of gray mist, our movements were slowed and our sense of direction was clouded. In this war of fog, there was no way of knowing who we were firing at. Too many times, we later learned that our guns were aimed at other Russians who were in a forward position. When it became too dark to move, we sought refuge in a shallow trench.

I wondered what had become of the fleeing German Landwehr. From everything we saw and felt, there was no retreat. Quite the opposite – we had come under heavy attack. Fewer than ten of us huddled in the trench that night. The unlucky who raised their heads lost them to Jäger marksmen trained to see in the dark. I continued to fidget with the bolt action of my *Mosin*, using my fingernails to try to free the movement. In the darkness, someone reached over and pulled the weapon from my hands. The dark figure of Luka began working on my dysfunctional weapon, which remained jammed. A mud-bound and sand-filled weapon seemed a fitting instrument for someone like me, who was said to have hands of rock.

Casualties had been high. The mythology of the indestructibility of the Imperial Army and the retreating Landwehr gave way like the sand beneath our feet. We didn't know this, but all of the messages sent from Samsonov to Warsaw had been unencrypted and intercepted, which hastened the decimation of the XV Corps and the Second Army. It was now clear that we were not only losing ground but were in full retreat.

From our shallow trench the next morning, we saw many dazed-looking Russians raise white handkerchiefs on the ends of their rifles. Others sat with blank looks waiting to be captured. Hours later, when it felt safe, we crawled out of the trench and slipped undetected into the afternoon fog. A small group of us ran forward, taking cover in a grove of birch. In the clearing, we saw hundreds of our comrades raising their arms and putting down their weapons. We lay motionless in the woods, holding our breath and watching our shattered comrades surrounded by the whooping cries of their captors. It was almost impossible to quiet my breath because of the constant blockage in my broken nose.

We were eight, maybe more, when we began moving again. There were no officers among us. Once it seemed safe, Luka and Glagolev took command, working in tandem to shepherd us through the woodlands and marshes. When he was certain that he would not draw enemy fire, Luka positioned himself to pick off stragglers among the victorious army. His long rifle glistened as single shots cracked from the barrel.

Few words passed between us. Vasily, with saber in hand, stayed at my side. In the remaining light of day, Glagolev looked at his map and motioned us to proceed south, away from Tannenburg, where the Second Army had been crushed. All the while, I fiddled nervously with the bolt action, optimistic that it was loosening.

When darkness fell, we remained shrouded in the forest but not immune to the scrambling sounds of men. Like us, others were trying to escape, only to become trapped in the surrounding marshy waters. If not for Luka, who guided us like a native warrior, we would have surely perished as well. From the dark woods, we continued to see columns of ghostlike prisoners, numbering now in the thousands, marching in the moonlight ahead of their German captors.

Luka spoke quietly, in three to four-word utterances. Only Vasily understood some of his fragmented Russian. For Luka Krestovic, the war was only about removing Austrians who had tormented his people for decades. In our retreat, most of us were trying urgently to get away from war. Only Luka was intent on heading into more battles. He told Vasily that he wanted to join the battle to drive the Austrian-Hungarian army from Galicia in the south. Though he was our guardian, there was something about Luka Krestovic that frightened me. His constant vigilance, deadly silence, and killer instinct sounded an ominous warning.

The light faded and there were no more woods to mask our retreat. Back on sandy, trench-filled roads, we hastened as we heard sounds of combat at our heels. The cacophony of artillery fire broke the dusky silence. Then, the loud clatter of voices charging from behind. Our quickened pace became a sprint as we made our way to the long trench fifty meters ahead. The squall of enemy rounds, "ZIFF, ZIP" thinned our tiny ranks, as the remainder of our group dove headlong into the closest trench. Luka positioned himself and began to return fire, while Glagolev moved to the far end to do the same. Loud sounds of shuffling boots and undecipherable screams grew louder.

As the fog of mayhem prepared to overtake us, I hunkered frantically trying to loosen the bolt action of my rifle. Now, with the full fury of bullets around us, the shouting grew louder. My stomach tightened and my fingers trembled. My nose had begun to bleed as I panted loudly. Bracing for imminent death, I feverishly worked the bolt of the *Mosin*.

The onrush of roaring voices had been too confusing to decipher. It had been a moment of terror, followed by an instant of panic. At the moment I saw soldiers appear at the edge of our trench, I reflexively lifted a rifle, closed my eyes, and aimed into the swirling fog!

In that moment, forever frozen in time, I thought I heard my name, "Anton!" as I fired a single shot – the only round I would ever fire during that cursed war. The blast from the end of my rifle ripped the air, and a man fell face down into our trench. The others around me continued to shoot and duck from incoming rounds. Gradually, the firing subsided. Like a wax figure, I remained still for what seemed like minutes. An eerie quiet descended on our smoke and blood-stained world.

Glagolev moved toward the motionless figure lying face down in our trench, and said, "He's a Russian Poporuchik; one of our own." In the cruel shadow of death and grotesque absurdity that had stained my life, I knew in an instant that I had just killed my brother. I saw his face and recognized his dead blue eyes, with the fixed expression, "Why?"

Luka turned the fallen soldier over to reveal a gaping hole in his chest and quietly mouthed the words, "*Pucano u leda. Ne front.* Shot back. Not front."

Without thinking, a speechless Glagolev finally said, "But a close-range shot could blow a hole in the chest like that." The corporal looked my way and added, "But we all know that war creates fog, and we end up killing our own. It happens, private. You did not know."

Not one to argue openly, Luka shook his head and muttered again, "*Ne front, ne front.*"

Two others in our ragtag band of six lay dead. Only Vasily, still holding his sword, knew of Chaim and realized what I had done. His eyes fixed on my frozen blank stare. "A…A-nton, I…."

My golden brother Chaim…always true to his word…had come looking for me.

On this day, our Second Army had been obliterated. Later, we learned by rumored reports that General Samsonov died from a self-inflicted wound, and that General Martos was captured while fleeing. But none of this compared to what I had done. Brother killer! The only shot I fired had found its way into my brother's heart. Vasily must have explained this to Glagolev and Luka for they watched me closely in the days ahead. Quietly, it was Luka who took the *Mosin* from my hands, concerned that I might turn it on myself.

Over the next several days, we continued to retreat. Down to only four, we traveled mostly at night, witnessing from the woods the familiar sight of captured Russian soldiers. Numb to feeling and thought, I moved mechanically as instinctual forces propelled me forward. Luka found food to sustain us, but I could not eat; I could not sleep. My mind had turned to stone. Glagolev, with his tattered map, led the way, while Luka Krestovic watched the road behind us. Vasily, with his saber in one hand and my arm in the other, walked silently by my side.

Soon, we passed by Neidenburg. We avoided the main roads because the German Landwehr had retaken the town. Traveling mainly by darkness, we found our way back to the small village that we had first passed through over a week ago. The surroundings looked vaguely familiar. Burned farmhouses and emaciated animals standing stuporously in the fields.

Then, we came upon the charred cottage where two small boys had stood over the body of their dead father. The older boy – the one Vasily had given his last crust of bread, because "he looked hungry too" – stood motionless in front of the ruin. Vasily recognized him, turned his head to the boy, smiled, and waved.

In return, the stony-faced boy coldly lifted a rifle and fired a round through Vasily's chest. Immediately, Luka raised his gun and killed the boy as he stood. I screamed hoarsely and lunged toward Vasily. Glagolev restrained me and grabbed my collar to drag me away. Luka walked backward, protecting our final retreat, as we disappeared once more into the fog.

And now we were three – a brave corporal who kept saving my life, a cunning Serbian survivalist, seeking to revenge his people, and a shadow man, numbed by unspeakable slaughter.

CHAPTER 7

The Madman in the Clock

It is said that early horologists did not have a method for regulating the turning wheel of a clock. They understood how wheels and gears could transmit energy, but had yet to devise a way to control the turning of the wheel. Then, they stumbled upon a simple device that changed everything. The mechanism consisted of a crown wheel, the *rencontre*, which was rotated by the power of weights. Tiny teeth gripped onto the pallets that were mounted on the stem. The device first turned in one direction then alternately in the other. This backward-forward movement, which turned linear into circular motion, seemed somewhat mad to the early horologists. How could time advance with movements in opposite directions? In their puzzlement, they chose the old French word, "*foliot*," or "little madman," to describe their invention.

When my mother disappeared, my *foliot* became stuck in a backward direction, moving the wheel of my life toward darkness. In the latter years of my childhood, after Papa placed his hand on my shoulder and invited me into his workshop, the movement was reversed; and I thought I'd found a sense of purpose and meaning. However, after Tannenberg, the reversal of my fate seemed once again fixed in a backward motion, leading me further into a darkness that I had never imagined.

Much of the time spent on the journey to Willenburg is lost to me, but some images remain clear. Scenes of dusty trails and rocky fields gave way to patches of gray forest. Trees still smoked in the aftermath of infernos that had previously engulfed them. The air had the thick, pungent smell of damp earth, burnt wood, and creosote. With dim recollection, my two saviors and I traveled east at night for one, maybe two days, moving cautiously so as not to alert German patrols in the heavily wooded area.

At Willenburg, we encountered other stragglers and fresh troops from the Fifth Army, all heading south to drive the Austrian-Hungarian forces from Galicia. The southern movement by train brought back memories of my first encounter with a band of bold and frightened men heading from Brest to Warsaw, months and lifetimes ago. Like intruders into a cloistered space, images of the innocent Vasily, the captivating Shev, and my golden Chaim made their unwelcome appearance. I quickly banished them with the silent words, "Doesn't mean anything. None of this does." Papa once spoke of removing, not adding, complications from a timepiece.

He would say, "Sometimes, it is best to make it simpler. Too many complications mean trouble for the watch repairman. You see, we just remove them."

And so, I did.

I don't recall exchanging words with either Glagolev or Luka, but they were never far from my side. I could feel their breathing bodies alongside mine, as we trudged our way south. It was clear that Luka intended to join the forces of the resolute Serbian general, Radomir Putnik, who were preparing to drive the enemy from their homeland. I assumed that Corporal Glagolev, being a good soldier, would march with the Fifth Army to reverse the defeat we had experienced up north.

When the train pulled into the station at Raya Russkaya, we shuffled onto the grimy platform. Glagolev placed his hand on my shoulder and said, "My duty is to the Imperial Army. Yours is to yourself, private. Join me, if you want to avenge our fallen comrades. Or, find your own way. I won't stop you." With this, he turned and walked away, not looking back.

I should have yelled to thank him for saving my life; but at that moment, I wished he had let me face the bullets and meet my fate. I knew I couldn't face another bloated corpse, hear another suffering horse, or watch another person I loved die a wretched death. The hollowness in my heart and gut grew as I watched him disappear into a sea of uniformed troops.

I turned, and standing before me was Luka. First looking down, he raised his head and peered deeply into my eyes. Then, he placed it in my hand. He must have known that I would face further battles, even if not as a soldier in the Tsar's army. "Take, yes?"

Though I didn't think I would ever fire another gun, mechanically, my *foliot* turned and lifted my hand to accept his offering. I knew I didn't want to touch his pistol, but I felt I couldn't refuse his offer. Something beyond reason led me to take the pistol and quickly stuff it in my knapsack.

What happened next stirred what little emotion remained within me. Master Sergeant Luka Krestovic, this hardened warrior, whose strength and power made me tremble, grabbed and hugged me tightly. "*Pucano u leda. Ne front…ne front*. Shot back. Not front." Luka turned and slowly walked away, looking back once. Now, I stood alone, as one.

In an ocean of men, who all seemed to move with direction and purpose, I was suddenly seized by a thought. To outsmart the madman in the clock, I had to reverse the backward motion of my *foliot* and return to where it all began, Zastavia. From there, I reasoned that I could undo whatever damage had been done.

A seed of excitement grew as I thought about rejoining Papa in crafting fine capsules of time. I would ask for nothing in return. I felt a budding warmth, as I imagined walking with Nadya again through the woods and helping her tend to little creatures who need kindness. I felt slightly amused by the thought that I would even greet old Kreusche and undo my brutal treatment of him by feeding his goats and cleaning his pigsty. Yes, with a growing sense of purpose, I realized that Zastavia was my home; and by returning, I would trick the little madman into reversing the dark movement of my life!

Before leaving the train station, I collected extra rations and found water to fill my canteen. Wearing a uniform allowed me to move without drawing unwanted attention. No one gave a second thought to a soldier standing in line to receive rations. No one questioned my asking for a terrain map, which I said was for my staff sergeant. As far as anyone, save Glagolev and Luka, knew, I was preparing to begin moving south with the Fifth Army.

When I had all I needed, I found a small alley to survey my supplies and check my precious cargo. Digging into the bottom compartment of my knapsack, I retrieved the carefully wrapped parcel holding my three watches. I was most worried about the condition of the Vacheron and Patek, the two "old ladies" as Papa used to call them, and whether they had survived. My stomach immediately sickened when I discovered a crack in the crystal of the Vacheron; however, I quickly determined that the inner workings of the piece were undamaged. I checked that I had my tools and the rubles Chazanovich had paid for the LeCoultre. I also carefully packed the pistol Luka gave me, placing in the top compartment.

I almost forgot about the other passengers I'd brought with me – my own crudely fashioned watch and the last of Mama's inkblots. As originally planned, I would give the watch to Papa, this time as a form of reparation.

And as for the old folded inkblot, I could not remember why I had decided to bring it with me. The parchment had yellowed and was frayed at the edges. Since it took up so little space, I kept it, this time, wrapping it around the watches. If nothing else, it provided another layer of padding for the more valuable contents in my knapsack.

After repacking my gear like the experienced soldier I was not, I looked at the map and tried to figure out directions. I would walk the distance to Zastavia. No more crowded and noisy train cars. Though I was not a hardened solider, I had grown accustomed to walking long distances. My feet had toughened and the weight of a single backpack paled in comparison to the heavy satchels I had carried for the last month. I thought about finding a medic for my nose, which continued to ache, burn, and seep but decided this might arouse suspicions and other unwanted complications. Besides, in three or four days, I'd be back in Zastavia, where Nadya would treat me with her herbs and potions.

I planned a route to avoid major roads and larger villages, to stick to smaller trails and, with the aid of a compass, to make my way through the woods. According to the map, I would need to pass through Radivilov, a large shtetl on the border, where I could resupply there before my final journey north to my home.

The woods east of the train station were unspoiled by the mass mobilization along the border. Gray skies, smoke, and fog had lifted, revealing an endless expanse of green fields, surrounded by tall pines. The grassy meadows were not littered with carnage. There were no smoldering fires, no charred buildings, broken wagons, or corpses left behind for the worms to feed on. Everything was alive and unspoiled.

❖ ❖ ❖

For the first time in more than a month, I was alone with quiet — no thunder of distant artillery, no panic-inducing crackling of automatic weapons, and most relieving, no heart-wrenching cries of men begging to die, or the pitiful moans of their suffering horses. As I walked, I began to feel something approaching serenity. The tightness in my jaw and gut loosened. My calloused feet carried me forward without the pain of leather on raw skin, and my back felt stronger. Even my breathing was less labored and painful.

After half-a-day's walk, I strayed off the road and discovered a secluded meadow. In the distance, I caught sight of black shapes moving against a background of trees. My nerves still frayed from unexpected threats, my heart began to quicken. Those blurred shapes had a foreboding quality; I had seen them too many times in my dreams. Now, I imagined they could be Austrian or Hungarian soldiers on patrol. Though I hadn't wanted to touch a weapon again, I suddenly felt reassured that Luka's pistol was sitting at the top of my knapsack.

Averting my gaze, I fished my hand into my knapsack to feel the cold steel of the pistol. Carefully pulling it out, I made sure it was ready to fire. When I turned back, all but one of the moving shapes had disappeared. I froze momentarily wondering what to do. I firmly grasped the pistol, which gave me the courage I normally lacked. I cautiously inched my way forward, squinting to keep the object in sight. At about 100 meters, the form of a large black horse emerged from the shadows. I let out an audible sigh. For the first time in weeks, a sense of dread and fear was replaced by curiosity. How beautiful and majestic he was, standing free and unfettered in nature. I slowly approached so as not to scare him. At 50 meters, I recognized the markings on the saddle. It was a Cossack steed somehow separated from its rider. Maybe the other shapes had also been horses, all of which had escaped their servitude. More likely, the sun had played tricks with the shadows and fooled me into thinking I'd seen many lurking in front of the trees.

This noble steed had probably known of my approach long before I knew of him. He stood, ceasing his restless motion and watching as I took small steps forward. Thoughts began to swirl. Though I had spent my early years drawing horses, I knew little about them. I would approach the stallion with care, offer him something to eat, and win over his loyalty. Then, I'd climb on his back and ride toward Zastavia. Imagine what Nadya would think when she sees her *Pidky* riding up on the back of a Cossack mount! Papa, in his predictable way, might issue a grunt of indifference; but he, too, might even be a little impressed and grudgingly welcome me back. No, he would not greet me as a hero, like Chaim, but as Anton, the sparrow soldier, who had dug latrines and burned shit, but still managed somehow to survive the horror. The thought of Chaim made me feel sick. For a moment, the sky seemed to darken. I didn't yet know what I would tell them about Chaim. They would surely ask. For now, I removed that complication from my mind. I slowly walked toward the mighty beast, trying to show him that I was not a threat.

Standing motionless, he locked his coal-black eyes on me. When I was almost 10 meters, I caught the toe of my boot in some roots and tumbled to the ground, discharging the pistol aimlessly into the air. When I got to my feet, all I saw was his hind-quarters as he galloped toward the woods. Even though there was no one else in sight, I looked around with embarrassment, hoping that not even the woodland creatures had witnessed such clumsiness. Humiliation gave way to faint humor, as I thought about Anton, the imposter, masquerading as fearless warrior. I was relieved I hadn't shot myself or the mighty steed. Placing the weapon toward the bottom of my knapsack, I vowed not to touch it again. After sitting in the field for several minutes, trying to calm my heart, I regained a modicum of composure. I decided not to let this ignominious incident upset my journey or my resolve to reset my arc of time.

I found my way back to the road and walked for the rest of the day. The sky was filled with starlings and other small birds I didn't recognize.

I watched them swirling gracefully. They were the essence of freedom, these gentle acrobats of the heavens. I stopped to adjust my pack and sip some water as I continued enjoying the starlings careening through the air. Suddenly, from outside my field of vision, a Northern Harrier dove and picked off an unsuspecting bird and carried it off. Startled at first, I was reminded that nature wears many faces.

As I resumed my trek through the brambles and brush, the incidents with the black shapes, the Cossack steed, my misfired pistol, and the predatory harrier passed from my mind. I marveled at the splendor of this peaceful afternoon. As the sun lowered, the clouds in the west radiated a pinkish-red hue. The silence and stillness of the air were ruffled only momentarily by a gentle, cooling breeze. I came upon fields where farmers had planted crops, rows of beets and potatoes far as I could see.

Ancient timekeepers relied on the movement of the sun and its resonant shadows to map the passage of time. They saw this same sun and sky I was viewing, which made me feel a connection to the horologists of old. This day seemed perfect. I mused how quickly things could return to a familiar rhythm, with few complications. In the end, fewer complications were better. No more bloody corpses, no more sounds of dying animals, and no one shooting at me. At these memories, my stomach tightened. But as quickly as they came to mind, I eradicated them. After all, I reasoned, it had only been a few months of my life. Better them than me. I didn't even *really* know them, so they meant nothing. Who was Vasily but some unfortunate boy, whose family did not love him? Mine loved me. And who was Shev? Who *was* Shev? I never even knew his name; but that was fine, too. And when Nadya and Papa would ask me about Chaim, I would say that he was still valiantly leading men in battle and would no doubt return a hero when his mission was complete. I reasoned that he was still alive, that the officer I killed that night in the trench could have been anyone. After all, who had really seen his face? I had instantly looked away and never identified this unfortunate soul. Yes, that was going to be my answer to them whenever they asked about my brother. This would also be the story I would tell myself whenever I was reminded of that horrible, foggy nightmare. Chaim could, no, Chaim *would* return to Zastavia a decorated officer and want to settle back into a peaceful life of watchmaking. It could be Zellinksy and Sons. To reset the time, I would gladly return to being the sparrow, who unpacked boxes and took his place in the back of the wagon with the chickens. I would return Papa's precious watches, and we would fix the Vacheron together. I had spent few of the rubles I'd gotten for the LeCoultre and would give the remainder to Papa, of course. We would go to Chazanovich and demand the return of that watch. I would explain to Nadya and Papa that I had not been in my right mind when I left. Maybe I would tell them I had gone to look after my brother. I would get on my knees and beg their forgiveness and atone for my sins against them. Nadya, always seeking wounded creatures to care for, would take pity on her *Pidkydannya*. I only needed to reduce the complications.

With these matters resolved in my mind, I lifted my face toward the sky. The sun felt warm on my brow. I breathed in deeply and noticed my nose didn't ache. My *foliot* maneuver had begun to work! Finally, peace and tranquility! I told myself that from this point on, everything was going to be fine. Yes, it would be fine… until later that night when Shev made his first visit.

Nestled in a little valley, I made a fire for tea and began eating my rations. I must have dozed while I was tending the fire, as the last of the day's light left the sky. Looking up through the glow of the embers, I suddenly saw Shev gazing down at me with his crooked smile. He was standing upright and whole, though there was a stain around his neck with red streaks down his shirt. I screeched loudly! Startled is not the word to describe my state, as I fumbled for words, "How…DID…but…YER…you can't….

"Yes, young Squire, the Lord called me forth. *Dominus vocavit me ad vos.* So many more complications ahead, I'm afraid. HA! A-head! And what have we here in this quiet glen but a mad watchman trying to make his way back home. Young Squire, did'ja hear about the time a foolish fool tried foolishly to fool the arc of time? No? Well after cleanin the shit off his boots and eatin his dumplins, in no time, he became twice the fool!" Then, as he stood bellowing out laughter, his red-stained head dropped to the ground. "Ha! Laughed me bloody head off." Seemingly unperturbed, he reached over searching for his head and plumped it back down on his shoulders. "Ah, that's much better."

Gasping a SCREAM, I jolted from this nightmare! Dripping sweat, I began to regurgitate my meal around the embers. The night was black; I was alone and surrounded only by the quiet sounds of cicadas in the brush. I was too rattled to fall back asleep. The day had convinced me that I was done with those unbearable times, but apparently, they were not quite done with me. The nightmare had felt real; but, I told myself, all unwanted nighttime visitations seemed that way. This was not real, only my imagination playing tricks with my senses, conjuring the dead, shit-burning monk.

The sky grew light in the east. I made some tea and decided to get an early start to arrive in Radivilov by late afternoon. After resting and replenishing my supplies there, I would make my final push homeward. But, an hour into my morning's march, I heard mumbling behind me; and, to my horror, there again was the unmistakable voice of Shev.

"They say, ya know, that trench warfare was a last-ditch effort. Oh, and after the war, little Shlomo asks his father, 'What did ya do in the great war, Papa?' 'Well, dear boy, I risked my life digging latrines for others to deposit their dirty deeds.'"

Catching his wink, as I turned to see him right behind me, I screamed without thinking, "LEAVE ME ALONE, WHATEVER YOU ARE! GO AWAY AND LEAVE ME IN PEACE!" Suddenly I realized what a fool I was. I glanced from side to side, hoping that no one, including the woodland creatures, had seen me squawking to myself. Suddenly, I remembered that Nadya once said that when black tea becomes old, it can ferment and play tricks with one's mind. Surely, that was all this was. But to my exasperation, the nuisance, Shev, hadn't finished his tormenting diatribe.

"With mirth and laughter aside, dear Squire, may I remind you of the Sufi poet Rumi, who said 'The act of trying to find the way home is what convinces us we are lost. We're not lost; we're not alone; and, we've never even left home.' But, in your case, young Squire, I think you actually are lost; but, do not despair for you are not alone."

Stopping in my tracks, I turned around to face this phantom of my imagination.

"I DON'T UNDERSTAND YOUR GIBBERISH, YOUR BUMBLINGS. NOW LEAVE ME BE!" I glanced again from side to side again and shook my head. "I AM NOT LOST! AND I AM ALONE! AND YOU ARE THE FERMENTATIONS OF THE TEA I DRANK!"

My eyes suddenly filled with tears and began to burn. My nose ached and became moist with seepage. "I WATCHED YOU DIE AND I DIDN'T EVEN KNOW YOUR NAME!"

Softly, Shev responded, "Ah…Now we have some truth from you, Squire. Something true from your heart, no? The language of emotion from one's heart never lies. That and the language of the bowel will never deceive us. Your mind will lie and try to trick you, but your heart cannot. Remember, The Turk Emre's words, '*Seni Gerçeklerden ayıran ne olursa olsun, at gitsin, bir şekilde yok olacak.*' Whatever separates you from the Truth, throw it away, it will vanish anyhow."

"ENOUGH!!" I covered my ears and broke into a run, taking one hand away to wipe the tears that had penetrated my numbness on such a calm and pure day like this. "STAY AWAY! YOU FOOL, STAY AWAY FROM ME!"

I was unaware of the two peasant boys, who looked up from the adjacent field where they were picking the last of the summer beets. Startled by the shrieking sounds that pierced the tranquil dawn, they beheld a stumbling madman screaming to himself along the road toward Radivilov.

Two hours later, I arrived on the outskirts of the shtetl. The roads reminded me of the deserted streets of Neidenburg, but here, there were soldiers everywhere. Some buildings had blackened mortar around their windows, with shattered glass strewn in the streets. Some soldiers were sitting in the sun, while others were drinking and whooping loudly. I overheard men talk about a great victory over the Austrians at Lemberg, where Luka had gone to fight.

Much of Radivilov appeared to have been destroyed. I walked by a row of buildings with broken windows and scattered debris. This was all that remained from the looting that had occurred in the homes and shops along the street. Drunken Cossacks, who had long been an unwelcome presence in Radivilov, wandered through streets, their pockets filled with silver bracelets, silk scarfs, and flagons of vodka.

On one street, several brutish soldiers pushed around an old man, while another one held a young woman, his daughter, I suspected. Their cruel debauchery escalated, as one soldier kicked the man in the stomach, and the other began to tear at the young woman's clothing. "Town's full of Jews, but their women will do." He belched a sickening laugh and continued to paw the terrified girl, as the two other goons picked through the old man's pockets.

Suddenly, I found myself standing two feet in front of them, as surprised as they by my unannounced appearance. Words spilled from my mouth.

"Ahem, good sirs….Di'ja hear the one about the Jews who entered the Tsar's bedchamber….?"

Then, I lost my voice, which had not felt like mine, to begin with. I stood still, and my knees began to shake.

The frozen looks on the faces of the brutes thawed, as two of them approached me, one asking in a menacing tone, "What have we here, a Jew lover? Are you a Jew, too?"

More words – this time, unmistakenly my own – poured out in frightened gibberish, "No, no, I don't look Jewish. I-I mean, No….No, I'm no Jew. XV Corps, 36th Infantry. A soldier for the Tsar, like you. Not a Jew."

The beefy man holding the girl smirked and said, "Then be gone, you rat of a soldier."

Then, from another goon, "XV Corps, eh? All of 'em dead or else cowards, who left their comrades to rot. Which are you?" The others laughed but were momentarily distracted by the cries of terrified children and screams of women from the building behind them.

Quickly, I backed up and scurried away. I tried to lose myself in the narrow alleyways of the shtetl, looking behind to make sure they had not tried to follow. Certain that I was safe, my breath finally slowed; and, my heart stopped thundering in my chest. I entered the remains of what had once been a marketplace with overturned stalls. On the cobblestone walkway lay broken baskets with decayed vegetables scattered about. I thought my bloodstained uniform afforded me the anonymity I sought.

Finding a well, I pulled up the bucket to fill my canteen. I gazed into the bucket and caught the reflection of a gaunt figure, with matted hair and dried bloodstains on his face. I *did* look like a rat soldier. I scooped some water and attempted to clean the soot and blood-grime from my cheeks and forehead. What was I thinking back there, to have risked my life getting involved! The old man and girl were strangers to me. It didn't matter. I was still breathing heavily and my nose ached when I heard the voice of Shev once more.

"Cleaning my cerebellum from your hair, I see. Young Squire, you nearly found what you felt you lost – your courage. I believe it was Marcus Aurelius who said that 'Everyone becomes brave when he sees one who despairs.'"

Then…another voice stammered an interruption.

"No, it was not M…M-Marcus Arelius, you old g…g-asbag! It was Nietzsche, who also said 'That which does not k…k-ill us makes us stronger.' Nietzsche said many things about your predicament, Anton, so you see. K…k-eep your wits. Think of the ancient P…P-ythagoreans. I want to tell you that numbers abound, Anton; they are all around us and c…c-ontain signs that will guide you, and so it is."

Now standing next to Shev was the youthful figure of Vasily, adjusting his mangled pince-nez. He was as I had last seen him – still holding the saber, except it was broken halfway down the blade. In the middle of his chest was a gaping wound that I could almost see through. By now, I'd grown hoarse from my startled screams. No longer capable of the shrieks and gasps, the protestations and the stammering shock, I simply muttered, "Now you?"

"Yes, m…m-e, or rather I, Anton," answered Vasily.

Quickly Shev interjected, "Our young Squire is confused and lost, and you've given him a rattle, with your mathematical jibber-jabber, my good fellow. You should leave him be, for the encounter with the ruffians back there nearly proved his undoing. And in case you did not notice, like St. Peter's denial of Jesus, the Squire just denounced his people and his heritage. He is accumulating a coterie of accusers, who'll be ready to condemn him of one such thing or another."

I finally spoke, momentarily losing sight of the farcical nature of this dialogue with apparitions, "What would you have had me do, Fight them!? I'm not a monk warrior, who fights like you. They would have beat me or something far worse. Besides, FOR THE SAKE OF GOD," my voice suddenly growing louder, "YOU'RE BOTH DEAD. GONE. SO, LEAVE ME IN PEACE!"

From across the square, a soldier approached. I looked up and saw a hollow-eyed figure looking down at me. "Comrade, what was yer company?"

Completely startled by his approach, I managed only to answer, "Whaat?"

In a quiet voice, he continued, "You don't look like the others around here. Looks like you've seen action, not like most of these sweet cherries…. And who in God's name were you talking to?"

First a quick denial, "No one." Then, my attempt to explain my situation and haggard appearance. "I was in the 36th Infantry, XV Corps. Most of us got wiped out at Frankenau, before we even got to Tannenburg."

He stared strangely at me and said, "I was with the I Corps at Usdau. Everyone blown up or shot around me…barely got away through the marshes. We were all starving and hiding til we finally found the Ninth Army heading south. Figured I'd had enough of all this. All my cousins… they're all dead….Thought I was done. Was headed home to Kobryn to farm with my papa and little brothers. I never wanted to be a part of this."

"Kobryn's north of where I'm headed," I said to the first living person I'd spoken to in days. "Zastavia's a little village where my family's from. Me too, I'm goin home."

The soldier continued to look at me queerly, his mouth moving but his eyes looked lifeless. "No….I was…. but not now. Not goin home. Figured nothin probably there. Gonna head west back to Raya Russkaya and find a division to fight with. Don't want no one thinkin I ran away from it all…. Plus…it's quieter."

"Quieter!?" I said, flashing back to the deafening sounds of incoming artillery, the screaming, and moaning. "Quieter? With all of that mayhem!?"

Again, looking through me as if his mind had somehow penetrated my own, he left me with these words, "Yeah….It's quieter out there."

As he turned and walked away, my two ghosts resumed their noisy banter.

CHAPTER 8

In the Shadow of Time

Before his shocking demise and after his disquieting return, Vasily had spoken incessantly about the mathematics of time. But whereas I had dabbled with the techniques of 18th century Swiss and German watchmakers, he sought to penetrate the mindsets of pre-mechanical timekeepers. As hard as I tried to tune out the chatter and fend off the unceasing raillery between Shev and him, I listened to Vasily with a third ear.

"You s…s-ee, Anton. I want to tell you, with only numbers to g…g-uide them, ancient horologists tried to decipher the unknowable forces of nature by m…m-apping onto the stars mathematical p…p-rinciples to create a predictable system for measuring the passage of time."

He explained how by attending to shadows and the position of the stars, Greek and Arabic timekeepers learned to chart the movement of time across the sky with mathematical precision. With such knowledge, I reasoned that the stars could guide me in my journey. Thus, after departing Radivilov, I decided to make the rest of my journey at night, while walking backward.

Traveling at night, though it slowed my pace, made logical sense. I was less likely to draw attention to myself, a ranting madman in a tattered Russian soldier's uniform. More importantly, like my ancient brethren, I could study the position and time patterns revealed by the stars. And the truth is, I could no longer sleep. That first night after I left Radivilov, I awakened from one nightmare after another. My childhood nightmares, which had never left me, were joined by a dreamscape of mind-shattering experiences from the last ten weeks. In my fragmented nightmares, I was walking dusty trails – with each aching step, frightened I would be unable to fill my lungs with enough air – then, scanning the horizon for movement of dark figures shadowing and closing in – and next, coming upon shocking scenes of bulging-eyed corpses wearing the masks of their sudden, deplorable deaths on what remained of their faces. I'd awaken soaked in sweat, drift off, and then dream of the suffering moans of petrified and putrefying animals, mixed with the sounds of a crying baby. In one of these nightmares, I veered off the road and encountered Captain Volkov, dining on his horse, as he directed his baleful gaze and angry rants my way.

"You have completely ruined a perfectly good Breitling, private; and you will dearly pay for your rock-handed incompetence!" When he lunged at me, his body broke in half; and his entrails spilled out.

Each time I awakened, I saw Shev and Vasily whispering and watching me. I nodded off again; but this time, I was terrified by the black form of Luka stabbing my guardian, Glagolev, in the back, while hissing, "*Pucano u leda. Ne front.*" Looking into my eyes, Luka then spoke in uncharacteristically clear language, "You turned your back on us all, and we will find you."

Badly rattled by this, I vowed to stay awake. Aided by doubling my ration of black tea, I managed to remain vigilant and defeat sleep's siren call for the next several days.

As for walking backward, this felt foolish at first; but I reasoned that it offered several advantages. First, I could keep the ghosts in front of me. My frayed nerves could no longer tolerate being jolted by one unwelcome voice after another. Second, my earlier theory about reversing my *foliot* had not been as successful as I had hoped. True, initially it seemed to have worked;

the arc of my life had improved, only to be jarringly reversed once again, as my past intruded in a most uninvited manner. I reasoned that by walking backward, I could enact a physical motion equivalent of the *foliot* reversal. This would hasten the re-setting of my own arc of time.

I made one more preparation for my travels. I had to do something about the unremitting clatter of voices that accompanied me. By stuffing tufts of grass into each ear and wrapping vines around my head, I convinced myself that this would bar the annoying claptrap of the ghosts. Walking backward, with ears full of grass, provided further rationale for making my journey in the dark of night. My descent into madness had not completely removed all sense of what a fool I must have appeared.

During the heat of the day, I looked for a hollow and the shade of a large tree, where I would sit motionless to study the changing lengths of shadows on the surrounding oak trees and sagebrush spires. Shev and Vasily kept up their commentary about my actions and the state of my health and moral rectitude.

"Squire, like the *Tradescantia Zebrina* spiderwort, you too, have become a 'wandering Jew.' Haha! Only that hardy plant thrives in thickets and wetlands, where you, my friend, will not last much longer in this state you're in."

"I would ignore his specious c…c-ouncil, Anton. It is r…r-ubbish indeed. I want to tell you that the monk has once more misnamed the species of a p..p-lant."

I achieved modest success ignoring them but would then interject an occasional protest and, in hushed tones, tell them to stop! During my afternoon vigils, I continued to catch glimpses of dark figures moving closer. Staring off in the distance, I felt sure that I saw these dark forms in motion and thought I'd begun to hear the wind whisper, "We will find you." One more reason I decided that it made sense to travel by stealth at night.

Late one afternoon, while swilling my black tea, I realized that the shapes had to be Luka and his darkly clad band of Serbian assassins moving toward me in the distance! The garbled words he offered when we said goodbye, which I first thought were meant to offer comfort, should never have been trusted. I became convinced that his true intent all along was to find and kill me. Of course, it suddenly *all* made sense now! At this moment of clarity, I decided to keep the pistol close at all times. The black forms tracking my movements and that hollow-eyed soldier in the market square, who asked questions about where I had been and where I was headed, now all fit together! I even imagined myself to be Luka's counterpart. Like him, I would walk backward in the dark of night with my loaded weapon, just as I had repeatedly witnessed him walking backward to ensure that we were not being followed. Only now, he was the hunter, and my task was to outwit him.

Any doubt or worry about my remaining sanity vanished the moment I realized the threat I faced. Shev and Vasily echoed this ominous warning, although the focus of their concerns was less clear. Shev quoted poets' views on madness; and while not to be outdone, Vasily relied heavily on words of scientists and mathematicians, who spoke of insanity in abstract philosophical terms.

On the third night of my backward journey, I noticed that two other figures had joined my ensemble – Glagolev, whom I had expected, and the old rabbi from Zastavia, whom I had not. With the addition of these two, the running commentary took on a more accusatory tone. I fought to ignore their allegations of sin, guilt, shame, misdeeds, atonement, ignorance, and cowardice. Shev brought up the Spanish Grand Inquisitor, Torquemada; adding that as Jew, I would have been burned at the stake for my idolatry.

"And yes, Squire, we must not forget the fires of inquisition, where Torquemada sought guilt in the innocent and proclaimed innocence for the guilty. But, alas, we have yet to determine which side you will join."

All that was missing from this derisive cacophony was the stabbing slur, "rock hands;" but soon, along with calling me "*schmutzie*," the rabbi reminded me that I would always have hands of rock.

The final night of the journey to Zastavia was surprisingly quiet. I walked backward along narrow roads that, even in the dim light of dawn, looked familiar. I passed small farms of the gentiles, where the Valeski brothers had grown up. For a moment, I wondered what had become of them. Had either survived or did they lie wide-eyed and large-eared among the corpses in the slaughter fields? Silencing those thoughts, I was distracted by the barren fields on my right, where many years earlier, I had built mudhuts as a strange homage to my lost mother.

The familiarity of the surroundings changed in an instant with the shock of what I saw. Many huts and cottages were badly burned, some houses completely destroyed. The roads in my village were deserted. There were no mules, cows, chickens, goats, or pigs. There were no signs of life anywhere. I turned and now walked facing forward, my mind unable to take in what I beheld. Everything had been burned to the ground!

In the spot where our house and Papa's workshop had once stood there was now charred rubble, blackened wood, and an old soot-covered stove. I stepped over the debris and found the space that had once housed Papa's workshop. I found the twisted, blackened remnants of the old Breguet and the ash heap of his workbench. All around were scraps of burned metal coils, tiny screws, gears, and springs. Then, I spied the remains of his books and journals with their scorched and blistered pages. I stepped on glass, broken by those, who had looted his remaining watches that had not been stolen by my earlier thievery. Like a granite statue, I stood motionless amidst the ruins and didn't even notice the woman who walked up behind me.

She spoke quietly, "They burned everything." Startled, I turned to see Kruehke's younger daughter, Esther, who continued to speak. "They're all gone. "They came and took them all," she explained, her voice soft and tentative, for surely I looked like a dangerous madman holding onto my pistol with tufts of grass dangling from my ears and vines wrapped around my forehead. "The soldiers were led here by gentile farmers, and they went from house to house gathering up all the Jews. They accused us all of being spies for the Kaiser….They took my sister and shot my papa because of his defiance." Her voice broke into a tearful lament, "He was a mean old man, but my papa, no? I hid in the cellar beneath the goats. They took your aunt Nadya and your papa too. Then, they took torches and burned the homes….I am so sorry, Anton."

She paused to compose herself and continued, "When your papa and aunt returned from Kamenetz without you and Chaim, they were so sad. You both were gone from their home, so suddenly. They believed you would both die, Anton." She stopped, turned, and walked away. I didn't know where she went; but when I looked up, she was gone.

And such was my homecoming….My grand plan to reverse the arc of my fate and return to a life with fewer complications….Burnt to the ground….They were all gone….

I dropped first to my knees and then fell back on my rump. I sat, dazed by the cauterized tomb that had once been my home. Nothing at all remained of my former life. They were all gone….My plan to return to Nadya and Papa, just foolishness….They were all gone….Ideas about reversing the course of my life had always been rubbish. My *foliot* was broken, and now it was *I* who had become the madman in the clock. There was nothing left now, no more family, nowhere else to go. I could not go on living.

❖ ❖ ❖

After several minutes of numbness in my mind, hollowness in my gut, and limpness in my arms and legs, I decided that I would fire Luka's pistol one last time, but now with purpose and intent. The only thing left to decide was whether I would aim for my head or my heart – whether to splatter my brains like Shev or to put a hole in my chest like poor Vasily and…of course…Chaim. I shut my eyes to weigh my choice.

As I rested the pistol on my lap, I heard whispers, "Do it. You have no worth."

I tried to recall the mourner's Kaddish, thinking that prayer would silence the tormenting voices before I joined the ranks of all who had fallen and been taken from me. As I sat in silence with eyes closed, searching for the words to El Maleh Rachamim, something unexpected happened….I fell into a deep slumber.

During what became a 30-hour sleep, I had a lengthy and puzzling dream that was not like the gruesome nightmares that had terrorized me before. To this day, that dream remains vivid and real.

In it, I am walking along narrow dusty trails, like before; only this time, I am determined not to look toward the tormenting sounds coming from the adjacent woods. I continue on the path that leads to a darkened village where I spot a house with lights coming from inside. Opening the door, I realize I'm home.

A fire burns in the stove. Everyone is there, everyone but Chaim. Nadya is seated at the table feeding Vasily, who is counting the pictures of horses he is drawing. He is smaller, and his feet barely reach the floor. He is sputtering random numbers as he speaks. I begin raising my voice, demanding to know why she is feeding him my babka and honey cakes.

Nadya looks mournfully at me and says, "But *Pidky*, he l…l-ooked hungry t…t-oo." Papa is in his workshop, his back to us. Mama sits at the table with Shev. She is speaking Hungarian while moving her inkblots around. Shev is sitting close by drinking vodka or ale. He begins laughing loudly and patting his belly, farting and preaching in a language that everyone, except me, understands.

Papa comes out and says, "Anton, I have a special gift for you because Chaim will not be coming back here." I anticipate the watch I had hoped for all along, but Papa hands me, instead, a rucksack filled with heavy rocks. His old clock is ticking loudly and blood is trickling from his nose.

Mama begins dancing and is now pulling me close. She whispers that she will share her secrets if I come to look for her. "You have to find me, my *Kicsi*. Your Uncle Andras knows where to look."

Suddenly, we're dancing, swirling faster and faster. I'm dizzy and my nose aches. The cacophonous sounds of a crying baby hover in the corners of the room, as dark shapes appear at the windows. The laughter grows louder, as the flames from the stove escape, and the walls of the room are engulfed by fire. Everyone runs out, grabbing Mama, who is screaming "*KICSIKEM*!...MY LITTLE ONE!...ANTON, FIND ME!"

I awakened with a start to the misty figures of Shev and Vasily looking down at me. The sun was high in the sky. I had slept for 30 hours. The first words that greeted me were those of Shev.

"Hark, our young squire emerges from the dark night of his soul; and neither head nor heart shows the mark of a hole. Welcome back. I see you've escaped the sentencing fires of Torquemada."

Not to be outdone, Vasily took his turn and stammered,

"Anton, n…n-one of this is your, so you see, your f…f-ault. I want to tell you this is not your t…t-ime to die. The numbers are not yours; the date is not right. Today is the t…t-enth, so you see, a number of order in the universe. It is the most perfect number, and the day that you cannot d…d-ie, Anton! Yesterday, your number was nine, your d…d-ay of pain and sadness. But, so you see, today, you have too much to d…d-o."

With uncharacteristic impatience, Shev proclaimed,

"Oh pish posh, you pop-eyed arithromancer, spare us your tiresome theories of making numerical sense out of nonsense."

Not to be silenced when he felt he had something vitally important to say, Vasily continued,

"And now we have more c…coprolite from the mad m…m-onk, and so it is. What would you offer, monk, more d…d-rivel about your gospels according to libations and flatulence?"

"Better a concerto trumpeted by my farts, than more of your numerological schemozzle," scoffed Shev.

"STOP!" I tearfully wailed. "THIS," motioning around me, "AND BOTH OF YOU ARE DRIVING ME MAD!….I believe that I have poisoned my brain with this tea that has gone bad. I do not believe either of you is real, but I fear even more that you might be. None of this makes sense. But…there is nothing here. THEY'RE ALL GONE! And I cannot stay and cannot listen to you poison my brain more with this talk of numbers and dead poets! Yet, I still fear there are those who wish to do me harm. Luka and his dark spies from Radivilov will try to find me. Glagolev knows where I am. We – err, I…can't remain here. I must go…but now, I know what *we* must do."

PART III

A SUTTAGO ROMANI

A solitary journey with one's ghosts makes for a crowded and noisy road
~ Nicolai Keloskovich

CHAPTER 9

Gypsy Song

Even without this dream to reset my course, I realized I had to look for Mama. I had no one – no Mama, no Nadya, no Papa, and…no Chaim. I had no purpose or direction. Except for the time I angrily confronted and questioned Nanya, I had never even spoken Mama's name. I had removed that important and painful complication from my mind. True, as a boy, I had wandered the village searching for her, thinking that by covering myself in mud, I could magically summon her back. Only by narrowing my focus and tightening the gears and springs in my mind did I manage to remove all thoughts, memories, and yearnings for her. Now, I *needed* to find Mama.

I planned to head north to Brest and then travel west by train to Budapest. From there, I would find a village called Felsögalla where I would look for my uncle Andras. I had no idea how I would find him or if he was still alive, but I had to try.

Traveling west frightened me because I would be returning to the eastern front, the land of death where I vowed never to return. I contemplated the dangers. Knowing that the dark Serbian assassins were hunting me, I feared traveling through the front would expose me to Russian, Austro-Hungarian, and Serbian killers. But, I had no other choice. Remaining in

|119|

Russia meant being taken by soldiers who saw all Jews as German spies. I needed to take the chance, but I was not without certain advantages. First, I had my uniform. It was tattered, dirty, and rank; but I could find a stream and wash it properly. I would wear that uniform when wanting to travel without attracting unwelcome attention. I also needed another set of clothes to blend in with regular folk who were not in the army. With the rubles I had carefully stowed in my knapsack, I would purchase suitable attire of a common man.

I decided that it was still safest to travel by night, and I felt most secure on foot. It would be a long walk to Brest, but I had become accustomed to lengthy marches. I didn't want to admit another advantage I might also have. Though I hated to think of "my ghosts" as assets – for they continued to annoy me with their chatter – I also found them a distraction and began to view them as companions. Sometimes, one or the other said something useful. I became less unnerved by their sudden appearance and less concerned if they were real or illusory. No longer embarrassed that others would view me as the village lunatic, I often openly whispered responses to Shev and Vasily's blather.

Walking backward no longer seemed necessary. It slowed my pace, and I was less concerned about keeping an eye on the ghosts. I continued to keep the pistol close because I was certain the Serbians were stalking me. Before arriving in Kamenetz, I went to the river to clean my foul smelling uniform and remove the war stains from my skin. Traveling by night gave me the whole day to dry my uniform by sun on the rocks.

Kamenetz looked much as it did the last time I was there. I knew where to buy food and other supplies. I found a tailor shop and bargained for damaged and flawed clothing. I thought of visiting old Chazanovich, who had tried to cheat me when I sold Papa's LeCoultre. I would go to him and demand its return! If the greedy old bastard refused, I would show him my pistol. My foolish bravado was quickly silenced by a useful intrusion of the ghosts. When the thought of threatening old Chazanovich with violence came to mind, I heard the voice of Shev.

"Young Squire, would you believe that it was Napoleon who said, 'There are only two forces in the world, the sword and the spirit. In the long run the sword will always be conquered by the spirit.' You and I have seen where the sword takes us, and we know that is not your path."

Like a wandering pilgrim, I continued forward until I reached the outskirts of Kamenetz. At the train station, I bought a ticket to Brest and planned to continue my journey to Krakow and Budapest. Memories of my fateful encounter with the foul-breathed sergeant at the train station reminded me that it was time to change into my military garb. In my weathered Imperial uniform, others would leave me alone, assuming I was returning to the front to fight for the glory of the homeland.

After replenishing my supplies, I boarded the train for the short journey to Brest. Upon arrival there, I puchased a ticket to Budapest by way of Krakow. As I approached the platform, I heard music and a soft, lilting voice singing in a language I recognized. A crowd gathered to listen. I saw a young girl wearing a long, brightly colored skirt. Long black hair flowed down her back; her dark eyes danced as her voice held me captive. I surrendered my attention, watching her sway while she played a balalaika. Deep within, the Hungarian words I had learned so long ago came back. *Idövel Jobban Leszeck.* Where had I heard them?....Then, I remembered, "I can be better with time." This was the song Mama used to sing!

> After a lifetime of losing the light
> It's hard not to feel like a bird without flight
> But I will be better tomorrow
> And I will be better with time
> Shedding my skin while praying
> For more

Watching my ghosts fall silent to the floor
In my house there is a tree
Her brittle limbs a reflection of me
She drops her leaves with every move
But give her time and new life blooms.
I will be better tomorrow
I will be stronger with time

When she finished, people moved away. An older woman put two coins in a tin and murmured, "Lovely voice but didn't understand a word." With tears streaming down my cheeks, I reached into my knapsack and fished out a hand full of ruble notes. I accidentally bumped the man next to me, and the notes spilled onto the platform for everyone to see. I quickly gathered them up and placed ten rubles in her tin. She looked and nodded gently in appreciation. As I tried to stuff the rest back into their hiding place, I spotted two brutish men moving toward the girl. The taller one with bad skin put his large paw on her sleeve and said, "A lovely little songbird but is she a tiger as well?"

Then the other one moved behind her and crowed, "Here, gypsy, come with us and we will make you sing songs of pleasure from our cocks."

I watched as she slapped the first man's hand away, while the other man grabbed her from behind. My mind went blank. In an instant, I was holding Luka's pistol at the back of the second man's head. This time, *my* words, *my* voice, spoke with an intensity I barely recognized as my own, "LET…HER… GO!"

By now, I had seen fear in men's eyes too many times. I glared at the frightened cowards as they backed away, just as the train pulled up to the platform. In the commotion, the gypsy girl disappeared into the crowd. There was nothing more to do but board the train for Krakow.

Once seated on the train, my ghosts engaged me in a lively trialogue about the events on the platform. First, it was Shev. "Your mama's song stirred valor in you heart and lit an inferno in your gut, young Squire. You *will* be stronger in time. Bravo!"

Then Vasily responded, "T…t-hat was very brave, Anton. I c…c-ould tell you were frightened, but the young women n…n-needed help too."

Shev added, "I think it took the magic of femininity to help our young squire summon his stuffings and stand up to the ruffians. Whatever the source for your spirit, I'm inspired by your courage, Squire."

With excitement in my voice, I eagerly whispered, "I don't know why I stepped forward. I hadn't planned. She was so young and there was something, I don't know what, so familiar about her."

"T…t-he song she sang, and that's what it is, Anton. I want to tell you that I c…c-ounted three verses. The t…t-rinity of the triangle of t…t-ime. Past, present, and future. You can become b…b-raver with time."

Oblivious to my surroundings, I whispered loudly with Shev and Vasily for much of the journey to Krakow. My spirited debate with the ghosts took on a dialectial quality, ranging from whether it was right to search for Mama or more sensible to rebuild my life in Zastavia; whether it was bravery or foolishness that led me to risk my life on the platform; and, whether the gypsy girl had finally awakened a humanity within, or, according to Shev, simply "stirred a longing in your loins, Squire."

When we reached Krakow, I knew I had an hour before finding my next train to Budapest. I thought it a good time to slip away and change my clothes. Better not to be wearing a Russian uniform as we entered the enemy homeland. I found a room in which to change and went to find something to eat. When I rounded a corner, I ran headlong into the two hooligans from the platform, who had apparently followed me off the train. With a quick jab, the bad-skinned one punched me in the gut, knocking me windless. I fell to my knees, as the other kicked me in the head, laying me out flat. I was barely consciousness but heard one say, "You saw all those rubles he has. We'll take those *and* his pistol. Then finish him off."

The other swine began to dump the contents of my knapsack to the ground and said,

" Let's see how brave you are now, moron!" All my worldly goods spilled out, as the two dropped to their haunches and sifted through my possessions. One stuffed my rubles in his shirt, while the other began to undo my carefully wrapped packet of watches.

While holding up the Vacheron, he claimed gleefully, "Shit, this scum is rich; and now, Deitric, so are we!" He put the watches in his pocket and then pulled out Mama's inkblot. Gazing at it quizzically, he tossed it aside. In a derisive tone, he sneered, "Just smudges of filth; he used it to wipe himself."

I tried to protest but couldn't speak. My left eye was swollen shut and my nose throbbed. Pulling myself up to my knees, I watched with one good eye as the bastards were suddenly halted midsentence, falling limply to the ground. It had been done silently and was over in less than a second. Both had silver daggers sticking out from their backs. Neither man moved. I'd seen that look too many times. They'd been killed instantly, surprised by the suddenness of their demise. I pulled my head around to see the young gypsy girl kneeling to pull the daggers from their backs, wiping the blood on the men's pant legs. As if speaking to herself, the girl spit the word *Gadje,* and said, "Two less bad mens to mistreat Romani."

I wheezed, "You…! The gypsy girl…playing the balalaika."

She helped me to my feet and, using a mixture of Russian, Hungarian, and Ukrainian words, softly replied, "Not gypsy, Romani. Not girl, em, woman. And not balalaika, mandolin. And you are welcome." She helped me to a sitting position, gathering my possessions and re-wrapping my watches.

She fetched the discarded inkblot, inspecting it closely. Motioning to the felled thugs behind her, she said, "We must go."

She asked where I was headed and took me to board the train to Budapest. Following closely behind me, she helped me sit and took the seat across from me. She pulled cloth from her satchel, sprinkled it with ointment, and dabbed the abrasion on my face. After a moment of awkward silence, I spoke, "I'm Anton, Anton Zellinsky. I'm going to find my uncle…. in a village called Felsögalla. Oh, and thank you."

She studied me for a moment, tilting her head the side. Narrowing her dark cobalt-colored eyes, she placed her hand on her chest and responded, "Katarina. Kata. *Nais Tuke.* It mean, em….'I thank you too.' And you, I think I call '*A Suttago*'." She smiled and explained in fragmented Russian-Ukrainian and Hungarian how she'd boarded the train in Brest after me. Watching from the back of the car, she assumed that my lively, hush-toned conversation must have meant I was with others. When she realized I was alone and talking only to myself, she decided to call me the "Whispering Man," "*A Suttago*." A moment of embarrassment silenced me, but I was also flattered that she had taken notice and adopted a pet name for my idiosyncrasy.

We sat together on the long journey to Budapest, stopping briefly at countless small towns along the way. During that time, I assumed the role that Vasily had taken the day we met. Yearning to connect and pour out my life to a living person, I shared a great deal, while she spoke very little. When she spoke, her words were filtered through five languages – fragments of Russian, with a sprinkling of Ukrainian, along with many Hungarian expressions that were beyond my comprehension. Mostly, she spoke in her Romani tongue, which was completely foreign to me. When we did not understand each other's words, we gestured and pantomimed. Despite the linguistic thicket, when my monologue shifted to more of a dialogue, we somehow managed to understand most of what the other had to say.

I found Kata enchanting and mesmerizing; yet her haunting opaqueness unnerved me as well. It is understandable that I might become quickly attached to someone who had just saved my life, but there was something more.

"The song you sang at the train platform, I've heard that before. When I was small, my mother would sing that to me. I remember now, *Idövel Jobban Leszeck*. Until I heard your voice, singing those words, I had forgotten it completely."

Kata smiled quizzically, "Your anya, mother, sang that song for you? Em…a Romani woman, no?"

I nodded slightly but couldn't say much more because I knew so little about Mama. I told about how she disappeared one night, how she had become strange after Papa and Chaim returned from Donesk. Then, I talked about Nadya, her love of small and helpless creatures, and how good she was to me.

"She called me '*Pidkydanya* or *Pidkya*.' Nanya told me it was a Ukrainian name, but I never knew what it meant. Mama called me her '*Kicsi*.'"

Kata squinted at the name "*Pidkya*," as if the word meant something to her. Then, her eyes softened as she softly repeated the name "*Kicsi*." "Ah… you were her small love. Em, her little one."

I told her about Papa and his watchmaking, about my golden brother, and how I had thought I wanted to be like Papa, a great watchmaker. But now, I was not so sure. I wasn't ready to talk about the trenches and the horrors of Tannenberg. Though she had observed my whispering, I wasn't ready to tell her who I was whispering to. Not yet. At some point, I grew wary that I had given too much away. I had forgotten that there were spies who had vowed to find and kill me. As enlivening as it felt to speak so openly, I suddenly feared that I had revealed too much to this dark-eyed stranger with her siren song.

We were instructed to get off our train in Ruzomberek because the tracks up ahead had been damaged by artillery fire. This meant securing tickets on a train to Bánska Bystrica, where we would have to spend the night before catching another train to Budapest. When we approached the ticket counter in the station, Kata, speaking Hungarian, initiated the transaction. A bored-looking ticket woman wearing an ill-fitting uniform processed our travel vouchers. Eyeing Kata suspiciously, the ticket woman moved her coin purse closer to where she sat. Her words had a derisive tone, as she addressed Kata in a cutting manner. When I stepped forward to ask how much this detour would delay our journey, she became more civil and said we should expect a day, maybe two, before they could repair the tracks that the "vile Cossacks had destroyed." Kata later translated this.

I was quieter during the short trip to Bánska Bystrica, in part because I began to feel the exhaustion of my autobiographical soliloquy, but more because I was convinced that I must be more careful. Though it was not a voice I recognized, I heard a whispering to "Be cautious, you rock-handed fool. Hold your worthless tongue. You've said too much already." Kata watched me, as if she had somehow sensed my sudden distance and reserve.

We left the train in Bánska Bystrica under a cloud-covered sky in search of a place to stay. This would have been the logical, and wiser, place to bid her farewell; but my attraction was stronger than my wariness. We walked side by side, and without exchanging words, found a small hostel where we reserved a room…together. I had more than enough money to pay for the room and motioned that I wanted to buy her a meal after she had saved my life. Kata nodded, her spangled gold earrings making a soft clanking sound, as she eagerly led the way to an inn.

The streets were crowded, filled with soldiers and couples out for a late afternoon stroll. It had been more than a day since my last meal, and I was famished. We approached an old inn, and Kata motioned that this would be a good place. "Not all inns, em allow Romani. This one, good."

Inside, it was dark and had an enticing and intoxicating aroma. We chose a small table just outside the inn. When Kata realized I could not read the menu, she motioned that she would order for us. She asked for a bottle of *pálinka*, which had a fermented., fruity flavor. The taste of the alcohol on my tongue instantly brought back images of sitting with Shev and Vasily that afternoon in Neidenburg, which seemed a millennium ago. Quickly ejecting the images before they blossomed as memories, I watched as a kindly old woman brought out dish after dish. We started with *lángos*, a fried, bread with cheeses and garlic bits. Another dark-complected woman conversed with Kata and smiled as she brought two large tureens, which she called "*halászlé*." This was a thick, spicy broth with chunks of fish. The heavy use of paprika gave the dishes a bright red color, but serendipitously, also acted as a salve for my aching nose and swollen eye. Kata motioned to the matron for another carafe of *pálinka*, which the old woman brought out with a thick vegetable stew called *lecsó*. The hint of cardamom instantly reminded me of stews Nadya used to make in the winter. The *pálinka* temporarily quieted my worries, making it easier to share more about my childhood in Zastavia. I even told her about drawing horses as a young boy.

Kata, who had shared very little up to this point, told me her parents had been killed. I didn't exactly follow the details but saw sadness in her face as she talked about her *anya* and grandmother, her *púridaia*. She told how members of her family were gathered up and taken to ghettos, where all Romani were made to stay. I thought of the shtetls in my country and how we were both part of a people, despised and reviled by so many in our own lands. Kata told me that she and her brothers eventually escaped from the ghettos. She'd lost all contact with them and managed to survive on the street playing music. Kata said that she'd learned long ago to protect herself from *gadje* seeking to hurt young Romani women. She saw that I didn't understand the word *gadje* and said, "*Gadje* people not Roman. They bad mens that hate Romani."

Along with another bottle of *pálinka,* the matron served *gúlyas,* another deep red-colored stew filled with meat and vegetables. With each bite of this savory meal, my clogged nose began to clear. With each sip of *pálinka,* I spoke more freely and began to laugh. Kata's face brightened. Her stern countenance gave way to a broad smile and playful laughter. After a momentary pause, she grew more serious.

"*A Suttago,* em, who your whispers are for? Who…follow you where you go? Tell Kata."

Too soon, I thought. Although the *pálinka* had loosened my tongue, I was not ready to tell her about Tannenberg, the deaths of Shev, Vasily, and my killing….

"They're mutterings to the wind. Nothing more. It's just what I do. When the timing of a watch is wrong, the movement of the tiny gears is off. My words are like that…off."

An uneasy quiet descended upon our table, as the old woman brought a moist sweet cake topped with chocolate, raisins, and walnuts, which she called *sómloi galuska.* With this dessert and a tray of cookies, she brought a small bottle of an herbal aperitif. Unfortunately, the honeyed layers of the *sómloi* and the bitter sweetness of the liqueur could not lift the curtain of discomfort that had fallen. Kata and I exchanged awkward glances while spooning the sponge cake.

Suddenly, we were distracted by sounds of music. We turned our heads toward an off key military melody in the distance. A small crowd had gathered on the street adjacent to our table to greet a twilight parade honoring octogenarian military heroes from the surrounding hamlets. Craning our necks, we saw a group of twenty or so old men and women dressed in uniforms, some too tight, others too loose, marching in shuffled cadence to the disharmonious sounds of a euphonium, tuba, and drum.

Out front, a somber-looking man wearing a bright colored sash led the procession. On a leash were his two small terriers, both dressed in matching military regalia. The scene had a surreal quality. We fixed our attention on the lead dog, which wore sergeant's stripes on his tiny military coat. Suddenly, the rascal broke loose, and the old man began chasing him around the procession. Soon, the other terrier was loose as well, running after his companion. All the while, the procession of old soldiers carried on as if nothing had happened, even though its leader was weaving in and out of the lanes. Then, the first dog in the sergeant's smock ran out in front of the old veterans, and, as if on cue, squatted to defecate in front of the procession. All marching stopped, as the little canine NCO finished his business. When the old man in the sash came over to grab the pup, he stepped firmly in the muck that his little dog had left in the street.

Kata and I turned to each other, and after a moment of stunned silence, exploded in laughter at the comedy we had just witnessed. I suppose there was really nothing that funny about the event – older patriots marching to the beat of a drum; a small dog dressed ridiculously as a soldier doing what dogs do. But any rational explanation couldn't stop the laughter that erupted in that moment. The contagion of seeing each other doubled over prolonged the hilarity of the moment, aided, of course, by the alcohol we had consumed. This small dog had provided a welcome respite from the heaviness we had felt moments before.

When our laughter subsided, we signaled to each other that it was time to leave. I had consumed so much alcohol that I stumbled out of the inn. Now, everything seemed funny – my staggering gait, remnants of the parade, and what was left of the little dog's deposit in the street. Our laughter carried us back to our hostel where I tripped on the steps and fell to my knee. The pain was instant, but the fall provided an additional source for my laughter. Kata steadied me as we entered our room, and I fell onto the hard bed. I watched her take off her boots and gold earrings, then remove the multiple layers of her flowing skirts. The room began to spin, and I thought I would be sick. I felt Kata removing my shoes and trousers, but that is all I remember before passing out.

My sleep was fitful, filled with nightmares that seemed to go on for hours. Marching down dusty trails, obnoxious music behind, suddenly interrupted by the sounds of incoming artillery. Running, stumbling, and tumbling into ditches filled with excrement. Running faster, picking up a rifle and stopping to fire it at the black shapes that were gaining on me. Each time I stopped to pull the trigger, the weapon would not fire. The battle sounds grew louder. Screaming men called out for their mothers; babies cried; and there were more ear-shattering sounds of enemy fire with branches cracking and falling all around me. Then, Chaim running up behind. I turn and pull the trigger and the rifle emits a horrible blast. More screams and explosions. "Run, run…RUUUUNNNN!! NO, NO…GET OUT!! I DIDN'T MEAN TO!! CHAIM…CHAIM!!

"Shuhh, Shuhh. Ok now, em, *Suttago*. Safe, safe…Anton. Shuuussh… Shusssh…*Kicsi*. It ok now." Kata held my head on her lap. "Shuuushh. Ok, Ok, *Kicsi*."

My shirt and bed coverings were drenched. Tears streamed down my face, as I sobbed wordlessly. "I…I….Kata…I…."

"Shuush, it ok. Sleep. Safe now, Anton." And she began to sing softly.

I woke in the empty room with the sun streaming in. My head pounded, my nose was congested, and my knee ached where I had fallen in my drunken stupor. Dried blood stained the bed covers. My trousers lay next to my boots. No sign of Kata. I sat up quickly, my head throbbing, and reached for my rucksack. Digging, I clawed through the few clothes and found the pistol, the wrapped watches, and Mama's folded blot of ink. At the bottom were the rubles I had attempted to hide. I felt a moment of shame for giving into the whispering voices warning that she would drug me and steal my possessions. At that moment, Kata opened the door, carrying a carafe of strong kávé.

We exchanged few words. Kata wore a look of sympathy and concern, while I avoided looking her in the eye. She had been to the ticket office and learned that the train to Budapest was still not running. "They say tomorrow maybe. Here, em, you drink and feel better." She pulled three leaves from her pouch and crushed them into the mug she passed to me.

The taunting voices were relentless that day, cursing my stupidity and warning that my life was in danger. The thickly accented voice whispering, "Killer…Killer…Kill er…Kill her…Kill her now before she kills you." I covered my head with the pillow to drown out the sounds. "NO! NO!"

Kata sat motionless and began to sing again, gently playing notes on her mandolin. I drifted off, dreaming this time of Shev and Vasily. We were sitting together talking; or they were talking, and I was listening.

"Squire, have you no trust? Mind the words of your countryman Chekov, who wrote that 'you must trust and believe in people or life becomes impossible.' You suspect all who show you kindness to be spies and agents. In so doing, young Squire, you insure that you will end up alone."

"Anton, I b…b-elieve the monk to correct. Remember, she s…s-aved you."

"No, no, no, no, NO!" I woke with a start and sat up, then fell back. Kata was still at my side. The sun was beginning to set. Slowly, she moved closer, climbed onto the bed, and curled up, laying her head on my chest. I smelled her skin, a rose-oiled scent, mixed with sweat from the heat of the day and night before. I matched my breathing to hers, as she drifted off. I put my arm around her. She awoke and inched even closer. I felt her beating heart, as she leaned her head back and gazed deeply into my eyes.

I had no experience with what I imagined was about to take place. Flashing back to distant memory. I was eight or nine and overheard Chaim's loutish friend Igor Blinovsky boast about his sexual discoveries; and how with a willing girl, "Your body will know what to do. No lessons; it's natural because we are all just animals, like old Kruehke's goats."

Igor was wrong. I did not know what to do. Yes, some things did happen naturally; but I needed Kata to show me what to do. And she did. She kissed my face and then my mouth. The taste of her lips lingered. What remained of our clothes fell to the floor. The touch of her skin was silken. The outline of her breast formed a tender arc in the dimming light. Then, our movements, which began tentatively and gently, became more certain, forceful, and passionate until a feverish explosion of pleasure. My body trembled, then she held me tightly, kissed my brow, and fell asleep in my arms.

Next morning we woke, dressed, packed our meager belongings, and walked to the train station. We bought some croissants and kávé and waited for our train to Budapest. We boarded and Kata sat across from me. With the motion of the train, she leaned her head against the window and fell asleep. I could still smell her on my skin. I watched her for several minutes, fighting the thoughts that were beginning to take form in my mind. I knew what I must do. When she awakened, I would tell her everything.

After she opened her eyes, I said that there were things I needed to tell her. Caught between a yearning to pour out everything about my life to this enchanting woman, and a fear to share anything at all with this dangerous stranger, I began to speak in a halting manner. Over the next hour, words would become caught in my throat at one moment, only rush out in the next.

I told her about my recurring childhood dreams of crying babies and distant black shapes that had been infiltrated by nightmares of the war. I shared stories about my mud-filled days after Mama disappeared, and how I tried resurrect what little sense of self I had by learning to make watches, hoping this would make Papa see me. I confessed that I had attempted to run away at the train station in Brest Litovsk, wanting the soldiers to conscript poor farm boys and leave me alone. I told her how my nose was broken and that I'd been assigned to dig latrines and burn shit. Finally, and with great difficulty, I told her about my irrepressible Shev and Vasily and how they had died horrific deaths. Then, I said that they continued to haunt and guide me.

"They are the ghosts I whisper with. They have tormented me with their noisy prattle, scared me with their phantom appearance, and made me believe that I have gone completely mad. But these dead voices have served as my counsel and constant companions. How mad and sad is this?"

Several minutes must have passed before I began speaking again. Kata remained transfixed. I told her how I had returned to Zastavia hoping to reclaim a life of innocence, pretending that I could reset the time to the way it was before all these terrible things happened. I recounted my backward steps to Zastavia, a lunatic traveling at night with vines wrapped around my head, and how Zastavia had burned to the ground. I told her I had decided to end my life that day but fell asleep instead and had a dream that Mama was calling for me to come find her.

I told her about my saviors, Luka and Glagolev, but how I feared they had turned against me and had dispatched spies to punish me.

"Punish you, *Suttago*? Em….For what crimes you make? Staying alive, while others get killed? Punish you for trying survive? What crimes you do?"

Suddenly, I was gripped by a fear that I had revealed too much to this stranger asking too many questions about my crimes. My mind was now in retreat, seeking a trench in which to hide and evade the searchlight of her interrogation. I felt a wall rise up between us. There would be no more confessions, no words about a lost brother, and nothing of that fog-encased night and a blast from the rusted barrel of that gun. No more whispers about my past. My crimes would remain my own.

My head hurt and nose burned. For the remainder of the trip, I scanned the horizon for dark shapes and heard taunting whispers accusing me of being duped by Serbian gypsies. I shut my eyes trying to silence the noise in and outside of my head. When I opened them, I saw Shev sitting next to Kata as she gazed thoughtfully out the window.

"Oh young Squire, how difficult that must have been to begin a confession to this young woman, only to stop yourself out of false fears. Your heart could surely be lightened, yet you refuse to release what you've kept hidden. Come now, *A Suttago*, what crimes you make?"

I began to protest; but, as quickly as he'd appeared, Shev was gone. The train suddenly came to a stop. Kata looked at me and said, "We, em, arrive Budapest, now."

It was midday, and the sun was bright. With a local map we found Felsögalla, 45 km northwest. Agreeing that we could make our way by foot, we bought some bread, cheese, and water for our canteens. I suggested it might be safer to travel by night, but Kata assured me we would be safe walking together in the light of day. That night, we found a place to camp. I made a small fire, while Kata strummed her mandolin. I closed my eyes and fell into a fitful sleep.

The following day, we reached the outskirts of Felsögalla as the sun began to set. The streets were deserted. I followed Kata, who seemed to know where to go. Winding our way through narrow alleys, I heard music in the distance. As we drew nearer to the music, people stood in doorways of small homes. The music grew louder, and soon we were surrounded by Romani of every age, all of them talking, dancing, or feasting. Burning torches emitted a flaxen hue, which illuminated their colorful garb.

We found a place to sit, then Kata pulled me close to her. She said softly, "*Suttago*, I want, em…help you. I know Romani people. I go ask to find Uncle Andras." I felt a confusing mix of warmth and wariness, gratitude and suspicion. I had allowed this dark-eyed woman, a stranger, into my life. I had opened my heart and spilled some of my secrets. Now, she was helping me search for the family I had never known.

Kata told me to wait for her there and then left. I sat as others passed by. People took note that I was a stranger, dressed differently, clearly someone from the outside. Yet, despite being a, what was the word Kata used, a *gadje,* my dark skin matched the coloring of those around me.

Minutes stretched into hours. The streets were nearly deserted when Kata returned with two young men following her. A tall man spoke words to his companion, who looked around furtively. Then, the taller man stepped forward, flashed a wide grin and placed his hand on his heart,

"*Vártunk az simensa." Fogadtatás."*

Kata looked bewildered, turned to me, and translated, "He say, em, 'Welcome, cousin. We been…*waiting* for you?'"

CHAPTER 10

Kiss of the Tschandala

I ask those reading to indulge a slight deparature. There was an evil man who changed everything. My story is incomplete without including him. Over the years, I've researched his personal background and family history. I traveled to his decaying estate, gained access to his library and journals, and spoke with his former servants. I have taken liberties in imagining this man – his appearance, demeanor, and the hatred he held in his heart so many years ago.

He rose at sunrise, as he always had, saying his rosary on the veranda while sipping his strong kávé. The silk cuffs of his plush, blood red velvet robe had become frayed and stained. His slender fingers with their long nails moved from one bead to the next, pausing momentarily to push back his thick mane of white hair, while his hounds chased rats along the floor.

On cue, Jazmin brought in a plate of buttered toast and three small sausages, his usual morning meal. She bent low to place the silver tray on the table, the fear in her eyes betraying what he always convinced himself was there instead – seductiveness and desire, no doubt. He watched as she refilled his chipped Lustre Pink teacup, his fingers moving up the rosary. Jazmin turned and quietly walked away as he traced her form with his pale, watery-blue eyes, moving from her dark hair to the chestnut-toned skin of her neck. Usually such images would give rise to unbidden thoughts that would linger until he quieted them with the leather strands of his cattails. But today was different.

He hadn't been able to silence his thoughts about the news he'd received the day before. A Russian boy, about 20, asking about the Vadoma family and the gypsy woman in Felsögalla. He had waited for years for news of this event, relying on his network of loyal minions in the villages around Bánhida and Alsógalla. Feeling certain that the day would eventually come when the child would return, asking about the "gypsy witch" and Hadik's son.

Thoughts of Tamás, his lost son who strayed and betrayed generations, filled him with shame and rage. He had not lived through a single day that the pain of his lost Tamás did not intrude and poison his mood. No parent ever recovers from the death of a child; but when that child has betrayed the family ethos, traditions, and moral values, the loss is intolerable.

That's how it was for his dear Liliana. How she grieved the betrayal by their oldest son, who succumbed to the song and lustful spell of that "gypsy whore," and then turned his back on his family. The grief over his death cut a deep wound in her heart, but the shame of having a son who impregnated and abandoned his family for a "filthy gypsy wench" is what finally killed. "My dear, Liliana," the old man whispered to himself, "but she was weak, like Tamás." She never had the strength to do what was necessary. He knew that one day that child might come looking for answers about his father, and the bitter old man would do what he had been planning for 20 years.

Count József Hadik lived on land owned by his family for generations going back to his great grandfather Field Marshal Victor Hadik de Rutak, who eviscerated the Prussians during the Seven Years' War. For generations, the Hadiks, with their Austrian brothers, had led the campaign to keep Sopron and the Burgenland free of "gypsy swine." But infestations are not so easily terminated, thought Hadik, and that's how it was with the gypsies in Hungary. They were worse than vermin. Genetically endowed criminals, they abducted children, swindled good Christians, worshiped the devil, and sent their whores to seduce weak men, like Tamás.

Hadik glanced over to the book he had taken from his mahogany bookcase yesterday after Djoivik brought him the news. Strindberg's *Tschandala* had become his bible, with its allegoric tale of a righteous man's triumph over "gypsy dogs." Hadik had placed Strindberg's masterpiece on top of his other literary guide, "Thus Spoke Zarathustra." Fully embracing Nietzsche's concept of the *Ubermensche,* Hadik viewed the gypsies as his biological inferiors. It was Strindberg, though, who touched his core. One passage, stood out for Hadik, after Tamás had fallen under the spell of the gypsy *szajha* whore. The book was opened to the passage that described the reaction of the protagonist, Master Törner, after his forbidden bestial encounter with the young gypsy girl. Strindberg's words spoke to him in a deeply personal way. Hadik had long ago underlined the passage

> He had embraced an animal, and after the embrace, the animal kissed him like a cat, and he turned away as if he feared that his soul would meet an animal soul on those lips, as if he feared breathing in impure air.

The Count possessed intimate knowledge of the degenerative lustfulness of which Strindberg wrote. His lost Tamás had come under that animal spell and had breathed in the impure air, only to exhale a foul cloud that suffocated his family with a shameful taint. But deep within, Hadik held an even darker secret that he'd concealed and spent at lifetime attempting to expel. Those few who'd learned the scandalous truth of his animal weakness long ago with his own tschandala, Zsófia, had been silenced forever. Hadik had seen to that, and his cattails were usually sufficient to banish distant traces of those sinful memories from his mind.

Soon Djoivik and Horvàt would come for plans and instructions. They were loyal lieutenants, who shared his hatred of Jews and gypsies. Like Hadik, they were men of action, who did what was necessary. Time and again, Hadik called upon them to control the pestilence in the surrounding villages and make sure that "gypsy vermin," whom Hadik was certain were spies for the Turks, stayed in their ghettos or, if necessary, disappeared during the night. They would carry out Hadik's orders and make sure that any trace of this genetic stain of a Russian boy, with his link to the Count, would be eradicated.

The sun was beginning to rise over the vast lands surrounding his estate. Count József Hadik pushed back his hair, finished his rosary, and muttered the words, "Thy will be done."

Familija Romani

After addressing me as his cousin, the first man stepped forward and embraced me warmly, repeating his greeting, *Fogadtatás*. He was a few inches taller than me. The son of a Greek Romani father and Portuguese mother, his full name was Zifploto Zitakis Szueta Zeekko, but everyone called him, "Zifi." His shoulder length hair was velvet black; his eyes, deep-set and cat-like. He flashed an eager, white-toothed smile that brought to mind a full moon rising on a dark night. He wore a scarlet and blue headscarf. From one ear dangled a large golden earring, which accented his strong, square jaw. Broad shoulderd and muscular, Mr. Zeekko wore a tight black vest against his bare skin. A thick brown belt fastened his green trousers, which ballooned loosely before tucking into his badly worn boots. He spoke rapidly in a deep, raspy voice, frequently grinning broadly and laughing a bit too easily as he spoke to Kata, while looking back at me.

His shorter companion was called "Tobbar." In one hand, he held the remains of a hand-rolled tobacco stick, in the other, a half-empty flagon of wine. He wore a black skullcap and a dirty, unbuttoned shirt, and baggy gray trousers. Tobbar was barefoot. Nervously glancing from side to side, I was struck by Tobbar's unusually outsized, widely-spaced teeth, which must have made secure closure of his mouth a lifelong challenge. His prominent front incisors were yellow and tobacco-stained. Where Zifi had smiled and warmly embraced me, Tobbar registered my outsider status and eyed me suspiciously as a *gadje.* Swigging from his bottle of wine, he tugged at Zifi's vest, motioning that they must go. Zifi repeatedly brushed his hand away, as he would a swarm of annoying gnats and said in harsh tones, *"Ne aggodi meg bugban,"* and then, *"Mennünk kell."* Kata whispered the translation, "He say, em…'Stop annoying me you bug.' He also say, 'We go now.'"

Later, I learned that Zifi was probably not my actual cousin, but that the Roma people considered anyone with gypsy blood a *simensa.* Because Papa was Russian and Mama Romani, I was technically a *poshrat,* or half-gypsy, but was considered extended *familija.* Zifi led us away from the open space where we'd met, down darkened alleys until we reached a small hovel, with a light shining from the window. We hesitantly followed him inside. He poured us wine and offered bread and fruit. Tobbar found a corner, stooped down on his haunches, and fixed his gaze on me, while sipping the remains of his wine. Zifi explained to Kata that it was not safe for us to be seen in open spaces. Romani had no trust for strangers, especially *gadje* and even *poshrat*, like me.

A look of concern passed Kata's face, as she further translated Zifi's words. "He also say that, em, bad *gadje* might be look for you, *Suttago.* He not say who or why they look, but he say they *gonosz*…em, how you say…evil."

Zifi told Kata they had to make some arrangements but would return tomorrow morning. My two Romani *simensa* bid us good night, leaving Kata and me alone in the dimly lit room.

❖ ❖ ❖

The whispering voices, even those of my ghosts, had been unusually silent over the past 24 hours, but that silence was broken by none other than the monk, who appeared and uttered the words,

"Aha! *Poshrat,* I always suspected as much, Squire, and now it appears that you might have found a new home. You've begun your new journey well, but remember, *Le the tacho pirrow an' its pars kaired.* 'Well begun is half-done.' Alas, sadly for me, Squire, that is the only Romani proverb I ever learned."

Then I heard the disembodied stutter from the ether, "B...b-ut, be alert, Anton. I want to tell you that the d...d-anger is real. People are like number patterns, as it is. They can fool you. Zifi seems friendly, b...b-ut his eyes are d...d-ark windows. You can't see in. And this T...t-obbar fellow looks cold and has a suspicious eye. But, do not mistake his sadness for unkind-ness. I know sadness in b...b-oys."

By now, Kata seemed to know when I was communing with my ethereal voices. I'd grow silent and look away, moving my lips and quietly muttering to the wind. The disappointment and concern in her eyes betrayed what might have been her wish that our blossoming intimacy would deliver me from my madness.

She moved to my side, and I pulled her close. We laid back on a small mat and fell asleep in each other's arms, but my dreams would not surrender to Kata's charms. I had also hoped the fever of my nightmares would be broken by what was developing between us. Shev's dead poets would have surely counseled as much. Yet, every time I succumbed to sleep, I was revisited by the cavalcade of unbidden images, dark shapes, and cacophonous sounds I had labored to stifle during the daytime. When my sleep movements became more fitful and my cries more audible, Kata gently reached for my hand, nudged me awake, and tried to quiet my anguish.

❖ ❖ ❖

Zifi arrived at sunrise with two different men at this side. He said these were his brothers, Vano and Timbo. He spoke at length with Kata, explaining his plan. Vano and Timbo looked like Zifi. Unlike the toothful Tobbar, Vano and Timbo Zeekko made welcoming eye contact, nodding a quiet greeting to their *poshrat simensa.*

After Zifi stopped speaking, Kata turned toward me; and with excitement in her voice, translated, "Zeekko say, em…he bring you to meet someone important. She, em, your mama's *nénike*….Her auntie."

Zeekko nodded eagerly at the word, *nénike*. "Baba Zsófia. We go."

A mile outside of Felsögalla, we came upon a small shack with a single window. Kata and I had followed Zifi and his brothers along a winding path, up a hill, and along a brook until we came to a clearing with this small wooden shed. A lone figure sat in a rocker on the tiny porch outside the hovel. Even from a distance, swashes of bold colors carved the outline of her scarfs and skirt against the drab exterior of her small house. As we drew near, the scent of sweet tobacco wafted in the air. She continued rocking, softly humming a haunting tune, while puffing white clouds of smoke from her pipe. She heard the sound of our steps well before Zifi announced our presence.

Baba Zsófia's skin was honey-colored and her hair snow white. The deeply etched lines around her eyes brought Nadya to mind. She wore a brilliant pink scarf with yellow, white, and pale green figures dancing throughout. The scarf became a pashmina that draped around her shoulders and fell to her waist. On each finger of her caramel-colored hands, Baba Zsófia wore large silver rings with various carvings. Like Nadya, deep veiny rivulets coursed the back of each hand. Rainbow-colored bangles circled each wrist; long beads, mostly white and gold, adorned her thin, weathered neck. On the left side of her nose was a pale-green gemstone.

She said nothing and only tilted her head slightly to the right as we stepped onto her porch. Baba Zsófia nodded as Zifi spoke but never looked directly at him. She continued to puff on her pipe and look into the distance. I moved closer and saw the milky whiteness in her eyes. Baba Zsófia was blind.

Zifi spoke to her at length, too quickly for Kata to translate his words. The old woman turned her head toward me and motioned that I approach. Hesitantly, I stepped closer. Zifi nudged me to bend down so she could reach my face with her gnarled hands. Moving her dry, rough palms around my face, her fingers tracing around my eyes, cheeks, nose, lips, and chin, Baba Zsófia sighed with a faint smile.

"So, it is you….Marina Vadoma's boy….Our *poshrat,* come home."

I was surprised that she knew I was only half Romani, that Papa was Russian. I was even more startled to learn that my blind, great aunt Baba Zsófia spoke perfect Russian.

"You must have many questions about your Mama, no?"

I quickly answered, "Yes….My whole life has been questions without answers."

After a momentary puff on her pipe, Baba Zsófia reached for my hand and said,

"Yes, my son. Yes, it is hard to live without knowing. This I know well. And because there is so much to say, I cannot tell it to you all at once. But, this is what I will do for the son of Marina Vadoma. I will tell you three stories over the next three days about your mama, who she was, and how she changed. One story each day, and then it is for you to decide what your path should be."

I looked back and motioned for Kata, who stepped forward. "Baba, will you allow my friend Kata to hear these stories?"

Baba Zsófia reached up with both hands signaling that Kata should lower her head so that Baba could touch her face. "This is only for you to say, my son, for it is your story, but yes, as you wish." Moving her hands over Kata's face, Baba Zsófia added, "She has a good mind and brave heart."

Over the next three days, we returned to visit Baba Zsófia. The Zeekko brothers accompanied us the first two days. On the third, it was only Zifi and Tobbar. Each morning, we visited the market and bought fresh fruit, salt, tobacco, and candied breads. After we arrived, the cousins took their places under a large black poplar tree adjacent to Baba's old house, while Kata and I stepped onto her small porch. Each story began with a ritualistic offering of our gifts. She would smile, put them to the side, light her pipe, and motion for us to step forward. Kata and I sat at her feet, as she rocked and spoke for hours. And so the story began on our first day.

"My son, to know your mama, Marina Vadoma, I must tell you about her family, which is your family, too, no?" Baba cleared her throat, puffed on her pipe and then continued. "You see, her mother, Evina, was my younger sister. Your mama had two little brothers, your uncles, Andras and Chal. Her papa, your grandfather, was called Danior. Though a humble blacksmith, he was a very smart, proud, and dignified man. In a different time and place, with lighter skin, perhaps, he might have even been a teacher or doctor. Who knows? When not working, he was always reading, reading everything he could find. Aye, there was not enough space for all Danior's books.

"Your grandmother was very loving and took care of the children. Marina and Andras were strong, like their papa. But poor Chal was born with crooked legs and could not walk, so your mama and uncle always pulled him around in a wagon.

"You want to know who your mama was? She was such a smart girl, like her papa. Her papa taught her to read when she was very little, so unusual for Romani children in our village. She wanted to know *everything*! Always asking, 'Why Mama?' 'What this for Papa?' 'What that mean?' Even when you gave her answers, little Marina wanted to know more.

"Then, your mama was a dancer, too. She danced even before she walked. When other little ones were taking their first steps, Marina Vadoma danced hers with the grace of a woodland nymph. Everyone expected that she would become a great dancer. But, what happened next made Marina want so much more than that.

"Your grandfather believed that Romani and *gadje* should live in peace as equals — no cruelty, no ghettos, only people living side by side. He made Roma people feel strong and proud. When your grandfather spoke in the public square, we cheered, '*Opre Roma! Opre Roma!*' This meant 'Roma Arise!' But the *gadje* saw him as a dangerous man. They tried to silence him with money first and then threats, but he said, '*Mashdar le gadjende leski shib si le Romeski zor!*' His words meant, 'Surrounded by the gadje, the Roma's only defense is his tongue!' He would not back down, your grandfather.

"You see, they feared your grandfather and said he was bad for making all Romani believe they were as good as non-Romani. One night, while everyone was sleeping, the *gadje* came to their house. They broke down the door, gathered up his books, and burned them in the street. Those devils dragged him out of the house, while your grandmother, Andras, and Marina ran behind crying. They cut out his tongue, beat him to death, and hung him from a tree like a goat to be butchered….Your grandmother, Marina, and Andras watched, choking on their screams and tears….

"Your grandmother never recovered. My poor sister was lost in grief that darkened the sun. There was only Marina and Andras to look after Chal; but, in time, he became sick and began to waste away. Healers from the villages conjured up potions of all types to restore his health, but nothing could bring life back into his eyes. Sadly, like his mama, poor Chal was lost. Within a year, we buried them both. With no one to look after the children, I brought Andras and Marina to live with me.

"All of this changed your mama. For a while, she stopped dancing. She spent her time reading the few remaining books that the *gadje* hadn't burned that night. She began to talk about becoming a healer. Some Romani girls want to be dancers or singers, but many want to become *drúkkeribén,* which means things like 'fortune-telling and spirit healing.'

But Marina was not content with old Romani ways of using charms and amulets, casting spells, or looking at gypsy cards to see into the future. No, she wanted to understand what secrets people kept hidden in their minds and hearts. It must have been because of the cruelty inflicted on her papa or the grief that took the life from her mama and little brother. Marina was determined to become a different kind of seer or healer. When she found old blots of inks and smudges, she thought that they could give her the answers. I don't know about that. Romani have used these things for many years, but your mama thought they could do more than tell someone's fortune. I think she spent her life trying to understand things about people that no one could explain.

"When she and Andras got older, I knew they would not stay. Felsögalla had too many ghosts and bad memories. They were restless, like young people get. Andras adored his big sister and would follow her wherever she went. He was interested in these things but not as much as Marina. But, he decided to go with her anyway. Marina wanted to go to places in Germany and Austria. She read books by professors who were discovering secrets in people's minds and hearts. Marina had to go learn about this, too. She told me that her blots of ink were more than tools for telling fortunes to seeing into the spirit world. She told me about a great Professor Freud who had written that the blots were tangled webs that might reveal stains and secrets inside a person's mind. This is what she wanted to know. So, they left for Wiesbaden. Like that, they were gone."

We had been listening to Baba Zsófia for hours without taking a break. Her voice grew weaker and we could see she was tired. Kata nudged me that it was time to stop. Baba nodded and replied,

"Yes, children. That was the first story of who your mama was. Come back tomorrow and I tell you more."

With that, she waved us away. Though her dead eyes did not reveal her emotions, her face showed that these stories had awakened a sadness inside.

We expressed gratitude, touched her hand, and kissed her forehead as we took our leave.

The sun was low in the sky, and the air had a chill. We walked back in silence. The Zeekkos mumbled to each other along the way. When we reached our shack, Zifi said he would fetch us at the first light of day so we could continue our stories with Baba Zsófia. There was ample wine, bread, figs, and assorted fruit; and while it was not the feast we had enjoyed in Bánska Bystrica, it was more than enough for us.

Listening for hours with rapt attention had made me weary, the emotion I felt too mixed and nuanced for words. I was grateful that Baba Zsófia had begun to introduce me to my mother, but I also felt sadness for her immense suffering as a child. I thought about Mama's song, *Idövel Jobban Leszeck,* which I'd heard Kata sing that first day on the train platform. I remembered the first verse

> After a lifetime of losing the light
> It's hard not to feel like a bird without flight
> But I will be better tomorrow
> And I will be better with time.

Mama's words captured how dark and sorrowful her life had been, but how she never gave up hope. I understood what this song must have meant to her.

Kata was unusually quiet that night. She played her mandolin, softly humming melodies that, by now, were quite familiar. There was no stove in the shed to keep us warm. The night air grew cold, so we moved closer together to warm ourselves. Our bodies responded to the closeness and touch of each other's skin. Soon, we enjoyed the harmony of a passionate embrace and the heat of the fiery dance that ensued. Later, as we lay together, the change in her breathing told me that she was asleep. I envied her for this. She lived life to the fullest; but when she closed her eyes at the end of the day, slumber came quickly, deeply, and was undisturbed, until my fitful thrashing and screaming awakened her.

That night, I hardly slept at all. My mind was awakened to so many stories and images of my mama. The scene of Baba Zsófia puffing on her pipe and telling such vivid tales about Mama – who she had been and how she changed – would not release me. But, there was something else, something on the edge of my mind that had been there even before we first arrived in Felsögalla and met Baba Zsófia….It was something about Kata.

I had opened the door and invited this stranger into my life, not only my private past and family, but to a deep yearning I'd never known was there. The thoughts and feelings it stirred brought the whispering voices, which called me a fool and warned not to trust. I waited for wise and comforting words from my ghosts. What wisdom would Shev proclaim? What sweet reassurance would Vasily stammer out? But, they remained silent. I feared I had gone too far with this sleeping woman next to me, trusted her like the innocent fool that I had always been. The sparrow was still just a sparrow. Little *Pidkya,* now inhabiting the body of a man and doing things that men did, was still the same lost boy, opening himself up and depending too much on others. In my final thoughts before succumbing to a brief sleep, with images of dark shapes and sounds of crying babes, I realized that I needed to leave Kata. I must stand on my own. The whispering voices were right. It was not safe to trust anyone. There was treachery all around. My grandfather might have trusted too much and look what happened to him.

The next day, we retraced our steps with the Zeekkos back to the small hovel in the clearing, where Baba Zsófia was waiting for us. We began again with our small offerings, which she gratefully accepted. Zifi said that he and his brothers had business in the village and would return for us later.

"My second story of your mama is from the time she and Andras returned four, maybe five years later. My memory is not what it once was. Your mama was no longer the skinny little, dancing girl, with a spark in her eyes. She came back a beautiful young woman, but the glimmer in her eyes was not there like before.

"Marina never told me as much as Andras did. He said they had first traveled to Germany, where they found a nephew of a famous doctor named Justinius Kerner. Andras said that this doctor had made and written poems about inkblots. He had preached that his blots could open doorways to the spirit world. Andras liked Kerner's nephew and would have been content to remain in Germany, but your mama grew restless. She was looking for something more and told Andras she could learn about telling fortunes and seeking spirits from old Romani fortune women.

"Marina convinced Andras to go all the way to Zurich, where she hoped to learn from Swiss professors and healers about truths hidden deep inside people's minds. She did not care about the spirit world but sought to find out what made us think our thoughts, feel our passions, and do things without knowing why. She told Andras about a great hospital with healers and men of science, who were trying to understand what went wrong in people's minds and hearts. This is where she wanted to go to learn.

"So, she left Germany; and of course, Andras followed. When they came to a place Andras called the Burghölzli, Marina wanted to become their student and attend their lectures. She heard they were interested in teaching women and believed her determined mind would convince them to say, 'Yes, you are welcome here.' But, Andras said these men laughed at your mama and said that there was no place for an uneducated peasant girl, much less, a gypsy. I think this broke her heart and crushed her spirit. Up to that time, she was such a fighter; but when they laughed and told her she was a 'silly gypsy girl,' this cut her deeply. So, she and Andras returned to Germany and eventually made their way back here."

Baba Zsófia closed her eyes and nodded off for a short while. When she awakened, she lit her pipe and continued.

"You want to know what happened when you mama came back to us? Well, I tell you. Her life changed itself around again. She began dancing and singing. I could tell that she was still not happy, but she started to live again and do things that other young Romani girls did.

"Andras lost his heart to the daughter of our neighbor Django Toth. Django had taken over as village blacksmith after your grandfather was killed. His oldest daughter, Elderia, thought Andras was very handsome. In a year's time, they married and started having babies. But, sadness seemed to follow the Vadoma family. All Elderia's and Andras' babies died when they were born. Only one son lived – Tobbar, your true cousin."

My head swirled at this news. Tobbar, the quiet chap with gigantic, tobacco-stained teeth, furtive eyes, and a half-empty flagon of wine? Not Zifi, Vano, or Timbo, but Tobbar was my blood relative! Why had he been so reserved? Zifi had embraced me warmly and welcomed me as his *simensa*, but not Tobbar.

"Many Romani men wanted to get close to Marina, but she showed no interest. Until one day, she met a young man. Finally, I thought, Marina can be happy! She had let go of her silly blots of ink and thoughts of studying secrets of the mind. She could finally be like other Romani girls – fall in love and have more babies for her Baba to take care of. Then, Andras told me an awful truth. Marina had fallen in love with the oldest son of a wealthy Count, who hated Romani. I knew the cruelty of this man, whose name was Hadik. He saw Romani as animals, vermin for his hounds to hunt. His son, Tamás, saw your mama dancing in the village market one day. If I hadn't known better, I would have believed that he'd drunk a potion to capture his heart. Whatever it was, Tamás was instantly smitten by your mama. *Gadje* did not enter our part of the village, but Tamás boldly came to see Marina every day. He brought her flowers and basketfuls of fruit and grains. Tamás did not see 'gypsy vermin' when he looked at your mama, only a beautiful girl with a sharp mind and soft voice."

Baba stopped at this point, swallowing hard. Kata got up to make some tea. I saw from the downward slant of the lines around her pale eyes that this next part of her story was going to be hard for her to tell us.

"It seemed like happiness for your mama was like delicate flakes of snow falling to the ground. They are so beautiful but last for such a short time. Then, they disappear. Her happy days with Tamás were like those exquisite snowflakes. He made her happy. But his powerful father would change all that. I *know* this man...."

Baba Zsófia stopped speaking again, pausing for several moments as if she were pushing something back into a box that had been opened.

"In his heart, dwells such evil. He was one of the men who dragged your grandfather from his home and killed him that night. When this evil man learned about Tamás and Marina, he was determined to destroy them both. But, it was too late. Their love had been sealed and your mama was with child. Both Tamás and Marina went into hiding among the Brothers of the Woodland, until your mama gave birth. The Brothers were men who lived deep within the forest, away from villages. Some were Romani. Some were ex-priests and teachers, old soldiers, and humble farmers. All had left their worldly ways behind seeking solitude and spiritual cleansing. There, they tended their gardens and practiced their spiritual ways in seclusion.

"Marina and Tamás were not safe. The Count had spies, who learned where Tamás and Marina were hiding and being protected by the Brothers. He sent his men to hunt them down. The *gadje* wolves found where they were hiding and killed many of the Brothers. Good fortune sent a blessing, for Tamás, your mama, and their baby son had escaped the night before. It was Sylvanos Zeekko, Zifi's papa, who came to tell them that Hadik's men were coming for them. He brought them two horses, and they escaped.

"What took place after that is hard to know. The Count and his men rode after Tamás and your mama with her baby. We can never know what took place. Stories have been told that Marina and Tamás outran their pursuers; but most believe they wandered into a den of hungry wolves. When I saw your mama so many years later, she would not talk about what happened. We can only guess that she and Tamás thought the dark shapes in the distance were Hadik's men, when might have really been gray wolves tracking their movements. All we really know is that poor Tamás did not survive."

It was clear Baba Zsófia was exhausted. She sat back in her rocker and shut her eyes. The second story was finished. We bent down and lightly kissed her wrinkled brow and quietly stepped off the porch. By that time, Zifi and Timbo had returned to guide us back to the village.

Neither of us slept much that night. We held each other tightly but did not share a passionate, heart-quickening embrace, as we had the night before. The weight of what we had learned was crushing for me, and I know that she felt it deeply as well.

I had a brother! Baba Zsófia had said little about this except that Mama and Tamás had left with an infant male child….Then, a long forgotten story floated to the surface of my mind. Suddenly, I recalled Nadya's story about how Mama had appeared long ago out of nowhere. I heard Nanya's voice, "One day, she was just there – a young peasant girl from Hungary with this tiny baby in her arms." I had a brother! I knew that this brother could not have been Chaim because we had different mama's. Somewhere, I had another brother! The excitement bled into confusion.

Kata had fallen asleep. As soon as I heard her heavy breathing, the whisperers intruded, mocking my stupidity, and warning me again that the wolves were out there, tracking me in their Serbian uniforms. They were coming. I must get away from this place and especially from Kata because the whisperers revealed that she had been sending encrypted signals of my whereabouts.

The next morning, I felt a hollowness in my chest. The ritual of going to the market, buying our gifts for the old woman, and trekking to her dilapidated hovel had grown tiring. Zeekko met us at the market, but on that third day, he brought only my cousin, Tobbar, who was smoking his tobacco and carrying a bottle of wine. When I saw him standing uncomfortably next to the effusive Zifi, I reached out to Tobbar, nodded, and said the words, '*fogadtatás simensa.*' He looked surprised but responded in kind.

Baba Zsófia appeared weary on our last morning with her. I couldn't be sure, but it looked like she had not moved from where we had left her the day before. She heard us approach and angled her head as we stepped onto her porch. With little fanfare and a terse greeting, she began her third story about Mama.

"Now, my final words about your mama, Marina Vadoma." She sighed heavily and lit her pipe.

"You have listened, my son, and are beginning to understand something about your mama. What I have to tell you now is not much, because I know very little. I did not see Marina for many years. What happened to her in all those years, who can say? All I know is that I became an old woman, who smokes too much tobacco. But, your mama did return again, many years later. She was not the same. Each time she came back, she was different – older, less joyful, burdened, and more distant. What more can be said. She came back, and Andras brought her to see me.

"She said, 'Baba, I must go. I have lost everything.' She cried that she had lost her *Kicsi*….Was that you?" The old woman continued without waiting for my response. "Your mama said that Andras was going to take her to find the Brothers of the Woodland once more and that maybe they could help her. I begged Andras not to go again. Though he had lost Elderia to the winter influenza, he still had a young son who needed him. But, it was no use. It had always been that wherever Marina went, Andras would follow. I think their hearts were bonded long ago after they lost their papa, mama, and little brother. In the end, they were all each other had in the world. They packed up and set out on foot in search of the Brothers. That was many years ago. Neither returned.

"Tobbar grew up without a papa. He lived with Baba until he left to live on the streets with other boys. It was sad to see him do things that give Romani bad names – drinking too much wine, stealing, and cheating people. Ayeee."

Baba Szófia wiped a tear from her eye. From the distance, Tobbar looked our way, as if Baba's sorrow had registered silently in his mind. Then, Zifi began barking something at him, knocked the bottle out of his hand, and gave him a slap across the face.

She continued, "Three stories about Marina Vadmom, your mama, in three days. Now, you know, my son. Now it is time to decide if this is what you were seeking or, like your mama, if there is more."

"And that was it, the last time I ever saw Baba Szófia. Kata and I each took one of her dried hands in ours, touched the top of her head, and bowed to gently kiss her cheeks.

I said softly, "*Nais tuke*, Auntie, my Baba. Thank you."

She looked up and said, "*Devlesa Avilan.*"

Kata's eyes spilled a tear, as she translated, "Baba say, 'It is God who brought you.'"

When we reached the village, I told Kata that I needed time to walk and clear my head. A look of concern appeared on her face, but she nodded in agreement. I wandered through the village, thinking, and trying to push it all from my mind. Where were the watches, the pins, springs, and tiny gears that helped narrow and focus mind? I needed these now, as I had 10 years ago when my mother disappeared.

My head was swirling. A brother! Mama left Zastavia one night. Why? I still didn't know why she left or who had taken her, only that she eventually returned to Felsögalla, fetched Uncle Andras, and left again. But where? What was she seeking? Baba Szófia had supplied many pieces of my puzzle. So many of my questions about my mama had been answered; but, in the end, I was left with more questions, more muddled swashes of dark ink. I remembered the words from my aunt Nadya, "Who can answer such things, *Pidkya*, who can really know."

I reached the end of an alley; and when I rounded the corner, I found Tobbar sitting by himself, smoking, and drinking a flask of wine. He saw me and stood up. Staring for a moment, he held out the flagon and motioned for me to join him. Because he had never spoken before, I had no idea that Tobbar spoke enough Russian and Hungarian that I could understand some of what he had to say.

Before this moment, I'd never imagined putting my mouth to a bottle that had touched his lips; but without hesitation, I accepted his offer for a swig of wine. It was warm, well marinated, and acrid in taste. Nonetheless, he was my cousin. The only cousins I had ever known were the faceless and nameless bunch from Rivne. But, here was Tobbar, my uncle's son. Tobbar finally broke the silence.

"Baba Szófia a wise spirit. She watch over me but not happy with Tobbar, em…what I do." Motioning to each of us, he continued, "Your *anya*, mama and my papa….You and me…*simensa*."

After a moment of uncomfortable silence to match his own, I spoke, "They left us both."

Tobbar looked away and drank more wine. "He go….Never say why…. Not say where, only that he must go watch over your mama, and I stay here with Baba. But that long time now." Shrugging and wiping his nose, he said, "Not come back to Tobbar."

Over the last year, there had been a handful of times when I found myself speaking with complete abandon. The words seemed to rush out – no filters, no anguished forethought, or rehearsal – just simple words. And this was such a moment.

"Then let's go find them. Let's find your papa and my mama!"

Tobbar looked stunned, as if the sky had turned as green as his teeth. I saw a smile in his eyes and an eager nod. "Yes, *simensa*! Yes, I go….We go. We look, your mama and my papa. We look together!"

And so a plan was hatched by these two lost boys, struggling to become men. I would have felt more confident if my true *simensa* was the bolder and seemingly more competent Zifi; but Tobbar was my cousin, and somehow, he would be my companion. We talked more about how we would set out in search of the Brothers of the Woodland, if such a group still existed. I had begun this journey after my dream in Zastavia, when Mama beckoned that I come find her. And this is what I would do.

I began walking back to the shack where I had left Kata. It was time to explain to her that I needed to continue my journey alone. For days, the whispering voices had warned me that I had to get away from her seductive charms because she would trick and betray me to the dark hunters, who followed our steps. Hadn't Zifi confirmed that they were hunting me here in Felsögalla?

As I walked, I soon realized that I was lost, going in circles. When I rounded the next corner, I was startled to see Shev sitting in a meditative pose like a statue of Buddha.

"Ahh, young Squire. There you are, my lost friend. There is so much you've ingested and still so much more to digest. The secrets that you've sought are beginning to reveal themselves, only you still manage to fool yourself, Squire. I've taught you before that the mind is a puckish rogue that can play tricks on you. But you listen to these menacing whisperers, who pretend to be your protectors. They badger you with the threat that you must get away from Katarina because she is so dangerous. They tell you that you must be hard, cold, and cunning and never trust. They tell you that she is but a spy, who will give away your location to the dark forces that pursue you. Danger, Squire, danger! But, your heart tells you the truth; and it is a frightening truth, indeed. It is not that this young woman is a spy, who will give you to wolves that chase you. No, Squire, it is because you are desperately afraid of the love you feel for her. Like everyone you have ever loved, you are terrified she, too, will leave you. That, my dear Squire, is what you fear most and why you feel you need to flee. That you might find your way out of this maze you're in, I leave you with words of Longfellow, who said that, 'Believe me, every heart has its secret sorrows, which the world knows not, and oftentimes we call a man cold, when he is only sad.' I fear that you are that scared and sad fellow, Squire, trying to turn a hard edge and a cold heart."

With those words, Shev was gone. His wise counsel dropped to the ground like stones before I was able to ingest and digest these mutterings from the wind. I resumed my wandering and eventually found my way back to the shack.

When I entered the small room, it was empty. I might have assumed that she had gone out to collect some supplies for the next leg of our journey. I had planned to tell her forthright that I must go on by myself, that we would simply part ways, and that the relief would be a salve for the pain in my heart. But, I realized that Kata had anticipated this all along. Over the time we'd spent together, she had watched and listened; she'd held my hand and comforted me at night when I awoke crying like a baby. From the beginning, Kata had known that we would say goodbye. I found a scrap of paper by the mat where we had slept together. On it were the words,

"*A Suttago, Nais tuke,* my *Kicsi.* Thank you. You be better tomorrow. You be stronger with time. I know this, dear Anton – K."

CHAPTER 12

Brothers of the Woodland

I noticed him before he saw me approach. There he was, stooped on his haunches, leaning against a red brick wall. A half-drunk flagon loosely held in one hand and a crooked tobacco roll in the other, Tobbar looked like a wretched soul. He appeared to have no clothes other than those that draped his gaunt frame, the ones I recalled him wearing the night I first laid eyes on him. He looked haggard and wore the same lost expression I'd seen in his dark and sad eyes that day. To my surprise, Zifi and his brother Vano rounded the wall and stood over Tobbar. When they heard me approach, Zifi turned and said, "Ah my *simensa*. A new day, no? Our friend Tobbar here say…em, you go together to find mama and papa. You know, Tobbar, he such, em…liar, so we come to see if true."

Tobbar took a swig and puff, while staring straight ahead.

"Yes, Zifi," I began, "Tobbar tells you the truth. We decided to go look for my mama and uncle, his papa. Baba Szófia told me where to look for them."

His eyes moved to my right and left.

"Em…where girl?"

"Uh…she moved on. Just went away."

A second or two ticked by before he broke into a broad grin, nudged me, while making an obscene gesture with this fingers. Then, he flashed a more sympathetic gesture and said,

"Oh well, my *simensa*, gypsy girls, they steal your heart like…like a thief rob you of, em…." He looked at his brother, who completed the sentence.

"Gold, jewels. My brother mean they rob your heart."

Slapping his brother's shoulder, Zifi continued. "We go with you then. We go with you…and this bug, Tobbar. It not safe to travel, em…without, em…." He stopped to flex his muscles and pointed to Vano beside him. "Without muscle boys. You need strong…like us! It not safe to go just with…little Tobbar. You can see, no? Tobbar not strong…cannot fight like Zeekkos. We fight like Greeks!" He suddenly pulled a dagger out of his belt and began waving it around. We greet you and girl when you come here and take you to Baba, no? We, em…fight bad men. Protect for you. Tobbar cannot do this, *simensa*."

I glanced at Tobbar. Somewhere between a shrug and a nod, he motioned his consent. It made sense that the Zeekkos would accompany us. Afterall, Zifi had arranged meetings with Baba Szófia and made sure we saw her every day. He'd brought us food and drink and provided a place to sleep. Other that my internal alarms warning me to trust no one, there was no other reason to doubt his word. I took another look at my cousin, Tobbar, who, by now, might have trouble standing up and walking without help. So, with a sharp nod, I said, "Ok, thank you. *Nais tuke*, Zifi, *nais tuke*."

It was cloudy that morning. There were no signs the sun was shining above the gray gauzy sky. We picked up enough supplies to last several days. A light mist fell as we left Felsögalla, heading west. I realized I was at the

mercy of my guides because I knew nothing about the Woodland Brothers, much less where they were hidden.

Vano walked proudly in front, serving as our trail leader. Zifi strode by my side, while Tobbar shuffled several steps behind. Zifi talked for much of the day, rarely stopping to catch a breath or wait for a response. Nevertheless, amidst trivial details about family members, repetitive stories of Romani and non-Romani women he'd had, and descriptions of important jobs he's held, Zifi revealed new information about Baba.

"Yes, Baba Szófia, she, em…very…" pointing to his head.

"Wise?" I inserted.

"Yes, yes *simensa*. She wise. But, she not tell you everything. Baba, I know her, ever since I baby. She act like old, em…*dinilo*, em, crazy, farm lady, like not know a thing. She sit and smoke her pipe and act like she not know things. She tell you your mama and grandfather Danior were ones that know books, that she not understand. But before Baba go blind, she read books, *simensa*. She read them all. No one read books like Baba. No one remember everything like Baba. She read all books of Danior, and she still see every word in her mind. Only…she, em, she…not let people know all she know. I think she not tell you all she know about your mama, *simensa*."

This was new information. Baba Szófia acted as observer, the one who watched my mama's and grandfather's quest for knowledge from afar; but she was learning everything with them. She acted as if the writers, scientists, and philosophers were just names she had heard, but she'd actually read and digested their works as well. She was truly wise and erudite, yet also wily. But I was puzzled by Zifi's comment about her not telling me everything she knew about Mama.

❖ ❖ ❖

Our first night under the stars was uneventful. Vano hunted small game, returned with three rabbits, which he gutted, skinned and roasted. Later, Zifi played a small harmonica, while Vano sang. Soon, they began to talk about who had more women. Tobbar sat quietly by himself. I moved over next to him. Communicating with my cousin was awkward. He had a decent mastery of the language, which must have come from Baba Szófia's tutelage, but social discourse was hard for him.

I said, "Its good that Zifi and Vano came on our journey. They seem to know the land and will help us if there is trouble. I think it's good, don't you?"

It took close to a minute for Tobbar to respond. I thought of all of those times when I'd count the seconds ticking from the old Breguet, waiting for Papa to answer a question.

Tobbar wiped his mouth and finally responded, "Yes, it is true. Zifi very strong. He smart, too. Good with trails. He help us find these *vashengo,* Brothers in woods."

Seeking reassurance for my nagging suspicions, I asked, "You trust him, don't you?"

Again, Tobbar hesitated and measured his words carefully. "Oh, sure… Zifi know *Romano Zakano,* gypsy code. Zeekko, we can trust." My cousin's words didn't match his expression. He was hard to read and even harder to engage in conversation, but, I'd learned from the day before that he spoke more easily when I shared his bitter-tasting wine. I motioned for his bottle and took a swig. Then, Tobbar startled me with the question.

"You know how Baba go blind?"

I shook my head, "no."

"This man Zifi say want to hurt you. You know this man? Baba tell you him? He a rich man who look to find you. He know many people who look, too."

I thought of the Count that hunted for mama and Támas. I recalled how Baba seemed to recoil when she said, "I know this man." I nodded for Tobbar to continue.

"His name Hadik. He hate all Romani. He hate Jews, I think, too." He kill our grandfather, Danior. Hadik take Baba. He take her. Don't know how you say. Romani word is *porradi*. It mean…she be taken and not want to. Hadik made her. He rip her clothes and take her! Then…he put poison weed in her eye to make her blind. After he take her, he blind her eyes. He say he afraid that Baba would make *jakhalo,* that mean curse with eye. But I think…I think Hadik never want Baba to see him with her eye and point at him. This man, he *gonosz.* Evil, I think you say, and *beng*…devil, is who he is."

Tobbar's story made sense. The way Baba Szófia had looked when she spoke of Hadik. He had blinded her so she could not identify him as her rapist. To accuse the respected Count of defiling a Romani woman would have brought shame to his household, perhaps even more than having a son who fell in love with a Romani girl. I had a sickening realization that my fate was tied to this wicked, *beng*.

Tobbar continued, as Zifi and Vano boasted of their manhood. "Baba good to Tobbar. She try make me good boy. She want me learn read her books, but she not able to see. She tried teach me to play *lavuta,* em…strings for music. But words and notes all backward for Tobbar. Baba sit and teach, but Tobbar head made of rock."

Those words immediately seized me, and I reached over to touch his shoulder. "No, no rocks. No rocks in Tobbar's head." And continuing silently, I said to myself, "And no rocks in Anton's hands."

We all settled into our blankets and slept under the few stars that peeked through the clouds. Then, my nightmares began. What does one explain to strangers suddenly awakened by your thrashing and screaming in the darkest part of the night? I'd only had that experience with the tender Kata, who responded with a soothing touch. The Zeekko's and Tobbar were catapulted out of their sleep by my shrieks, "NO, NO, NO, RUN, RUN…I DIDN'T KNOW!"

Tobbar who came forth to gently shake me to my senses, while the Zeekkos watched in bewilderment. When I caught my breath and regained my senses, I told them that I'd been a Russian soldier, not by choice, and saw many men die. They fell back asleep, but I remained awake stirring the dying embers in the fire.

Our second day proved longest and difficult. We passed into Austria and were beginning to see signs of the battle-scarred earth. Many of the fields surrounding us were brown and trampled. We passed wreckage of wagons, remains of useless equipment, and groves of burned trees that were fitting tombstones for the lives that had been lost. Throughout the day, I caught the others glancing at me, trying to gage my reactions to the carnage we passed. Disturbing dreams from the night before were fresh in my mind. I kept my head down, watching my feet marching step after step. I was suddenly transported back to the long, blistering marches in the heat of the day, as we headed to the slaughter fields of Tannenberg. Memories of endless marches stirred brutal images that I needed to banish.

Zifi walked astride his brother, while Tobbar continued to lag behind. I was left alone with my thoughts on this monotonous march. Trying to distract myself, I looked back at Tobbar. What did I *really* think about this pitiful soul? He seemed so lost and overlooked. The Zeekko's swatted at him like a bug. When I saw him that first night, he seemed odd and off-putting, everything that the charming Zifi Zeekko was not. Yet, I was puzzled by my growing affection for him. Why had my feelings changed? True, he was my cousin, perhaps the closest relative I had to Mama, and we were both left by parents who never returned. Tobbar felt he couldn't learn because he was "rock-headed," while I fought against the belief that I was "rock-handed." Then, there was his awkward manner and halting speech, which made me think of Vasily. I recalled Vasily's words – if the words of a ghost are to be believed – about knowing "something about sad boys." Though there was a world of difference separating them, Tobbar, like Vasily, had certainly been a sad boy. But something else about Tobbar, some other quality kept him on the edge of my mind. Then, I realized it had to do with learning that I had a brother! I think I saw Tobbar as my unknown brother. Maybe he looked like Tobbar. Maybe, instead of being like the golden Chaim, my other brother was like sad and lost Tobbar, who I would want to take care of. Tobbar, my cousin…maybe like a brother or another sparrow.

My thoughts were swirling and becoming confused, so I tried to distract myself again. But in the empty space I'd created, there suddenly appeared an image of Kata. For two days now, I had managed to keep her from my thoughts, a talent for removing complications I'd honed over the years. But there she was. Kata…Katarina. I saw her face, her jawline, the soft creases around her cobalt eyes. I heard the slightly throaty timbre of her voice. I smelled her hair, the rose-oiled perfume of her skin, and the sound of her breadth as she lay next to me. STOP! I silently commanded. I had to devise a way to divert and refocus my mind.

Gaining momentary clarity, I decided to picture and inventory each part of a watch I'd memorized years before. First, the balance spring, then the balance wheel attached to the mainspring. After that, there is the barrel with careful placement of the jewels. I need to carefully handle the escapement, "hold it like it is a baby, my bubelah." The placement of the escapement always brought back Papa's words to Chaim, as I watched from the door to his workshop. Chaim, again, intruded into my thoughts! I pushed the image to the side and continued to inventory the parts of a watch.

When I had exhausted all of the parts, I set about listing all of the tools and their functions. When I'd completed my list of specialized screwdrivers, tweezers, and calipers, I decided that I would construct a watch in my mind. After all, this is what I had done for all those years after I emerged from my mudhuts – building watches to drive out painful thoughts, memories, and their unwanted emotional stowaways. So, for the remainder of that day and for much of the next, I began to construct, in my mind, a beautiful, intricate timepiece, but one with few complications.

As the sun began to set, we came upon a shepherd tending to his flock in a grassy meadow. Zifi approached him, motioning for us to stay on the trail. Vano indicated that he was asking the shepherd which trail we should take into the forest to find the *veshengo*. Vano began speaking spontaneously about the Brothers of the Woodland.

"These *vashengo* lived hidden in forests for many years. Some from far away in Hindustan, but most Romani from different places. They know mystical ways. They healers but some once warriors, too. When they hid your mama and uncle, many died."

Zifi returned to our group and indicated that we were getting close but should set up camp and try to find the Brothers the next day. The shepherd told him that no one had much contact with the Brothers because they stayed hidden from people. He said we would look for them in Joglland, a thickly wooded area in the mountain. We had a steep climb ahead of us before we entered the forest.

That night Zifi was not his usual smiling and laughing self. He appeared more distant and preoccupied. He and Vano played no music. We ate the remains of the rabbits from the night before, along with some potatoes and beets they had brought with them. I tried to engage Zifi to tell me more about the Brothers, but he waved me off and said I would find out.

As usual, Tobbar said very little. Never one to initiate conversation, he kept to himself, often with his back turned toward the fire. With nothing more to do or say, we nestled in our mats and fell asleep. By now, my traveling companions had grown accustomed to my fitful sleep and nightmares. When I began to thrash and cry out, one of them would reach over to shake me with words like, "It ok. Just sleep now. Not real. You here. Safe now. Sleep."

The morning climb proved not to be difficult. The slope of the trail was gradual but became rocky and required attention to footing. Tobbar lost his balance once or twice and fell hard against the dry earth. I helped him up and saw that he had bloodied both knees and began to walk with a limp. Each time he fell, neither Zifi nor Vano slowed or looked back to see if he was alright.

The terrain changed significantly from broad plains and rocky trails to rolling green hills. The trail ended as we walked through a meadow with long grasses and brush. Ahead lay a line of pines marking the beginning of the forest. When we stopped for a short rest, Vano walked back to tell me that we were in the heart of Austria proper. He drank from his canteen and said,

"If there are Brothers, they be there. So we look. But they not want to be seen, so we go quiet. Walk soft and stay quiet."

Stepping into the forest was like entering another world. The sky disappeared, hidden by a dense, high canopy that rose far above our heads. The ground was entangled with leaves, vines, and brambles. We were surrounded by lush and verdant hues covering the ground and in leafy formations climbing the enormous pines. The air was cool but humid, and the rich perfume of loam and mulch teased our noses. The moist air soothed my nostrils and eased the unremitting pain, when walking the arid trails. We heard only the sounds of our steps upon the leaves, an occasional bird overhead, and the buzzing of dragonflies as they glided intermittently across our path.

After an hour or so, we stopped to get our bearings and sip water from a gurgling brook. It was at that moment we realized Tobbar was missing. We craned our necks and began calling his name, first in loud whispers and then in louder voices. Afraid that we would lose each other if we separated, we retraced our steps. After more than an hour, we reached the forest's edge and found no trace of my cousin. I noted more annoyance than concern in the faces of the Zeekko brothers and understood some of their side comments.

"He is of little worth, this Tobbar. No more sense than a *moaker*. Most probably stumbled off cliff from drinking stale wine," said Zifi, his words laced with contempt.

Vano nodded and said, "Right, brother. Tobbar is a *moaker*. That mean 'mule,'" as he turned his head to translate Zifi's words for me. "Your little *simensa* has no sense in his head. That you agree to take a journey with this fool mean you, too, a fool. No, *simensa*, joke, you, of course, are no *moaker* like Tobbar.

I could do little more than shrug at Vano's cutting words. I was baffled by Tobbar's sudden disappearance but also felt concernd. Tobbar had told me that he was never able to learn to read. How had he put it? "Words all backward for Tobbar." Maybe his sense of direction was backward, as well, and he hadn't been able to follow us as we walked through the forest.

Despite my concern, I understood the Zeekkos' annoyance. By the time we got back from retracing our steps, we'd had lost two hours. The little that light filtered through the thick canopy was fading. It was too dark to continue. Vano gathered wood and made a torch, then a small fire before he headed off to find food. Zifi sat by my side, tending the fire.

"Hey, *simensa*, what if, em…never can find mama? She disappear many time back. She could be gone, maybe dead too."

Long on charm, Zifi had already showed there was little room for empathy in his world. I wondered how Shev would have described his dearth of compassion. I remained silent for a moment or two then responded,

"I don't know Zifi. If there is a chance, I want to take it….I'm grateful that you agreed to come with us —err, me. I wouldn't have know where to look. You do, and for that, I'm indebted."

"Oh sure, *simensa,* sure…sure. Like I say, em, you need Zifi and Vano. We try look. Maybe, em, we find mama, maybe not. And…maybe she dead, no? Who know. Not Zifi."

Vano returned with more wood, some roots, and another rabbit. He was a skilled hunter. I imagined what my fate would have been had I wandered into the forest with only Tobbar. Who knows what ravine I'd be lying at the bottom of with my skull cracked open. With Tobbar as my guide, the vultures surely would have feasted on my carcass.

After eating, the three of us positioned ourselves against the huge trunks of surrounding trees and tried to get some sleep. I managed to pass through the night with minimal thrashing. I woke early as the light creeped through the trees. I heard whispers that I had once again misplaced my trust and would surely perish at the hands of the dark shapes wearing Serbian uniforms. I slapped the side of my head to silence the whisperers and awakened Vano, who looked over at me.

"You ok?"

I nodded and waited for Zifi to wake up and make a plan for the day. I wondered if they would invest anymore time trying to find the, "bug," Tobbar. And, what I would say if they decided he was not worth their time? When Zifi woke, we ate more of the yellow, bitter-tasting roots that Vano brought the night before. I asked them both where they thought we should go.

"This way. Over there," answered Zifi.

By mid morning, we arrived at a small clearing. Still troubled by the disappearance of Tobbar and lack of a plan to find him, I finally spoke up,

"Zifi, Tobbar is, as you called him, a *bugban*, but he is my true *simensa*. I think we should look more to see if we can find him. He might have fallen. He might be hurt."

Zifi eyed me for several seconds, then, with a brush of his hand, responded, "Naw. Tobbar, he ok. Just fine like me and you. He may have, em, head like mule, but Tobbar live on street and can take care of Tobbar hisself. Now, we go this way to find *veshengo.*"

We had been trudging through the woods half a day when we reached another clearing, only this time, it looked like there were two paths through the woods on the far side of this meadow. I followed Vano and Zifi down the path on the right. We proceeded slowly around another bend where the path was obscured by overgrown ground cover and low hanging branches. The path opened up to reveal what looked like two, maybe three figures standing at the far end.

We instantly stopped and watched these figures, who appeared to have been studying us. After a momentary pause, we inched forward. What we saw was both relieving and ominous. There was Tobbar kneeling between two tall figures. As we neared, I saw that his hands were bound from behind. Flanking Tobbar were two tall thin men dressed in gray robes, each holding a long Hussar saber. The one on the left wore a long black beard, his comrade had scraggly white hair. The bearded figure motioned for us to approach. When we were within earshot, he spoke in a thunderous voice. I could not make out the language, but Zifi responded. Turning toward me, Vano said, "They're Greek."

Vano translated the exchange that Zifi had with the man. "They say they find Tobbar wandering through forest. He hungry and had wild look." When they bring him back to where they live, they feed and give him water. But then he try to leave and rob them. They not believe in killing but he a thief. They ask if we want him back."

When I saw that Zifi shrugged, I stepped forward and nodded my head. "Yes, yes." I motioned toward Tobbar and pantomimed that we would take him. The two men looked at each other and indicated agreement. One bent to untie him. Tobbar had a sheepish expression and avoided looking at me or the Zeekkos.

I placed my hand on Zifi's shoulder and said, "I think we found the Brothers. Can you ask about my mother and Tobbar's papa, Uncle Andras? Maybe they can tell us something." Zifi motioned agreement and spoke at length to the bearded figure in Greek. After a short back and forth, Zifi turned to me and said, "He say we follow them."

Vano made sure that Tobbar walked in front of him as our group followed the two Brothers through a thicket of narrow trails. We entered another clearing and saw several small evenly spaced huts. The two tall robed figures pointed to where we should wait and disappeared into one of the enclosures. In 20-minutes time, four figures emerged from the enclosure – the original two along with another tall man and a short man hunched over a branch he used as a cane. The old figure with the cane wore a white robe, with a peculiar circular symbol on one side. The bearded figure spoke more with Zifi, who then motioned for us to put our knapsacks and satchels down. Zifi then waved his hand for us to approach, as the hunched figure hobbled forward and spoke.

"They tell me you've come a long way with many questions." His Russian was clear, not as fluent as that of Baba Szófia, but I could make out every word. I could not guess his age, but he must have been in his 9th decade. Strands of white hair sprouted from his bald head. He had large ears with fine tufts of hair like old Kruehke. His nose was crooked. On one cheek was a jagged scar that climbed to the bridge of his twisted nose. The old man's eyes lay hooded under drooping lids, which belied the sharp, penetrating quality of his gaze. He moved closer and whispered, "I might have some things to tell you, come this way."

I followed him to a smaller hut, while the Zeekkos remained outside with the other robed figures. Cousin or not, Tobbar had been a bother. The Brothers found and cared for him, and he returned their kindness by stealing from them. I would listen to the old man and then decide whether to share anything more with Tobbar.

Inside the small hut was a sparse, single room. On the floor lay a thin mat, with several low stools along the perimeter of the sodden walls. The room had a musty smell, not unpleasant, but old and earthy. Adorning the walls were pictures of symbols like the one he wore on his robe. Each was a circular structure with splashes of color, characters from different languages, and small figures of various sizes and shapes. He motioned for me to sit on a stool and carefully positioned himself on another.

"Your colorful friend out there tells me that you seek a Romani woman and her brother who came to us so long ago. He tells me that you are her son!" His eyes lit up as he fixed his gaze, a slight smile on his slender lips.

"Yes, my mother was Marina Vadoma. They said she came here with her brother. I was also told that she came here once before when men were trying to kill her and a man called Támas."

"What they have told you is true. It is sad…but all true. Your mama came to us twice, first as a young woman, seeking to escape evil men who hunted her and a young man. She was with child then and gave birth in this room. We help those who have lost their way or need shelter. When your mama and this man came, we offered protection, but it came at great cost. Many gave their lives trying to keep them safe.

I nodded and asked, "And you helped them escape before the men came?"

"Yes. Then, many years later she returned to us, but she was not the same. The light in her eyes had gone out. She spoke of many things, the books she had read and of the mysteries for which she sought answers – things that none of the elders knew about. All we knew was that she was not right. At night, she would have long impassioned conversations with unseen others. She laughed, cried, and threatened. With all that knowledge, she could not even care for herself. She needed your uncle's help. All we could offer was solitude and healing that comes from herbs and spiritual practices. Though we fed her and saw to it that she rested, her mind remained unsettled. Your uncle could not tell us the source of her ailment or what it was she was looking for. We tried everything to reach her, and finally, we taught her to draw these." He pointed to the symbols that covered the walls.

"We used the ancient practice of the mandala as a way to focus and still her mind. You see these gates surrounding the center circle here? They are to help one find a center point for the spirit, to find and know oneself. The mandala quieted the storm in her mind and brought comfort to her restless spirit. So, she began to draw them. She drew and drew; and when we had no more parchment, she painted them on my walls.

Then your mama began to talk of a great secret she had learned from her drawings. It was as if she felt the mandala spoke to her and told her where she must go. Sadly, what had been settled grew more troubled again. She began to speak of her books, the writings and teachings of doctors and professors in Vienna and Zurich. Her mind became fixed on Zurich and seeing a professor there. She talked all the time about this man and how she must return to see him again, as if she had been there before. No one understood what she was saying, and no one could tell her anything different. She insisted that she must find this doctor named Jung. All she spoke about was the message that she must get to him."

The old man poured some water to moisten his throat, which had become dry from talking. He offered me a cup and paused several minutes before continuing.

"I could see how weary your uncle had become trying to help her find balance again, but she would hear nothing he said. She insisted on leaving. I remember Andras as a kind man, who loved her deeply. No one doubted that your uncle would have followed her to the depths of hell, but he told us he was tired and that he had to return home where he had a son. It was with great sadness that he realized he could neither heal your mother nor follow her any longer.

One morning, we arose and she was gone. Your uncle had planned on returning to his village, but he became ill. As we had discovered with your mama, there are sicknesses deep in the forest that our potions and prayers cannot heal. Andras might have consumed some poisonous plants or vegetables. But, truly my son, I believe that his heart became sick at having to choose between his sister and his child. He didn't last long. Again, our healing failed. Your uncle died right over there many years ago."

The gripping weight of this information brought me back to Baba Szófia's porch, where I had listened to one sad story after another. Once again, I found myself in the presence of another wise old soul, who provided heartbreaking answers for questions about my mother, and my uncle. I fought back tears, which I also saw forming in the old man's eyes.

"You see…I knew her father, your grandfather Danior….I was there that night they took him from his home, dragged, and beat him to death. He was my friend. But the night they came for him, I ran and hid, frightened they would come for me too. I left Felsögalla the next day and have been with the Brothers ever since. The shame from that night still stains my soul. I think that is a reason that I couldn't guide your mother's healing. Perhaps the dishonor I felt was too deep for me to see what she really needed…." We sat in silence for several minutes.

What happened next will always remain a blur, a kaleidoscope of single images jumbled together, moving slowly. For years, I have tried to piece together what occurred that afternoon; but to this day, I cannot be certain I know.

❖ ❖ ❖

My sacred silence with the elder Brother was suddenly disrupted by loud shuffling and shouts from outside. We moved quickly to the doorway and saw several armed men standing in the clearing, surrounding the Zeekkos, Tabbor, and the three Brothers.

Then, came crackling of gunfire. Two of the Brothers fell to the ground. In an unimaginable treachery, Vano pulled a knife and rammed it through his brother's belly, leaving the shocked look of fraternal betrayal as the last expression on Zifi's handsome face.

Tabbor stood motionless, his eyes flashing terror.

A stout man in a black tunic, his long brown hair tied behind his head, stepped forward with a pistol in his hand. He looked up at the only remaining Brother and shot him in the face without a moment's pause. Then, surveying the small cluster of huts, he barked the commands,

"Horvàt, make sure that there are no others! The Count made it clear. This band of woodland priests shall cease to exist."

The large man then walked toward the fratricidal Vano Zeekko, who nodded slowly and said, "As we'd agreed, Herr Djoivik, I've given you the Brothers and the *poshrat*. Plus, I throw in a bonus for the Count – my own tiresome gypsy brother." And pointing to Tobbar, he added, "And this worthless little *bugban*, more food for the worms. Now, you make me payment as agreed, and I go. You have what you want. These last nights, I make sure you could follow our trails."

The one called Djoivik smirked at Vano's words.

"Yes, you carried out your task admirably. I'm sure the Count will want to reward you himself."

On cue, from the trees another old man in a dark cape stepped forward to Vano and Djoivik. His long white hair was oiled and fell to his shoulders. He carried beads in one hand and a sharp dagger in the other. The blade of his knife glistened in the remaining sliver of sunlight. His long fingernails moved up the beads, while he wordlessly mouthed something to himself. He passed Vano, who looked up as if to speak; and without pausing to address Vano, the caped man drove his blade forcefully into Vano's gut, leaving another dead Zeekko with a shocked expression of unanticipated betrayal.

Tabbor stood, shaking visibly, his head down. He broke loose and ran toward the forest. Horvàt aimed and fired his pistol, as Tobbar fell face down.

The white haired man in the cape walked to the old Brother and said,

"Ah, Damion, did you think I would forget?" With another thrust of his blade, the old Brother doubled over and fell to the ground.

The white haired man glared at me with hatred burning in his eyes. He spat in my face and slapped me to the ground, as he spewed the words,

"The cursed seed has returned at last."

I fell by my rucksack, dazed. Driven only by instinct, I reached inside for Luka's pistol.

The wild-eyed old man approached, as I fired a shot, blowing a gaping hole as large as my fist in the middle of his chest.

Horvàt moved in quickly and drove one of his boots into my stomach and another to my face, breaking my nose once more.

It was over in a matter of minutes. Before darkness descended and I lost all consciousness, I saw that no man had been left standing. The last of the Brothers of the Woodland had been eliminated. Both Zeekkos lay lifeless – brothers in birth and one betrayor in death. Then there was poor Tabbor, whose hope of finding his father was but a flash of light in his otherwise dark world. And an evil Count, eaten away by ancient hatred, was splayed out on his back, his pale eyes frozen open and a massive bloody hole blown into his chest. Among the carnage, I was puzzled to see that both Horvàt and Djoivik lay face down in the dirt. Both had been killed. But how? Everyone else was already dead….Though I didn't know it then, their deaths would remain a riddle that I would never be able to solve….

❖ ❖ ❖

My mind broke that afternoon in the Joglland Forest. A dormant volcano, suddenly erupted. The image of one brother killing another and the sight of a gaping hole in a man's chest unearthed a sickening reality that I had buried deep within my mind….I KILLED CHAIM! That the Count would have surely killed me mattered nothing in that moment. All that I could see was that I had blown a hole in another man's chest. Like an over-tightened spring, my mind just snapped, spewing one unbidden and muddled fragment of sound after another – "come my *Kicsi*," "just flap your wings Sparrow;" *"oh Pidkaya,* draw me a nice picture;" *"schmutzie!"* "but his hands are like rocks;" "the Tsar will takes pigs in his army;" "I see, I have a special job for someone with your technical skills;" "young Squire, seems a Hussar named Rheshevsky;" Anton, b…b-ut they looked hungry t…t-oo;" *"Ne front;"* "you will never be better tomorrow because the wolves will catch you;" "come *Suttago,* tell Kata;" "Anton, I will cut out your tongue;" "we will p…p-unish you;" "a message for Jung; I must get a message to Jung…."

I had only a vague sensation of movement, as I felt the vibration of wheels on a dirt road beneath me. Everything else was darkness. Thoughts were spinning in my head when I suddenly seized upon the idea that there was danger in movement. Action….Movement….I concluded that movement, of any sort, had caused all of this. Movement was danger! Movement was destruction! It became clear that a long chain of my movements and actions since I'd left Zastavia had led to one death after another….

Stillness would now be my refuge. No movement. Of this, I was certain….The world depended on it….Time passed in this void of darkness and motionlessness. Then, the stillness and silence were disrupted by the sound of a muffled voice speaking German words that I could decipher.

"Looks like another case of the Praecox, but this one's frozen like a statue. Don't know where he came from. Was just left by the outside gate. Can't leave him here. Bring him in; put him with the other loons. Doctors will want to have a look."

BEYOND THE BURGHÖLZLI

In the circle of life, mysteries abound and then confound, but alas, most journeys end with not all answers to be found
~ Nicolai Keloskovich

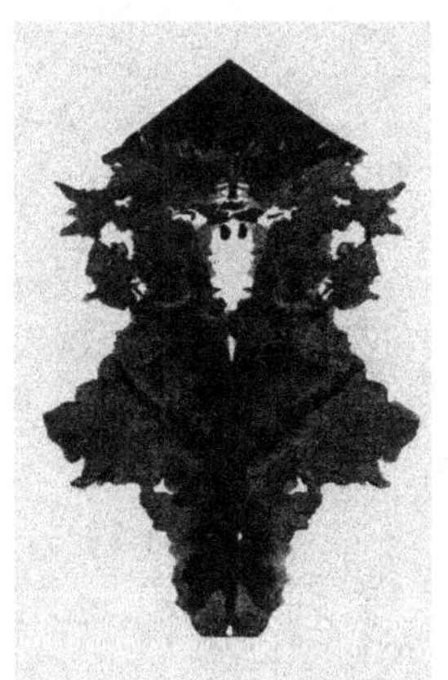

CHAPTER 13

At the Gates of the Burghölzli

For those who read my story, understand how the events of the next weeks and months remain, to this day, a blur. Despite having reviewed my old medical records, interviewed staff who saw to my care, and the considerable effort I have devoted to reconstructing the sequence of events at the Burghölzli, I cannot attest firmly to their accuracy. The details I describe are based on spotty memories, recollections of old staff members, entries in my records, and inferences I've made. With this disclaimer duly noted, here is what I have been able to piece together over the years.

I believe I was placed on some kind of restraining device with wheels and taken into the main building by several attendants. Much of this I recall from the sensations of movement and the voices of the matron and her nurses, who arranged for my examination by the admitting physician. You see, I relied primarily on auditory and somatic cues because I'd spent the first weeks in the asylum with my eyes closed in darkness. The records also indicate that I didn't speak, move, or eat voluntarily, so I had to be fed by the aides.

I'd apparently assumed a frozen pose. They called this an "acute catatonic dementia." I have vague recollections of snickering comments from the attendants who said that I resembled the face of a clock with its hands in a 3:00 position. Caspar Fleishman was one of those attendants I tracked down years later. Fleishman agreed to speak with me. When I described the timeframe and my condition upon arrival at the sanitarium, his eyes widened. Then, with a wink, he said, "Ja. 'The clockman,' is what we called you. No words, no movement, only 3-o'clock all the time. Ja, I remember now. Tick tock. Ja."

I have a vague image of an old matron who oversaw my daily activities. I believe that she was a heavyset woman; yet I've been unable to recall her face. I remember how she once raised her voice and angrily chided two younger aides whom she'd caught repositioning my arms, as if reseting the face of a clock. She shooed them from my room but left my arms in a new 4:10 position.

I remember attendants taking me to warm baths. Afterward, a therapist came in to reposition my arms and massage my extremities, back, neck, and sides of my head. The records documented a few occasions that I became agitated and needed to be restrained. Caspar Fleishman recalled how I once poked him in the nose during one of these frenzies. When I became agitated, I was placed in cold wet sheets and swaddled like baby. I can remember an unexpected calming effect after the initial shock from the icy wetness of the sheets.

The hospital records showed that the matron charted my nightmares, including my physical agitation and screaming, which occurred several times a week. It was noted that the night nurse and her attendants would then administer treatments, including tonics and cold wet sheet wraps at such times.

My medical records also detailed a procedure to treat the chronic inflammation in my nose. That treatment and the daily ointments they applied worked because my nose began to heal.

Each day, I was hoisted from my bed, placed on a wheeled cart, and then pushed by one of the aides around the grounds. I felt vibrations from the chair, felt the warmth of the sun, and heard idle chatter and singing birds. One day, I opened my eyes and was struck by the beauty of the immense grounds. I recall my first visual impression when I looked at the span of white buildings, situated on a bluff over a lake, and how it offered unparalleled serenity for an asylum such as this.

The number of Russian doctors working at the sanitarium surprised me too. Although I could understand more German than I would have imagined, I frequently caught snippets of side conversations in my native tongue.

I was assigned to a young female physician in training. My records identified her as Orina Minkowski. She performed her examination and checked on me daily to determine changes in my condition. Reading my medical records brought back the memory of her asking if I spoke German? French? Russian? I can picture her eyes brightening when I nodded at Russian. From that day, she conducted all of her medical business with me in Russian. I imagine that since I remained mute and frozen like a stopped watch, the doctor's visits were brief.

My records documented the day I began to speak. The matron summoned Frau doctor Minkowski to my room. I remember the matron talking quietly to my doctor, saying something like, "Frau doctor, this man has said the strangest thing! When he opened his eyes, he simply uttered the words, 'I have a message for Jung.' I tried to find out more, but he fell silent again. That is when I summoned you."

Dr. Minkowski encouraged me to begin speaking. Detailed notes of her interview that night appeared in my hospital record. The doctor asked my name and about the circumstances of my sudden appearance at the gates of the asylum a month earlier. Our brief exchange went like this,

"Tell me, do you have a name?"

….

"What are you called?" she repeated.

After a long pause, I whispered, "Anton." I can remember the burning in my throat after not having spoken for several weeks.

Frau doctor's attempts to broaden our dialogue proved fruitless. Her notes indicated that she left "the patient" after being unable to get him to speak again. Then, her chart entry noted,

"The patient suddenly spoke again as I was about to depart his room. He murmured in a low hoarse voice, 'a message for Jung.'"

The records showed that I began to speak more the following day. I can still feel a jolt of fear in my abdomen when I remember the terror I felt about moving my arms and legs. Though I was convinced movement of my limbs would result in destruction or death, motion of my eyelids and limited movement of my vocal chords felt less threatening. Unfortunately, in that constrained and frozen stillness, I could not escape the steady stream of intrusive whisperers warning I had been captured at last, and that my fate was somehow tied to this person named, "Jung."

Entries in my record helped piece together the events of the following day. When I was returned to my room after hydrotherapy, I saw Dr. Minkowski standing with two older, distinguished-looking men in white coats. She stepped forward to speak, and I the conversation went something like this:

"Here is Herr Dr. Maier, and this is our Director, Herr Professor Bleuler. They have come to speak with you, Anton. I hope you can find some words for them as they have taken time from their busy schedules."

I still picture the Director bowing his head slightly, and then allowing the other man to speak first. This man's tone was cordial but professional.

"As your physician has told you, I am Dr. Hans Maier. Tell me, do you understand if we converse in German?"

I slowly and softly replied, "Ja."

"Good, good. Perhaps if it becomes too difficult then the good Dr. Minkowski will assist with translation to your native language. Do you find this suitable, Anton?"

"Ja."

"Good. Can you tell us what happened to you and how you got here?"

This was too much. I couldn't explain what had happened. So much remained a blur. I had no idea how I'd been brought here. To this day, that remains a great mystery. But I do recall how, in that moment, the whispering voices chided me not to give these enemy doctors too much information.

The doctor spoke again. "Alright, then Anton….When some people come to Burghölzli, they hear voices talking to them, giving warnings and commands. These may be voices that others cannot also hear. I wonder, Anton, do you experience such things?"

Written in the medical records was my response, "…Nein."

I remember thinking there had been too many questions that felt dangerous to answer. Nonetheless, my lengthy pause and grimace certainly told these doctors as much any words. Maier said, "I see. Not something you're prepared to answer. Very well."

I still have the image of him glancing at the older man with the long, well-groomed beard. This man now moved forward, as the others stepped back. Something about my interactions with this man stood out. His voice had a warm, resonant quality.

"Anton….Now, that is a fine name. I believe you have traveled here from a great distance. We have many guests who have come from afar, and like you, cannot tell us their stories and what has caused such pain in their lives. I believe this is the case with you. But, it is our hope, Anton, that we will be able to help you while you are here. We certainly will do all that we can to ease your pain and make you more comfortable….I am curious though, your good doctor and the matron, here, have told me that you came with a special message. Is that correct?"

My records documented my halting response to his question. "Ja….A message for Jung….My mama had a message for Jung,"

I recall how the men looked quizzically at each other. I couldn't discern what their look conveyed – concern, intense curiosity? They then thanked me for answering their questions. Herr Bleuler added that I seemed to be showing signs of improvement already.

The doctors huddled outside my room, while the matron signaled the aides to change my bed linen. I overheard Maier and Bleuler talking in hushed tones. Although their German was too fast for me to comprehend completely, I understood bits of their conversation. I have a memory of Maier speaking first.

"So it is true. He speaks of 'the prince,' our brother Jung. If we could coax our eminent colleague to meet with this patient, perhaps in a teaching session for our students, we might gain a deeper understanding of the patient's delusions. Carl Gustav has not lectured here for several years. It would be good to have him return. He has always brought distinction to our institution." I still picture Herr Bleuler flashing a look of uncertainty, to which Maier quickly added, "I know you had concerns about those circumstances under which he left Burghölzli, but most of the time he has brought honor to psychiatry in Zurich."

Bleuler paused and spoke slowly, his beard moving in harmony with his words. "I cannot say I agree completely with your idea, Hans; but, on the other hand, having Jung see this fellow might yield diagnostic information. Carl Gustav is no doubt a gifted clinician; and while we might disagree about many things, he could help shed light on the delusional basis of this man's message. If nothing more, having Jung in front of him might be a catalyst for this young man to reveal more about "his message," whatever it might be. I can speak with the scheduling secretary and have her contact the eminent Professor Jung, to see if your 'prince' might agree to grace us with his presence."

A week or so passed. My records showed that Frau doctor continued her daily rounds. I remember how she spoke in Russian and seemed less discouraged that I responded in so few words. She persisted in asking me if I heard voices or feared that others were plotting against me. Each time she asked, I turned away, which communicated more than a verbal denial would have.

My medical record identified the day I was taken to see Jung. The matron entered and said that they would be taking me to the grand amphitheater for the teaching rounds with a famous Professor. When she mentioned the name "Jung," my ears perked up. I was taken to the baths and then wheeled around the grounds before being brought to the grand amphitheater.

My first impression of the amphitheater remains fixed in my memory. The theater was like a pit with a small stage in the center and steep circular rows of seats. The stage was illuminated and the rows of seats were dark. I sat in the glare of the lights, my arms still frozen in the 4:10 position. I remember seeing scores of faceless young doctors wearing white coats. They entered from the back and filled the amphitheater. Two attendants sat behind me as Herr Director stepped onto the stage. I have always remembered his words.

"For the students and residents, we have a special training session today. Our patient is a young Russian man named Anton. He has been at Burghölzli now for six months. We have asked our renowned colleague, Professor Carl Gustav Jung, to examine our patient. Hopefully, he can bring his wisdom and clinical expertise and help us understand this man's illness, its nature and source. As many of you know, Herr Jung was my second assistant until six, seven years ago. He is now in his own practice and heavily involved in the Swiss Psychoanalytical Society. May I introduce Dr. Jung."

With a loud applause from the dark rows of seats above, a stoutly built man stepped out of the shadows and onto the stage. Carl Gustav Jung was not how I had imagined him. To this day, my initial impressions of him remain vividly fixed in my mind. This "Jung" fellow had inhabited my thoughts as a much darker and more sinister-looking figure, somehow connected mysteriously to Mama's disappearance. Though I found his countenance to be stern, the professor did not look sinister. I remember he was impeccably dressed, wearing a tailored pin striped jacket and vest, dark trousers, a crisp white collar, and dark tie. He presented a dramatic contrast to the sea of white-coated doctors and students, who populated the rows above. His closely cropped hair was graying, his moustache neatly trimmed; and above his nose, he wore a pair of small spectacles. His dark blue eyes were razor sharp.

Detailed minutes from Jung's interview and examination were included in my medical records. Before conducting his examination, Jung made inferences about the circumstances of my arrival at the gates of Burghölzli. The following information was taken from the minutes of his Grand Rounds:

"Before we conduct our clinical examination of this patient, let us ask ourselves, how this poor man came to Burghölzli in the first place? What do we know? Well, his records tell us that this wretched soul was left at the front gate – no one with him to explain his symptoms, nothing written about his disease, his origin, or the necessary background information required to make a clinical diagnosis. So, without this, we are left to make a series of disciplined inferences. How could he have come to be left at the main gate? Well, of course Occam's razor would urge us to assume the simplest explanation first. The man might have walked here on his own accord, seeking assistance for his illness – that is the simplest possibility. But we know that this cannot be true. Why? Because we also know that he was in a severe catatonic state, making all voluntary motor activity impossible. So, what else….Well, we must conclude that he was brought here by a good Samaritan or by someone who knew him. If so, why did this person or persons not remain to explain his condition? Why simply leave him? Those who left him or, should we say, abandoned him, might have not wished to become involved. Such is often the case with our species – we do not like to become involved. Why? Well, for now, we must put this line of inquiry aside. Perhaps we will know more after we examine him."

Jung commenced his clinical examination. Initially focusing on my facial characteristics, he explained how race and ethnicity provide valuable clues about a patient's culture, most importantly, the myths and religious traditions that could contribute to various types of psychotic symptoms and associated complexes. Here is an excerpt from the minutes:

"Now, let's proceed with the physiognomic analysis. Let us look carefully at his facial features. From the pigment of the skin, we note a Mediterranean complexion, yet the features themselves have a Hindus quality. So, we have a wide range of possibilities existing outside the Aryan race. Observe the patient's broad and flat nose, the spacing of his dark eyes and their position in relation to his ears. If we infer that he is of a non-Aryan race, then we can begin to investigate the social constructs and mythological structures in his society, namely the readiness of these people to believe in magical and spiritual forces that they use to explain the symptoms of their illnesses."

Dr. Jung turned next to the symptoms of my illness.

"Now, we understand catatonia, from which this patient most certainly suffers, as a secondary symptom of dementia praecox, or what the eminent Director calls "schizophrenia." Certainly, this motoric symptom is founded on a delusion, most likely based on the myths of his primitive culture, that the world will come to an end should he move about freely. We can also assume that he is communicating with hallucinated voices and harbors paranoid beliefs that others intend to do him harm. Let us now question him to probe to basis of his delusional beliefs."

At that point, Professor Jung motioned to one of the attendants to move a chair next to me. I was facing forward and did not look directly at him. According to the record, Jung began to inquire about my symptoms.

"And now, young man, be sure to speak loudly enough so that they can hear you in the back of the theater. I see you are from Russia and are called Anton. Is this right, young man?"

The notes indicated that "the patient nodded his head and spoke the following words.

"My papa and brother…they took what was mine. My watches, the foliot correction is what is needed to stop the time from moving."

Jung addressed the audience, "As you can see, this boy speaks unintelligibly in a word salad. He uses invented language to express what cannot be clear to us."

Turning back to me, Jung asked,

"Now young man, please tell us something about the voices that you hear. Is it but a single voice or are there many?"

Notes of the interview described how "the patient tried to turn his head away from Professor Jung, who then instructed the audience of the significance of the patient's action."

"Ah, see, we have our first clue. With the catatonic, we do not expect a verbal response, but young Anton, here, tells us through his actions that my question has created anxiety, most likely related to the charged content of my question. Thus, it is reasonable to assume that he has provided an answer – he *is* hearing voices. I dare say we would observe this same sequence of evasive, motoric defensiveness had I questioned him about his paranoid fears."

The interview continued. The minutes captured his words and my terse responses. Each time I responded, Jung reached conclusions, which he explained to the audience. After conducting his clinical examination, he demonstrated a special procedure, which he said he and a colleague had pioneered when he was at Burghölzli. He described this as a "word association technique," which would help him "deduce the presence of underlying complexes that will aid in our clinical diagnosis of the patient."

Jung motioned for two aides to bring the equipment from the back of the stage. The device reminded me of the inner working of a clock. He supervised as they moistened two pads, and affixed them to my hands. Turning to the audience, Jung explained,

"The word association method has been used in scientific studies for quite some time, but I've elevated it to a diagnostic procedure. Here is how it works. As you see, we have connected our patient to this psychogalvanic meter to monitor the electrical reactivity in his epidermis. When we read the stimulus words, we can measure his somatic-emotional responsivity. I hold here in my hand a precise timing device to record the latency of his responses. The longer it takes him to respond, the more evidence we have of a repressed complex, which has disrupted the associative process. The word has triggered an unconscious response, revealing the patient's complex, which will help us diagnose the roots of his clinical psychopathology."

I remember that Jung held a rare and expensive Blanchpin pocket watch that he used to time my reaction speed. I had seen this piece in one of Papa's catalogues many years ago.

Dr. Jung wound the crown and proceeded to read his word list, to which I was supposed to respond with the first word that came to mind. Most of the words were neutral in tone and connotation – words like "head, cold, window, water" and so forth. The records indicated I either did not respond at all or gave banal, predictable responses. However, there are noted here several of my associations, which seemed to evoke a reaction from Professor Jung, who then promptly asked that I provide additional associations. My added responses to his queries were generally quite spare. Verbatim examples included,

Jung's Stimulus Word	**My Response**
dead	…Chaim
father	rocks
sad	sparrow
penis	schmekel

The records showed that after responding with "schmekel," Jung stopped the procedure and asked that I associate to the word "schmekel," to which I responded,

"D'ja hear the one about the biology teacher who drew a cucumber on the blackboard?"

There was muffled laughter from the dark rows above, but Jung was not amused. He interrupted and cautioned that I was to provide only single-word responses. It had not been my intention to make light of this procedure, but truly, Shev's "schmekel" story was the first thing that had sprung to my mind. The professor proceeded with several other words before this final interaction, took place. Jung said the stimulus word, "mother," and I did not respond. He waited and repeated, "*mother*," this time more loudly. At this, I turned my head, which up to that point had been frozen in a forward position, toward him and responded in a louder voice,

"Yes, my mother…She said that she had a message for you….Did you know her?…. Did you?"

Jung appeared startled both because I had again broken set and not responded with a single word, but also because I had turned toward him and, with a fixed stare, and asked a pointed question. He studied me, narrowing his blue eyes veiled behind spectacles.

The procedure ended at that point. Jung quickly shuffled his papers and addressed the audience regarding the word association procedure and the unconscious complexes that he believed had been revealed by my responses. He noted my unusual fixation with my mother and how I had viewed him as a rival, a "rock-hard" father substitute. He noted that, in addition to my oedipal complex, my associations revealed a strain of mania because I was unable to contain my responses to a single word and seemed intent on making a mockery of the procedure. He concluded with the following summation,

"In conclusion, we know from his catatonia and other secondary symptoms of psychosis that this patient suffers from dementia praecox with elements of mania. I believe his condition is endogenous, that there is an organic basis for this psychosis and his incomprehensible jumble of words. I suspect a chronic, deteriorating course. His treatment should aim to contain his symptoms with somatic therapies. He is not an appropriate candidate for psychoanalytical treatment, much less analysis. Sadly, gentleman and ladies, the prognosis is rather grim."

With that, the teaching rounds were concluded. The audience applauded. Several in attendance approached Carl Gustav Jung to shake his hand and ask their questions. He nodded curtly at the Director and walked through the door without looking back at me. An entourage of white-coated physicians trailed closely behind.

This completed my encounter with Carl Gustav Jung and my delivery of a "message for Jung." I realized I had neither a "message" nor any idea what that meant in the first place. The aides detached me from the galvanometer and wheeled me back to my room, where I spent the remainder of the afternoon and evening in bed.

The following day, I had a surprise visit from the Director, who was accompanied by the matron. Dr. Bleuler sat by my bed. "Ah, Anton that must have been quite something for you. Herr Jung is considered, by many, a genius in our field here in Zurich and among colleagues in Berlin and Vienna. He is gaining quite a reputation, but he can be forceful. I hope you were not too, how should I say, bruised by the examination."

He said he had given a great deal of thought to Jung's diagnosis and prognosis. "I must say, Anton, that what Dr. Jung said makes a great deal of sense. This catatonia – the frozen posture you assume – *is* diagnostic of schizophrenia, and what Jung said about the endogenous or constitutional basis for this disease is often correct….but, something tells me this might not be the case with you, Anton. I am not seeing the underlying structure of this disease process, only secondary symptomatology. Perhaps, there is an exogenous explanation. I am wondering if something horrendous happened to you, maybe many things – events that had catastrophic effects on your mental functions. Think of it this way, a sudden disruption of the earth's surface can be caused by convulsive forces deep within, leading to what we know as an earthquake. But, it is possible, that something could crash onto the earth's surface from the distant skies, like some heavenly body falling from above. Yes, Anton, this is what I am wondering about with you. Are your symptoms the result of traumatic events and not an organic collapse of your mind from within?"

At the time, I had difficulty understanding the meaning beneath his comforting voice and manner. It felt quite different from what I had experienced the day before in the darkened amphitheater. The Director continued. "I don't think you should remain at Burghölzli. Although we have the finest physicians in the world, too many are swayed by the strength of charismatic personalities. I fear that Jung's grim prognosis has prejudiced my staff to view you through a narrow lens, limiting their openness to exploring other possibilities. I would like to send you somewhere else, Anton. I know of a brilliant young psychiatrist at the cantonal asylum in Herisau, a small province, 80 kilometers to the east. His name is Dr. Hermann Rorschach. He trained here, and I had the pleasure of supervising his dissertation. I think this man who might be able to help you. He is an independent thinker, with a particular interest in the study of movement and psychoses. I should also mention that his wife, also a physician, is herself Russian, and that Rorschach lived there for a period of time before returning to Switzerland. He has a love and respect for the Russian culture. Most importantly, I know this physician establishes a gentle and caring rapport with his patients. Too often, we physicians see only the disease. I believe that Rorschach sees the person *with* the disease. Yes, Anton, I believe this is best. I will send him a telegram later today, and we will see about arranging your transfer to Herisau. *Gut Sein,* Anton, farewell."

That evening, the attendants brought my supper tray and tried to feed me. As usual, I had little appetite. Absentmindedly, they left the tray by my bed. Later, Shev and Vasily startled me with their appearance. Although the taunting whisperers had continued, my ghosts had not made an appearance for some time. Vasily stood behind Shev, but, now, his form appeared more diffuse and indistinct. Shev's words rang forth,

"My dear Squire, what a sad and sorry state you've been in. Your travels have been long and hard. You have become frozen by unanticipated treachery and pain. Others have guided you faithfully, while there were those who betrayed you to the devil. You have been aided by wise counselors, but, still, there are those who would lead you astray. You feared that all was done, that all had been lost. But, best to remember Khayyám's words from the Rubiayat – 'The moving finger writes; and having writ, moves on.' Your journey, though stalled, moves on. It has by no means come to an end, Squire."

As I listened to the monk, I glanced down and saw my finger moving, as I reached for the tray of food and began feeding myself the remaining morsels on the plate.

CHAPTER 14

Drawing with Rorschach

We set off early the next morning. The aides and nurse matron were pleasantly surprised that I had use of my arms and was able to feed myself breakfast. They assumed my improvement was connected with my session with Professor Jung. I overheard the matron whispering to the senior attendant, "I've seen Dr. Jung perform similar miracles with patients far more afflicted than this young Russian. Pity, they asked Professor Jung to leave his staff position here."

Buoyed by my improvement, they urged me to try to stand and see if I could walk. When I stood, my legs didn't hold me, and I fell. Dr. Minkowski made her morning rounds just in time to see me collapse. The others told her I'd miraculously regained the use of my arms, and they thought that I might be able to walk as well. Minkowski quietly said,

"Herr Director informed me that you'll be going to a small hospital in Herisau, Anton. I know Rorschach. I think the Director made a wise decision sending you to him, but I shall miss being your doctor here." With those words, she leaned down and gently hugged me. The warmth of this gesture was both surprising and comforting. She instructed the matron to pack my few belongings and ready me for the journey to Herisau. An honest and decent woman, the matron ensured that my watches and inkblot parchment were carefully wrapped and stowed in my backpack. As for Luka's pistol, that had long since been confiscated upon my admission to the sanitarium.

Before I left, I was taken to the baths for my final hydrotherapy. There, the nurses encouraged me to move my arms in circles to "promote circulation." The aides all beamed with pride that it was their therapy that had restored the use of my arms. But rotating my shoulders caused great pain. As I winced, they reassured me that pain was to be expected after having not used these muscles for so long.

They wheeled me to the coach to take me to Herisau. I took a final look at what had been my home for nearly a year. The leaves had begun to fall and the air was cooler. A nurse and aide were sent with me on the journey east. We rolled by pastures with sheep grazing in the sunlight. I grew sleepy as we passed through the bucolic countryside with rolling hills and farmland. The fields lost some of their summer luster, as colorful blooms on wildflowers had faded. I awoke with a start as the coach suddenly stopped, and the aide announced that we'd arrived.

The canton of Appenzell Ausserrhoden was a scenic rural community, made up of an insular local population. The main hospital, called the Krombach, was perched on a hill to the west of Herisau. The hospital grounds resembled a country park with several small buildings that housed male and female patients separately. We'd stopped in front of the main hospital building, where I was wheeled in and ushered through the admissions process. The nurse was engaged in a long conversation with administrators regarding my transfer to Dr. Rorschach, per orders of Herr Director Bleuler. After a lengthy course of filling out forms, I was finally brought to a large common room. There, the nurse and aide bade me a cordial farewell and left me at a table by myself.

I was not alone. Seated at other tables were patients, eating and writing, some in quiet conversation, while others sat with empty expressions on their faces. I noted one or two fixed in rigid postures, reminiscent of my own frozen days at Burghölzli. Most of them wore white gowns or colorless shirts and loose-fitting trousers.

I watched as a dark-eyed man moved gracefully from table to table, quietly speaking with those who were seated. He had a casual air, dressed in an open collared white shirt with a woolen vest. Several other men and women in traditional medical coats followed him from table to table.

"Ah," I thought, "So familiar. The doctors are observing an agitated patient as he prances about. I've seen this before. They're making notes about his aberrant behavior, which they'll report to the senior physicians."

I was distracted by commotion from the far end of the room, where other patients with loud voices were seated in the common area. Over my shoulder, I had not seen the vested man approach me. He suddenly appeared, carrying a tray of food. As he sat down across from me, he pushed the tray forward and he said,

"My name is Dr. Hermann Rorschach. I'm to be your physician. I've read the notes from the Director. Welcome to our humble hospital – nothing like Burghölzli, but I believe you will find it a comfortable setting in which to heal. Here, I brought you a tray of food."

I was taken aback by the discovery that the man roaming the room was not an agitated patient but none other than the Rorschach fellow the Director had sent me to see. I was also startled by his unsolicited offering of food. I sputtered,

"But, but, I didn't ask for any food."

To this, Rorschach replied with a faint smile,

"Yes, but you looked hungry, too."

I felt a distant stirring and was puzzled why his simple words brought a moist stinging to my eyes. However, I was aware that this man with dark, sensitive eyes had taken note of my silent reaction to his words. Hadn't Shev once said that the body never lies?

Rorschach added, "Eat first, then we talk."

At this, he got up and moved to other tables with his white-coated entourage following in tow.

The following day, I was wheeled back into the common room and seated at a table with two other patients, an older man and younger woman. The woman said little and never looked up; but the old gentleman, who called himself, "Schmeegle," jabbered throughout our noontime meal. He spoke German, mixing in words with a bizarre, inventive quality. Schmeegle talked about his scientific discovery of a new form of "odorless energy," which he called "mercrozenium." He looked suspiciously around the room, leaned close to me, and whispered a spittley message that his discovery could connect people's thoughts with each other.

"So, you see that with mercrozenium, all the world can see into a single orb, removing the very essence of speech itself, leaving our species to evolve. My discovery must remain a secret, young man. Swear you'll share no word of it."

I nodded hesitantly at the moment that Rorschach approached our table. He handed each of us a parchment paper and placed a box of multi-colored charcoal sticks in front of us. The others began drawing on cue. Old Schmeegle mumbled under his breath and began drawing dark circles with lines connecting each.

Rorschach mused, "Good, Herr Schmeegle, good. You've gotten right down to work today I see." Turning to the quiet woman, he said, "And same for you, Daunet." Rorschach looked my way and gestured for me to draw as well. I sat motionless. "Anton, right? I see that you are Russian. I happen to speak some Russian. My wife, a physician herself, is Russian and gives lectures to our patients with slideshows about life and culture in Russia. I think you'll find these quite interesting. Would you like me to use your language, or do you also speak German, Anton?"

I indicated that I understood some German, to which he replied, "Then I'm sure we'll be able to find each other with our words. But I would also like you to do some drawings for me. You see the others are working on their drawings. We find that drawing frees the mind to express itself, unencumbered by words. We encourage art as a creative activity here at our small hospital. Some of our patients improve as a result of their creative pursuits, Anton. So, here. I think you'll find art can be quite healing."

He moved paper and the charcoal sticks in front of me and watched. I sat and did nothing for several minutes. Rorschach made other encouraging comments. I hadn't drawn anything for longer than I could remember and had no intention of doing so again. Finally, I gazed up at my doctor and shook my head. Rorschach nodded and said, "It can be hard to begin, I understand this, Anton, and will respect your wishes today. Tomorrow, maybe you'll feel differently. You need time to adjust to your new life here."

Days stretched into weeks, then months, as life at the asylum became more routine. Each day, I was wheeled into the common area for a morning meal. Later, some patients were organized into work groups, while others formed small choirs under the direction of the nurses. The hydrotherapy baths and gardens at Herisau were modest compared to those at Burghölzli. Every day, aides attempted to get me on my feet; but each time, I fell.

Afternoons were time for drawing therapy. Rorschach and the other doctors wandered from table to table encouraging patients to draw what spontaneously came to their minds. Each day, Schmeegle seemed to seek me out. When he entered the common area, he scanned the room until he found me. Pushing other patients aside, he always headed straight to my table and took the seat next to me. If it was occupied, he paced nervously until the other patient relinquished the seat. Oblivious to my hints that I preferred to be alone, old Schmeegle leaned his face close to my ear and echoed the details about his important discovery. Each time, he had me swear that I would not divulge the contents of our conversations.

In the evenings, Rorschach often returned with silhouette puppets made out of cardboard. The figures depicted men and women, staff, patients, and doctors. There was even one resembling Rorschach himself. The joints on the arms and legs were hinged so that the characters could be manipulated into various poses to capture different forms of movement. He explained to the patients, during these "puppet shows," that movement was an "expressive form of experience that reflected imaginative processes within the mind and allowed us to understand what others were feeling." His words made little sense to me, but I was amused by his playful spirit in staging his puppet shows. During the days, he continued to gently offer paper and charcoal sticks but would patiently accept my refusal with a polite nod.

After I had been a patient for two, maybe three months, he increased the pressure of his gentle offering by professing, "As your physician, Anton, it is my medical opinion that your treatment must begin by finding an expressive outlet. Especially for the catatonic, who has been terrified of movement, drawing is a first step toward recovery. So, today, Anton, I am asking you to draw."

The sparkle in his dark eyes communicated something, though I was uncertain what. All I knew was I felt calm in his presence. His thick brown hair was neatly brushed back. He never wore a white coat like the other doctors. He rarely donned a jacket at all; and when he did, there was always a pipe sticking up from the front pocket. He had the faint aroma of tobacco, which brought memories of Baba Zsófia. On that particular day, I succumbed to his gentle request and began to draw with Rorschach.

❖ ❖ ❖

I continued drawing each day. All my drawings had dark horses, no other colors, just charcoal black. Rorschach seemed pleased and offered encouragement. "Ah, good Anton, a fine drawing. Continue."

It turned out that drawing quieted my mind, which had been unsettled since coming to Herisau. At night, I continued to worry that I was not safe. I dreamt of explosions that ripped through tranquil, blue-sky days – the quiet, punctured by screams, which unleashed rivers of blood flowing up to my knees. As I attempted to escape, I was chased by dark figures, whispering my name. Several times a week, I woke up on the floor, huddled in the corner or lying under my cot. The nighttime aids would rush in and, at times, had to fend off my blows, for I believed they were the dark figures who had come to kill me.

Strangest of all was that I missed the visitations of my ghosts, Shev and Vasily. Though it had been longer than I remembered that I had seen or heard the voice of Vasily, I particularly missed the annoying presence of Shev. Once or twice, before I had fallen asleep, I thought I'd heard his voice but could not make out what was saying.

During the day, I continued to draw. Placing the charcoal stick on my paper, I allowed my hand to move on its own. All my drawings had horses, nothing else. One day, Rorschach took a seat next to me and said, "I'm pleased, Anton, that you seem to enjoy drawing. I wonder what your drawings might tell us about your bad dreams."

Until that moment, Rorschach had not said anything about my nightmares. He had not asked me any questions about my life before I appeared at the gates of Burghölzli, but clearly he knew more than he'd chosen to share. He continued, "These are such powerful horses that you draw every day, Anton. And they are always black. I wonder what leads your mind to this avenue of expression. Why these horses? And how curious…

Anton, your drawings have no people….So, I must ask myself, where did they all go?" A simple observation turned into a question, which he repeated softly, "Where are the people, Anton?"

After a frozen pause, the unexpected upsurge of emotion was immediate. I suddenly broke down and began to sob, quietly at first but then more forcefully. Choking on my tears, I sobbed,

"They're all gone….ALL OF THEM…GONE."

Rorschach moved next to me and remained silent as I wept. He placed his hand lightly on my forearm, handed me his handkerchief, and softly encouraged me. "Let if out. Let it come, Anton. I think you've carried this alone for far too long. Just let it out now. We have much work to do. I will leave word with the nurse to bring you to my office tomorrow at 9:00 AM. Now, I think we can begin.

His office, a modestly-sized room, was crowded with books, charcoal drawings, and papers. A large window opened to the Säntis, one of the highest mountains in northwest Switzerland. Sunlight streamed in providing a warming glow; the air was fresh and cool. Rorschach motioned for me to sit across from his desk, while he lit his pipe and reached for a notebook and pen.

The walls of his office were adorned with drawings, which I later learned were the creations of the psychiatrist himself. At the far end of the room was another table piled with stacks of paper, charcoal sticks, paint brushes of varying sizes, and liter-sized bottles of ink, mostly black. On the table, I saw pieces of the silhouetted puppet figures that he would later join together to make moveable joints.

Seated across from me, my doctor asked if I'd like to try drawing more pictures. As I shook my head, I suddenly began to blubber again, the very sight of paper and charcoal triggered in me a reaction I could not control. Rorschach leaned forward, passed me a handkerchief, sat back, and began making some notes, which later turned into sketches. After a minute of silence, he said, "We have time, Anton. I believe that the affect, your emotion, will lead the way. We cannot force this work. I am here when you are ready to talk."

I wasn't ready to put words to my sobbing for many days. Each morning, the nurse brought me to his office, where the sight of him, the art on his walls, and the aroma of his tobacco made me sob. Rorschach sat patiently, occasionally passing a handkerchief or offering me water. While waiting, he moved to his table with the parchments and ink bottles and dribbled droplets of ink onto white cards, which he would then carefully fold in half.

After a week of this routine, I finally spoke, "I began drawing horses when I was a small boy. I had bad dreams with horses, and my aunt told me I could become the master of my dreams by drawing them."

Rorschach asked me where in Russia I was from. I described Zastavia, and told him about Papa, Mama, my brother, and dear aunt. "My papa made beautiful watches. My mama was a dancer, and my aunt cared for small creatures that needed food and shelter. I had a brother, Chaim, who was very strong. I used to call him 'my golden brother;' he called me 'Sparrow.'"

And so, our dialogue, my monologue, began. Much as I had opened up and shared stories about my life with Kata, I began pouring out a jumble of details about my home and family. When I paused, Rorschach would ask, "What were you thinking at the time?" or "Can you recall what your deepest feelings were when that happened?"

For days, I talked about Papa's workshop and how he'd wanted Chaim to become a watchmaker like himself. I said that Papa never looked me in the eye. Even when he finally allowed me to begin making watches with him, he never really saw me. I told Rorschach about Mama, how different she looked, how she gripped my hand tightly, and how Papa's family ignored her. I described the love I'd felt from Nadya, who called me "*Pidkyana*" or just "*Pidky.*" I recalled how Nadya said Mama just appeared one day in the woods around our village, carrying a tiny baby, and how Mama had used ink drawings to tell fortunes for the villagers. I began weeping again when I told Rorschach how she changed, how Mama grew strange and distant.

"One night when I was ten, she disappeared. That's why I finally went searching for her and somehow ended up here."

We spent months talking about my life in Zastavia, before and after Mama disappeared. Rorschach was curious about how I went from drawing horses to smearing myself with mud, only later to sit beside Papa, focusing my mind on tiny metal pins, springs, and coils. I told him about making a crude timepiece for Papa, how I had foolishly believed that he was making a special watch for me, only to learn that it was for my "golden brother" instead of his "rock-handed" younger son. I found it was easier to talk about my accidental conscription and involvement in the war than about Mama's disappearance. I described how I'd left my home, and in a bitter state, had stolen my father's precious watches, only to be forced to join the Czar's Imperial Army as I tried to escape from Russia. I recounted my job as latrine digger and excrement burner and how I had managed to use my watch repair skills to escape the world of piss and shit. Rorschach asked about my fellow conscripts and soldiers. After initial hesitation, I talked about Shev and Vasily and our afternoon of drinking and story-telling amidst the death and ruin in Neidenburg. Rorschach encouraged me to say more about these encounters. "In the darkness of those days, you managed to find light in these two fellows, who, were far more than they seemed. You haven't said what became of them, Anton."

By this point in our sessions, my well of tears had run dry and had become replaced by an arid reluctance to give up more. I simply shook my head and turned away, which was a transparent clue to Rorschach that we were done for the day and that there was more left to explore.

Between sessions, the rhythm of my life became comforting in its monotonous predictability – daily meals, morning sessions with the warm, yet inscrutable Rorschach, treatments at the baths, group gardening activities, and evening drawing sessions.

Each day, when we were brought to the large common room, old Schmeegle would search the room for me. After a period of trying to evade his hungry eyes or ignore his frothy efforts to engage, I succumbed to the reality that, like many of the misfits I had encountered in the Imperial Army or in Felsögalia, my fate was inextricably bound to this assemblage of characters that now was part of my daily life. After some time, my annoyance and aversion to Schmeegle began to soften, and I found myself almost looking forward to our daily encounters. As I reflect back on my year at Herisau, I realize that his mad rantings about discovering a secret source of energy that would "connect human minds" was really no different than my own misguided attempt to reverse the course of time so that I could find my way back home to reconnect with my family. In his amusingly crazy way, he, too, seemed to be trying to connect with a home of his own, only to become lost in his delusional ramblings.

During our evening drawing sessions, I used grayish tones to draw Papa at his workbench, with his back turned. I made crude drawings of Mama and used bright oils to color her long skirts and flowing scarfs. I chose browns for Nadya but found light colors for her eyes. On some days, I drew watches, focusing my tired mind on bits and pieces of cold steel.

Sessions with Rorschach continued into the next year. I saw him each morning at the same time, as our dialogue continued. One day, he said that the trails leading to Säntis were quite beautiful this time of year, and that it was a pity I didn't have the use of my legs so we could have our sessions while strolling outdoors in the fresh air.

He added, "The curious thing about your legs, Anton, is that the nerves and muscles are quite intact. Physicians who've examined you cannot explain a somatic cause for your paralysis. It's as if you've become a wounded sparrow that convinced itself that it cannot fly. Flight and movement through space must have unsettled you, so you remain a flightless bird. So, I must ask myself, why is this so?"

Something about his words angered me, but I couldn't do more than fall into a petulant, stubborn silence. Rorschach leaned closer and explained, "Sometimes, there is an earthquake inside the mind, with subterranean fault lines that badly damage the psychic apparatus. I believe this happened to you, that the fissures in your mind are the result of your crushing losses and terrors, some of which you have told me about, but much of which still lies hidden in those subterranean caverns of your mind."

I turned further away and brought my hands up to my ears.

"You see, Anton, I believe that to shelter yourself from the earthquake of cataclysmic psychic shocks, strains, and losses, you attempted to reconstruct a world within yourself to replace the one that exists outside. Somehow, you came to believe that you could protect yourself and prevent further catastrophes by restraining all external activity – all forms of movement – and by freezing your mind to the meaning of all that you've lost. Like all catatonics, you convinced yourself that to move is to die or cause further death and destruction in the world. Like Atlas, burdened with the weight of the world on his shoulders, you have condemned yourself to bear this burden."

I don't recall when I began to regain movement in my legs. I remember more the pain I experienced when I tried to unbend my knees and straighten my legs. My nascent movement caused a stir among the nurses in the baths, who again, assumed that their massages and hydrotherapy had cured my paralysis.

Rorschach's reaction to my movement was understated. Clearly pleased, he took care not to draw too much attention to the fact that I was able to stand and slowly take my first steps. After several weeks, we took our first walk together in the snow.

In the brisk morning air, we strolled through a grove of silver fir trees. The air was crisp, and soft flakes of snow clung to our hair and eyebrows. My legs ached, but he gently encouraged me to keep moving. As we walked, I thought about the interminable hikes toward Tannenberg. I recalled marching with Shev and Vasily and finally told Rorschach about the horrific ways in which they were killed. We had to stop as I dropped to my haunches and wept silently. When I had composed myself, I confessed to Rorschach that I continued to communicate with them.

"Such hallucinations are understandable reactions to horrible events that overwhelm the psyche. As you heal, they will pass."

"But, I'm not so sure," I said. "When they first began, I feared they were signs I was losing my mind; but over time, I've come to believe they were something else."

"What else could they be, Anton?"

I shrugged and said, "Annoyances…ghosts…maybe, guides, I don't know."

I did not wish to reveal more about my "conversations" with Shev and Vasily, or how, at times, I'd felt my private insanity was the only thing that had kept me sane, so I changed the subject. I told him about my journey back to Zastavia and how I'd been convinced I was being hunted by dark Serbian forces. Rorschach listened as I told about wanting to die when I discovered the ruins of Zastavia. I described how my strange dream led me on a quest to search for my mother in Felsögalia. I painted a verbal portrait of the haunting Kata and the meaning of her gypsy song. Before then, I hadn't spoken about how she had given life to a well of confusing feelings. I tried to distract myself by refocusing on my lost cousin Tobbar and the arrogant Zifi Zeekko or by describing the wisdom of Baba Zsófia and her tales about Mama's sad life. I told him about our trek to find the Brothers of the Woodland and of the bloody events that followed, before some mysterious stranger brought me to the gate outside the Burghölzli.

"You're painting an ever expanding picture of your life with finer details," Rorschach said, "but I can see that there are still things you would rather me avoid and leave for another day."

Although the whispering threats and nightmares became less frequent, I was not free of them entirely. Often, before drifting off, I thought I heard low voices outside my window warning me to stay silent. It had also been months since my last encounter with Vasily or Shev. From time to time, I heard Shev's laughter or caught glimpses of him walking behind me on woodland trails outside the hospital, but I no longer heard Vasily's stuttering voice.

One night, I had a vivid dream. I was watching a line of passengers preparing to board a ship. I spotted a man who looked like Vasily. He wore a prominent pince nez. He was surrounded by children, several of whom wore spectacles and carried books. As they made their way toward the gangway, I attempted to shout his name. Only a stuttering sound would come out. Suddenly, before Vasily made his way up the platform, he turned my way and raised his hand to wave. I watched as he mouthed the words, "Find your peace. Farewell, Anton."

❖ ❖ ❖

As my legs grew stronger, the length of my walks with Rorschach increased. During one of our walking sessions, he observed that I never drew pictures of Chaim and had said almost nothing about him. "You've begun to draw pictures and tell me about your papa, mama, and your aunt but nothing about Chaim, except to refer to him as your 'golden brother.' Like the precious metal itself, Chaim must have been truly magnificent in your eyes. You called him 'golden' yet you mentioned that he referred to you as 'Sparrow.' It seems that your family all had these little names for you, Anton, *Kicsi, Pidkydyanna,* and, Sparrow, as if you were a small, fragile boy, like the helpless creatures your aunt would find in the forest."

After a long pause, Rorschach asked where the name *Pidkyana* came from and whether I understood what it meant. I explained how my aunt often used Ukrainian words or expressions that I did not understand. Rorschach reminded me that his wife was Russian and was familiar with Ukrainian.

"Anton, though I do not discuss my patient's private matters with my wife, she knows the Ukrainian language well. So, I asked if she had ever heard the word *"pidkyana."* She said that it was the word for foundlings, babies who were abandoned, found, and cared for by others. I find it puzzling that your adoring Aunt Nadya used such a name for you, Anton."

As was frequently the case, Rorschach did not allow silences to linger for long before he began speaking again. "You told me disjointed stories about how your mother had fallen in love with a man and escaped with their baby from men who were trying to kill them. You also told me that your Aunt Baba said they were attacked by a pack of wolves and that your mama had somehow arrived in Zastavia with an infant in her arms. Am I remembering this correctly, Anton."

I nodded.

"Who, then, was this found baby, Anton?"

"…I…I have an older brother somewhere. Not Chaim, but another brother. That's all I know. I will find him someday."

Rorschach stopped to relight his pipe. He turned toward me and said firmly, "Maybe you already have, Anton. Sometimes, we protect ourselves against certain truths by pretending that we cannot see or hear what is there in front of us…*Pidkydyanna.* I believe you were the baby that Aunt Nadya found in the forest by your home that day. Such an endearing name, *Pidky,* which always held the truth about you….And, as for the black shapes and horses that have always haunted your dreams, I must ask myself if these are but ancient images stored in the mind of a tiny baby whose parents were fleeing on horseback from a pack of Siberian wolves?"

He certainly realized he'd said more than I could take in because I did not leave my bed for the next several days. When the nurse came to escort me to my morning sessions, I responded that I was feeling too ill to attend. I refused to go to meals or participate in other hospital activities. I looked for Shev among the shadows in my room. I even spoke his name, but all that remained was deafening silence.

I gradually emerged from this period of dark solitude. To this day, I don't know what shook me from my stupor – the feel of spring in the air, Rorschach's respectful distance, or simply noticing how Schmeegle began drawing faces on his connected circles? Whatever it was, I began to think more clearly about the story Rorschach had told of my life – how Mama and I were "found" by Nadya in the woods; why Papa would not look at this foundling who was not his son, and why I always had nightmares about terrified horses, dark shapes, and babies crying. The hollow feelings in my stomach gave way to sadness. I resumed my sessions.

"You have come far on your journey here, Anton. The arc of your story has broadened so that we can see in many directions, but there is still something that troubles me…Chaim, your 'golden brother.' What became of him? Whenever he comes up, you cleverly change the subject, throwing out one tantalizing story after another. It has taken me some time to catch up with you and understand your evasions. Early in your work here, you said that 'everyone was gone.' I know about your mama, papa, about Nadya, your comrades in the war, and the Romani girl, but what became of your golden brother?…Eh, Sparrow?"

His stinging words, calling me "Sparrow," were provocative, perhaps by intention. He would not let this be! My heart began to pound, and I suddenly roared,

"THERE ARE SOME PLACES IN MY MIND WHERE YOU CANNOT GO! WHY CAN'T YOU SEE THAT AND LEAVE THIS ALONE?! WILL YOU ONLY BE SATISFIED WHEN I CONFESS TO THE WORLD THAT I MURDERED MY BROTHER?!"

I could see that my angry tone and booming voice had not deterred my doctor. Rorschach quietly listened and motioned for me to continue.

My chest felt like it would explode as I blurted out, "YOU WANT ME TO CONFESS THAT THE ONLY TIME I PULLED THE TRIGGER ON MY RIFLE WAS TO KILL CHAIM?!…To blow a hole through his chest as he came to find me?"

After a pause, he looked into the distance and said, "You keep using the word 'confess' as if you have been accused of a terrible crime and are on trial, Anton. Sadly, the courtroom exists in your mind; and you have taken roles of prosecutor and judge, only your prosecutor is more of a persecutor, who hunts and haunts you."

After several minutes, I began to calm down. I was drenched in sweat and out of breath. I spoke slowly about our retreat with Luka and Glagolev from Tannenberg that night. I replayed the moment that I blindly fired the

Mosin into the darkness, as my brother dropped lifelessly into our trench. I echoed the words that Luka as repeated, "*Pucano u leda. Ne front.*"

Rorschach asked what those words meant, and I translated, "Shot in the back, not the front." Rorschach was curious why I hadn't believed the seasoned warrior, who was trying to tell me that I had *not* killed my brother. He queried that, as a soldier, I'd surely learned that the exit wound left a much larger hole than the entry point. He continued, "Somehow, you ignored this man, who you said protected and ultimately embraced you. You could not accept the truth that Chaim was shot from behind, that you did not kill him. You pronounced yourself guilty of fratricide and turned your Serbian protector into a hunter…I must ask myself, why this need, Anton? Why this need to punish yourself for something that you did not do, unless…."

A torrent of words rushed forth, as I shouted, "HE MEANT EVERYTHING, BUT I HATED HIM, HATED WHAT HE TOOK FROM ME!!"

I had long since lost count of the number of times our sessions ended in a pool of tears, but I still remember this time. Rorschach motioned that we sit on some rocks in the shade of a large beech tree. When I stopped sobbing, I told him how much I'd adored my brother but how his golden hue became darkened by my jealousy and resentment. I suddenly recalled watching Chaim walk away from me when he had found me digging a latrine and then hearing the words, "good riddance," echo in my mind.

Rorschach said that I clearly hadn't killed Chaim, but that "a forbidden wish to rid yourself of your brother took the form of a crime in your mind. You lost the distinction between an unspeakable wish and a physical deed. What complicated all of this, Anton, is that you also never stopped loving your brother….Now, I believe that it is time for you to forgive."

Through my tears, I wheezed that I *wanted* to forgive Chaim.

"Good, but that's not the forgiveness I was thinking about. His crimes, if he committed any to begin with, were quite minor. The crime of having *his* father love *him* more than he loved *you*. No, I'm thinking of forgiving yourself for the crimes you believe you committed in your heart. That is the task and road ahead of you.

It had been over a year since I was brought to the hospital in Herisau. Some of the patients had left, but many remained. Schmeegle passed one night in his sleep. The next morning, I learned that he'd had an unexpected visit from his son the night before he died.

The season had begun to change again. The cool fall air gave way to wintry frosts. I slept soundly. I no longer had nightmares. One night I awoke and saw Shev sitting across the room. He was dressed in a brown robe that made me think of the drab-colored smocks Nadya used to wear. He stood and finally spoke, "Yes, Squire, it has been quite a journey of exploration. The moving finger writes and continues to write or, should I say 'right', your story."

"You haven't been around for a while," my comment sounding more like an accusation than an observation.

"You haven't needed me, Squire."

I continued, "They say you're not real. That none of this was…. Rorschach called you something like a 'reflex hallucination.' He said it was my mind's attempt to repair the fissures or something, and that all of the words from you and Vasily were memories embedded in my unconscious from that drunken afternoon in Neidenburg. He said I've kept replaying all that in my mind."

The monk smiled enigmatically. "It could be that, or it could be this, or it could be something magical, Squire. Your Herr Rorschach is very wise indeed, but like many learned men of science, his sight may be blinded by trying to discern what is real from what provides meaning in our lives."

As I watched him walk toward the door, I said, "You look like you're dressed for a journey."

"Yes, a pilgrimage, for like all of us, I am but a pilgrim making my way, Squire."

"But, wait," I blurted out. "I never knew your name!"

"You never asked, but since you are now, I am Nicolai, Nicolai Keloskovich, but those dear to my heart have always called me 'Nike,' as in Nike of Samothrace. You will always remember me, Anton. To paraphrase our own Dostoyevsky, 'there is nothing higher, stronger, and more wholesome for life in the future than having some good memory; and if a man carries even one such memory in his heart, then he is safe to the end of his days.'"

With a final wink, Shev, Nicolai, turned and disappeared into the shadows. Gone.

I called his name, "Wait, WAIT! Nicolai, Nike…SHEV!"

Suddenly, the night nurse opened the door and asked who I was talking to. She wondered if I had had another nightmare and whether I was alright.

I crawled back under my covers, closed my eyes, and quietly replied, "I was just muttering to the wind. I'm fine. Good night."

As the light in my mind grew dim, I recalled words from Mama's song *Idövel Jobban Leszeck*, which I'd heard Kata singing on the train platform,

Shedding my skin while praying

For more

Watching my ghosts fall silent to the floor

I sensed that my journey at the canton hospital in Herisau was drawing to a close. My sessions with Rorschach were no longer scheduled on a daily

basis. I spent increasing amounts of time away from the hospital, tending to the gardens and assisting other patients on their day-trips into the town. Rorschach informed me that my progress had been remarkable and that I would be discharged in the months ahead. I was given passes each weekend and encouraged to rent a room in Herisau, where I was to spend time getting used to the freedom of life away from the institution. The plan was for me to continue periodic follow-up meetings with Rorschach after my discharge, while I was living in the community.

I discovered a small watchmaker's shop in town and obtained part-time employment assisting with simple repairs. The watchmaker was an elderly gentleman with an awkward gait, named Otto Kooch. He soon saw I had more than a modicum of knowledge and skill with timepieces and allowed me to sleep in the small room behind the store.

The room was small, but larger and brighter than the hospital rooms I had inhabited for the last two years. As I unpacked my few belongings, I discovered Papa's watches I had carried with me all these years, along with the tattered and yellowed inkblot I had saved from the fire so long ago. I also found the watch with the ink-stained face that I'd begun to make for my father. I suddenly felt inspired to finish the piece and give it to Rorschach as a token of my appreciation for all he had done for me. I glanced at the back and recalled how I'd started to engrave, *From AZ to H.* I would finish engraving it, clean, and present it to Rorschach as a gift. Otto was kind enough to allow me to use his tools, and gave me advice about using his stylus.

After several months of returning to the hospital for sessions, the nurse met me outside his office and hinted that this was to be my final appointment. Rorschach greeted me warmly. I noticed that his hands were stained with ink and saw that he had been working on his art table with his folded parchments and ink bottles. He inquired about my job in town and seemed pleased that I was adjusting to my new life. After a pause, we began speaking at the same time. He said there was something he wished to discuss with me but invited me to speak first.

I reached for my rucksack and tilted it to get the watch I wanted to give him. Suddenly, Mama's tattered inkblot fell out and floated to the floor. Rorschach fixed his eyes on it and asked what I had brought with me. In our many hours together, I had talked about Mama's use of pictures to tell fortunes, but never described much about her strange method. I picked up and gently unfolded the cracked parchment and displayed her old, faded inkblot. I told him how my mother used these blots to help people understand things about their lives. He asked to hold it, his eyes growing wide. "Remarkable. *Klecksographien*! Just remarkable."

He excitedly told me of the research he had been conducting with inkblots as a means of investigating the human psyche. He mentioned work he had done while a student at Burghölzli under the supervision of Director Bleuler. Rorschach stood with the inkblot and said, "So, it seems that your mother was interested in the same thing, Anton! You've told me how she was a seeker and journeyed, possibly even to Burghölzli, but now I see she was a pioneer of sorts. Fascinating, the way she constructed this blot. There is more to this than dropping random blotches of paint on a parchment and folding it over. No, I can see that your mother knew something about that. This could not be a more chance and fortuitous event, Anton! I am conducting my own inkblot investigations and would like you to become one of my research assistants. This is what I wanted to ask you! Your progress has been astounding. You are capable of living an independent life; and now, with the discovery of this inkblot, it is all the more reason that I would like you to assist in my scientific experiment!"

I was stunned by his emotional reaction to Mama's inkblot and honored by his invitation to become one of his research assistants. I eagerly nodded my head and felt this was the right moment to show my appreciation for his faith in me. I reached into my rucksack and brought out the watch.

"Herr Rorschach, my skills as a craftsman are lacking, but this is my attempt to show my deep appreciation for your helping me find my story. Please accept this."

He unwrapped the watch, turned it over and read out loud the inscription,

"*From AZ to HR. Le Chaim.*" His eyes were glossy as he turned it over and said,

"Oh my, Anton. There is a klex spot on the face." Pointing to the small smudge on the face of the watch, he said, "See, you signed it with an inkblot. Perhaps, it was your way of carrying your mama with you all these years. Thank you."

If I thought I had shed my last tear in his presence months before, I had been mistaken.

CHAPTER 15

Interpretation of Accidental Forms

found it difficult not to stare at his drooping right eye and the sagging corner of his mouth. When I averted my gaze, I'd notice his misbuttoned shirt and mismatched shoes, often on the wrong feet. I followed him, his slow shuffling gait making it difficult not to step on his heels. When he opened the door to his tiny workshop, cascading memories were awakened by musky smells of oils and leather and rusted displays of metal pins, gears, and coils.

Otto Kooch's kindness belied his comically sad appearance. Oblivious to his grooming and the peculiarities of his attire, Otto seemed most concerned in making me feel comfortable in my new surroundings. When he spoke, he often paused, searching for a word to complete his thought. Sometimes, he reversed his words like he reversed his shoes. In spite of his odd appearance and difficulties communicating, Otto had a natural affinity for humor.

"This, then is my…shopwork, ya know, where the magic happens. I bring da pieces back here and kaphflunken! I fix em up. Been doin this for oh, about 600 years I expect. It was my papa and Uncle Karl which provided the…interrogatories to master the technique. If you're interested, I could accommodate an instructional assistant."

Unlike Papa's meticulous workshop, Otto's "shopwork" was cluttered with parts and pieces jumbled together in a large box under his workbench. The grit of metal filings and gears littered the wooden floor and crunched under my feet with every step.

"Yes, Herr Kooch, I accept your offer. The first thing I will do is clean and organize your shop and bench. I did that for my papa many years ago."

"Oye no. No, that is not…not…in the requirement of p… p-ossibilities, young man. If you did that, then kaphflunken, how would I find what I need? I can use yer…assistantship with my customers and some of the…rep…fixing up the pieces and what not. Do you have a name young man?"

I told him again that I was Anton.

"Yes, yes. That's right," he said, pointing to his noggin. "Yes, I'll remember that, Antonio. Is that a Greek name? I once knew a Greek, Constantine or some such. Did you know him? Never liked him much."

Somewhat amused, I replied, "No, not Greek. I'm Russian."

In the jumbled and mismatched world of Otto Kooch, I was surprised how much his few customers adored him. Along with their array of old timepieces, they often brought baked goods for the old man. He would motion me to the front and introduce me to his customers. Each time, he called me a different name.

"Oye, such del… lutriciously good looking bread! Thank you dear, and meet my new apprentice, Arthur"

Things were never as they appeared with Otto. Even more surprising was the technical expertise of this bumbling, stumbling old man. His right hand was of little use, other than to steady the pieces he was working on. But, the fingers on his left hand move deftly as he dissembled clocks and watches and then fished through the box beneath his bench for the piece he needed. When he found it, he'd proclaim, "kaphflunken! Got you now. Can't hide from Otto. No that won't do."

When I reminded him that I would also be assisting a doctor at the hospital with his important research, Otto smiled with the functioning side of his face and said, "Ah, that's right Ashmont, such research is of great…importunance. Yes, you might make great discoveries and kaphflunken, you can find ways of helping people who have needs and…afflictuations like Otto's."

As I walked to the hospital for my first meeting with Rorschach to learn about his inkblot experiment, I decided to stop at the café for tea and a croissant. I was nervous about who else would be attending this meeting, and if I was really the right person for this job. Most of all, I was rattled at the prospect of entering into an unfamiliar relationship with my former doctor, who knew everything about me. This time, I would be entering his office, not as his patient, but a member of his research team. The fact that his research focused on inkblots, which had consumed my mother and created havoc in our lives, weighed anxiously on my mind.

I was distracted thinking about the meeting, as I walked toward an empty chair by the window table. Suddenly, a neatly dressed woman with chesnut hair bumped into me, causing me to empty a full cup of hot tea onto her pristine white blouse. Certain that she had not been paying attention and was the one responsible for this mishap, I expected an apology; but instead she shrieked,

"FOOL! Watch where you step!"

I expressed my regret about the incident but said that I thought it was she, not I, who hadn't been looking. I pulled out my handkerchief, which she grabbed, muttering "thank you" and then, under her breath, "This is brand new, and now it is ruined!"

Stunned by the chance encounter and taken aback by her beauty, I said,

"Please accept my apologies for this accident, madam, but I don't think you saw me."

With tears forming in her eyes, she threw the handkerchief in my face and quietly fumed, "*Slaboumnyy.*" At this, she turned sharply and left the café. I stood motionlessly, mouth agape from this word she had just spoken. This stunningly beautiful woman had just called me an "idiot," a "lummox," a familiar slur I understood clearly. In an instant, I realized she was Russian!

Walking briskly in the fresh morning air helped me regain my composure but also recall my apprehensiveness about the meeting. I assumed I wouldn't be the only one present but didn't know who else would be there. In the midst of my angst, I felt reassured by my trust in Rorschach. He had patiently and faithfully guided me from my wilderness. Surely, he believed that I could contribute something to his research.

Upon my arrival, a nurse escorted me to the doctor's conference room. I was relieved that we were not meeting in Rorschach's office, which held too many unsettling reminders. When she opened the doors, I saw Rorschach sitting at the head of a long table with several other men and women seated at his sides.

I entered tentatively. Rorschach greeted me warmly, "Ah, now we are almost a complete set. Just one missing. Welcome, Anton. This is the young man I was speaking of. I believe that he will bring a fresh point of view to our endeavors. Please take a seat and meet everyone."

Seated to his immediate left and right were two distinguished-looking, middle-aged men. Rorschach introduced them as "the Emil's," his friends and colleagues, Emil Oberholzer and Emil Lüthy. Cousins and both psychiatrists, Rorschach said that they shared his keen interest in psychiatry and art. Each doctor politely nodded his head. He then introduced two young women, Martha Schwartz and Johanna Schtimhultz, both eager to help in the Rorschach's experiment. The women acknowledged my presence and went back to writing notes. Finally, Rorschach introduced the last member of the group, a young man he called "Hans…." The young man quickly pronounced his last name "Behn-Eschenburg."

During these introductions, an elderly gentleman was escorted into the conference room. Rorschach's face lit up as he greeted and introduced as Oskar Pfister, who was founder of the Swiss Psychoanalytical Society. Rorschach later added that Pfister was both a pastor and an analyst.

Rorschach stood and began, "Now as you all are aware, this experiment consists of the interpretation of accidental forms, that is forms that are chance and lacking in specificity. The experiment is really a simple one. In fact, it is so elementary that common and learned people, alike, will shake their head, just as all of you might have done, when I first introduced the idea of an inkblot experiment. But, I believe it's apparent simplicity masks an unimaginable richness in what it may reveal about a person's mind. Perhaps, it will aid us in the diagnosis of our patients, but even more, possibly serve as a wellspring of information about basic determinants of the individual personality. But, not to get ahead of ourselves, there is much work to be done to see if any of this is scientifically provable."

Rorschach sketched out a plan and rough timetable for his experiment. His medical colleagues would serve as professional consultants, helping him sharpen the theoretical underpinnings for how the use of inkblots could reveal things about the human psyche and eventually, applying the method to samples of patients and nonpatients in the surrounding communities. The assistants, myself included, would work with him in the production of the blots.

The older Pfister reminded Rorschach of the need to complete research on the religious sects. Looking at the younger assistants and then up at

Rorschach, he said, "I'd like remind the good doctor and those of you new to the world of science, we are also keenly interested in studying the Swiss religious sects. Hermann, you said that this would also be part of what your assemblage of assistants would be deployed to do. I'm sure you recall your intention to send some of your assistants to the Staatsarchiv archives in Zurich to gather more information about the mystic cultist Binggeli and his Forest Brotherhood."

"Yes, correct Herr Pastor. I was going to mention that, in addition to assisting the production of inkblots, we will simultaneously be pursuing a detailed study of the Swiss cultists. In fact, I was thinking that Anton and Miss Schtimhultz might be suited to this work for reasons I can explain later."

The first meeting ended with aides serving coffee and pastries. The physicians chatted with Rorschach, leaving the research assistants to converse awkwardly with each other. The women spoke about their backgrounds and how they first learned about Rorschach's work. One of the women smiled warmly, while the other, who wore large spectacles, had a bookishly stern countenance and did not look up from the notes she was writing. Hans Ben-Eschenburg had a friendly manner. He turned to me and asked how I came to become involved. Nervously, I responded that I wasn't really certain. Recalling something that Rorschach, or was it Shev, had once said about truthfulness being the key to freedom, I responded, loudly enough for the women to hear, "You see…many months ago, I was a patient here….Dr. Rorschach believed in me and thought I had something to offer. Beyond that, I cannot say what this is. But, I am here."

The silence was drawn out. Martha was the first to speak, shaking my hand and telling me that she had complete trust in Rorschach's judgment and that it would be a pleasure to work with me. The others nodded in agreement and promptly changed the subject.

We planned to meet three times a week for the next several months to plan the different phases of Rorschach's experiment. Together with

Hans and Martha, I was to assist Rorschach in making his blots. My other assignment was to accompany Johanna Schtimhultz to the Staatsarchiv archives to gather information about this figure called Binggeli and the Forest Brotherhood cult. I imagined that because of Mama, Rorschach thought that I knew something about the construction of inkblots, which was not at all the case. And I thought that his knowledge of my fateful encounter with the Brothers of the Woodlands suggested to him that I knew firsthand about Swiss cults. I wondered if he'd thought that the Brothers, and Mama for that matter, were somehow connected with the cults he wanted to study.

The next several months passed quickly. My days were occupied with meetings at the hospital, learning about Rorschach's technique for constructing the inkblots, and assisting Otto in his small shop. In the basement of the hospital, Rorschach set up a small laboratory with a large table filled with parchments, paint brushes, and liters of different colored inks. Rorschach mentioned to Martha and Hans that my mother knew the right way to create the blots, explaining that she had been an early pioneer in this method. He said that the blots were not as random and arbitrary as they seemed, and that he had in mind particular configurations in making them.

"Too much complexity is not good. Too much simplicity does not serve a purpose either. No, each blot must conform to a particular format. I will teach you."

And this he did. Rorschach worked with the energy of ten men. He spoke while showing us the difference between random puddles of ink, the "muddy refuse," as he called them, and the kinds of figures he was trying to create. All of us became accustomed to ink-stained hands. Over the course of six-months, we assisted Rorschach in creating over 40 inkblot cards.

Assisting Otto around his shop was easy. I had grown comfortable with his mismatched ways and appreciated his kindness. One day after finishing early at the hospital, I entered the shop and saw a short young man with slicked back hair standing behind Otto's cash register. Otto was leaning against the wall and seemed happy to see me when I entered.

"Ah, Andrew, this is my brother…no, my son's brother. Oye, kaphflunken, my nephew, Hein…."

The young man, clearly impatient with Otto's affliction of words, said, "Heinrich. I'm the old man's nephew, and you are who?"

I explained that I assisted Otto around the shop in exchange for allowing me to live in the back room.

"I see. My dithering uncle has taken in another stray. You should be paying us rent."

Otto tried unsuccessfully to protest, but his nephew held up a hand and rudely interrupted, "Enough, my uncle *dummkopf,* just make sure you have more francs in the cash register next time I come by to collect. We wouldn't want strangers like Andrew, here, to take advantage of my dear uncle, would we?"

He patted Otto on the head, stuffing the francs in his purse and exited before I had a chance to respond. Otto looked up sheepishly and tried to tell me that Heinrich was really a "good boy" but had not been treated kindly by his sister and her husband when he was a lad. He said that Heinrich was looking after his interests and would come by once a month to make sure that the shop was in order. I could tell that Otto did not believe what he was telling me.

Several days later, walking home after working on the inkblots, I saw the Russian woman who had bumped into me several months earlier. Walking toward me, she looked up and quickly crossed to the other side of the narrow avenue to avoid passing directly by. I stopped to watch her pass. As she walked by, she turned, revealing a faint smile. My heart quickened at the thought that she had taken a second look at me and liked what she saw. This splendid woman's annoyance with me had given way to an…interest? Perhaps, dare I imagine, even an attraction?

I walked the rest of the way home buoyed by my interpretation of her second glance. I must seek her out and get to know this lovely woman, whose smile had seemed to betray an interest in me. As I walked up to Otto's shop, I glanced at my reflection in the window, seeking to reassure myself that I was a handsome man, after all. To my chagrin, I saw in the window the reflection of a man with dark smudges of ink streaked across his cheeks and forehead! In my haste to leave the laboratory, I had not cleaned my hands with the towel but inadvertently wiped them on my face. I looked like a spotted animal, a comical hyena-man walking the streets in broad daylight. So *this* is what had brought a smile to the Russian woman's face – not my good looks but my silly and clownish appearance. It would be several weeks before I had the pleasure of another chance encounter with this captivating woman.

Rorschach sent Johanna Schtimhultz to Zurich to be the principle researcher on Swiss cults. I was to remain in the laboratory helping with the construction of inkblots and then later travel to the Staatsarchiv to assist with cataloguing records about the religious cultists. Rorschach was particularly interested in understanding this figure Binggeli and the power he seemed to hold over his followers. He also told us that Binggeli had once been institutionalized at the Münsingen, where Rorschach had been a staff physician before coming to Herisau. He said he believed that Binggeli was psychotic and that many of his teachings reflected his dark delusional beliefs. An infirmed old man, Binggeli was said to be living with his children and grandchildren. Rorschach, said that his research now centered on trying to understand "black blots and black souls!"

On my first journey by train to Zurich, I was reminded of previous encounters in train stations that had changed the course of my life. I boarded the car and sat opposite a frail-looking elderly gentlemen, impeccably dressed in a banker's three piece suit that seemed somewhat dated. He sat clutching a large leather valise, which was oddly chained to his wrist. He eyed me suspiciously. Assuming that my darker complexion made me stand out in the sea of Aryan faces on the train, I averted my eyes to others entering the car. The old man continued to hold me in his gaze until our train stopped for our first transfer. I followed him onto the platform and began searching for the train to Zurich. I watched the old man suddenly stumble, then collapse onto the hard surface like a branch dropping from a tree. Shockingly, no one rushed to the man's aid, so I moved quickly and bent to help him. The wariness, visible in his eyes only moments before as we'd sat opposite one another on the train, softened. He quietly thanked me. The pallor of his skin blended with the color of his starched white collar. His lips were dry and his forehead dampened by perspiration. He had a small cut above his eye. I helped him to his feet and onto a bench, handing him my handkerchief to hold against the lesion on his forehead. Making sure that he was alright, I got him a cup of water from the coffee vendor. I joined him on the bench and sat in silence for a few minutes, until he began to speak.

"That was a kind and decent act, young man. I have been having these spells. My physician says that it is my blood pressure and that my trips outside of Zurich must stop, but I believe he is a charlatan, hired by my greedy offspring. Truth is, we have a business name to uphold and I cannot fully trust it to the youth. But thank you, young man. I don't know what would have happened if you had not helped me. I have fallen before and not been able to find my feet."

At that moment, I heard a final announcement for the connection to Zurich. I could run and try to catch the train, but I felt concerned about this elderly gentleman. He spoke again, "Were you going to Zurich, too? I'm afraid we've both missed our train and will have to wait two hours for the next one. Undeserved consequences for a good Samaritan. Unfortunately, the doddering ways of an old fool have waylaid you, young fellow. Perhaps, I could compensate you for your kindness with these old *Konkordanzbatzen*. You see, I have not fully placed my faith in the viability of the French franc."

With gnarled fingers, he reached inside his vest pocket, pulled out an exquisite gold timepiece, then retrieved and offtered me several old bronze coins. I refused, but he insisted that I at least take one with me for my troubles.

After moistening his mouth with another sip of water, he said, "Jean Karl. I am Jean Karl Vacheron, and whose company do I have the pleasure of enjoying, young man?"

I shared my name, and that I was traveling to the Staatsarchiv to do research for a project. Suddenly, I wondered if I had heard his name correctly, "Vacheron," and whether he might possibly be a member of the legendary Swiss family, who for centuries crafted elegant timepieces. He appeared somewhat surprised and a bit alarmed when I asked about this; but I quickly added that I had once apprenticed under my father who had been a horologist in Russia. I told him that my father was also a collector, who had "given" me a 19th century Vacheron Constantin pocket chronograph, cast in yellow gold.

Jean Karl's eyes sparkled with curiosity, as he told me that, indeed, his great-grandfather had been none other than the founder, Jean Marc Vacheron, and that he had been involved with the company all his life. He said he would love to see the timepiece of which I spoke and encouraged me to look him up whenever I was in Zurich. "We always have use for those with knowledge about crafting and caring of our timepieces. I'm afraid I have little faith in my sons and nephews. If you tire of your research, young man, please come find me. Oh, and bring the pocket chronograph as well. Perhaps, we could make you an attractive offer."

Of Rorschach's research assistants, I was least familiar with Johanna Schtimhultz. Tall and willowy, she wore her hair tightly braided in a bun and always draped her shoulders with a white lab coat, which showed her name beside the lapel, embroidered in ruby-colored thread. Her round spectacles magnified her eyes, which rarely gave way to the natural reflex to blink. More unsettling, however, was her heterochromatic eye coloring. With one blue and one green eye, it was difficult not to stare as she gazed wide-eyed at me.

Johanna Schtimhultz was not warm, like Martha Schwartz, or easy-going like Hans Ben-Escherburg. Instead, she exuded an intensity that made me uncomfortable. Rorschach had sent her to Zurich several months before to compile research on Binggeli because she was doing a dissertation on the early Swiss cults. I was to serve as her assistant in this part of his research.

When I arrived several hours late, she impatiently cut me off as I tried to explain the reason for my delay. "You're late. Regardless of the reason, we have work to do."

I kept my distance, quietly following her to the room where she had been working around the clock for months. A pile of clothes on a chair, in the corner of the room, made me wonder if she had actually been living in the Staatsarchiv. With great intensity, she told me she'd uncovered alarming patterns in the movements of the cults and had found disturbing evidence that they'd taken keen interest in Rorschach's research on their leader Binggeli.

"Something's up with this. I have unearthed documents suggesting the cultists in Binggel's group want to put a stop to Rorschach's research. I think they're dangerous."

First confused, then startled by what she to be saying, I found my voice and asked what evidence she had for these conclusions. Without pausing for a breath, Johanna Schtimhultz's spoke for the next 30-minutes showing me detailed notes and a large chart of names and photographs, where she had drawn lines crisscrossing across the page, connecting one name to the other.

"We have to warn Dr. Rorschach. He is not safe!"

Though I had no training in the methods of conducting research, I thought her interpretations bore a great deal of speculation. Nonetheless, it was clear that my questions were irritating to her, so I kept my observations and thoughts to myself. Several more times over the next six months, I boarded the train from Herisau to Zurich to assist Frau Schtimhultz. I entertained some doubt about whether her interpretations were based in fact or the embellishments of an overly active, possibly troubled, imagination.

I next encountered the Russian woman quite by chance one evening in Herisau as I went to a small bistro for a meal with Ben-Escherburg and Martha. Over the course of our work in the lab, we had become friendly and would on occasion share a meal. I was to meet them after assisting Otto in the shop. Trudging through the snow, I entered Lugasso, a fine bistro known for its German and French cuisine. My eyes adjusted to the cozy firelight, which immediately warmed my chill. As I walked toward the back looking for my coworkers, someone called my name. I looked around and saw Rorschach sitting with two women, one of whom was the Russian beauty. I waved, but he motioned for me to come to their table. The two women watched as I approached. I thought the older, dark-haired women must be his wife. Nervously, I glanced down at the other woman, who wore an unreadable smile on her face.

"Ah, Anton. How nice to see you. You have chosen a fine bistro. The food and wine are excellent. I don't think you've ever met my wife, Olga." Turning to her and speaking in Russian, he said, "This is the young fellow I've mentioned before. He is part of our team now."

I bowed my head and greeted her respectfully in my native tongue, which seemed to delight her.

"And this is my wife's cousin, visiting us from your homeland as well. Greti, meet Anton. Anton this is Greti, Greti Nonyenka Matveyenva."

The woman offered her hand and nodded. I took her small hand in mine and shook it gently. She remained seated and said, "It is a pleasure, Anton; but pardon if I don't get up for I am wearing a new blouse and cannot risk another mishap of kávé or ink stains."

The awkward silence ended as Greti laughed and explained our two chance encounters. I apologized profusely, accepting responsibility for the first encounter and sharing my embarrassment at the second. Rorschach invited me to join them, but I said that my colleagues were waiting for me in the back. Before making my exit, I had another of those moments when my courage snuck past my reserve. "Perhaps, Miss Matveyenva, you would care to accompany me on a stroll someday. I know a charming trail that leads toward the Säntis."

She nodded and said that would be lovely. The fate of the moving finger brought good fortune into my life that evening. Another in a series of accidental occurrences had led to this moment that brought Greti into my life.

For the first time in many years, perhaps in the entirety of my life, I felt a sense of peace and gratitude. I felt strong. I had meaningful work. I knew people who cared about me. My courtship with Greti provided the background music that accompanied me where ever I went. I thought about her while in the laboratory as Rorschach was finishing his blots, deciding which to include in his final set. I thought about her when I was working in Otto's shop, even when the loathsome Heinrich made his rounds. Greti was in my thoughts on my weekly trips to meet the idiosyncratic and overly zealous Johanna Schtimhultz, who obsessively spun conspiratorial theories about the Binggeli cult and the need to warn Rorschach. Greti was my first thought in the morning and my last thought before falling asleep at night. Finishing up my work with Schtimhultz, I would rush to meet Greti and spend the next day or two with her.

Greti had a small apartment in Zurich where she taught art to children. She was also a pianist and gave concerts for the small Russian community in Zurich. Greti was passionate about children and animals, explaining that it was the creatures who could not fend for themselves that captured her heart. She was an artist, a musician, and a devoted friend. As I came to know her better, her radiant physical beauty was illuminated by the depth of goodness in her heart and soul. One day, she announced that she had decided to move to Herisau. The Rorschachs had arranged for her to teach music and art at the hospital. Greti had eagerly accepted. My life felt complete.

Though I loved her name, I chose to refer to Greti with something more private, a special name that no one else shared. I loved the sound of her beautiful middle name, "Nonyenka," so I began calling her "Noni."

The decision to ask her to become my wife came easily. There were no bright bursts of light, no rainbows in the sky, only the deep certainty that I loved her and wanted to spend my life with her. One evening I nervously dropped to my knee and proposed. I assured her that I was saving my meager income to buy her a fitting engagement ring. Greti eagerly accepted, then smiled and said she would have been happy with a new blouse. The other, she said, "Remains stained with some pattern only your inkblot research could discern." I told her the meaning was clear: that we would be permanently joined someday." "Yes, permanently," she repeated. The joy of her acceptance was something that I'd never known in my life. It was all too good to be true.

Rorschach made his final selection of 10 inkblots. His colleague Oberholzer, joined by others, began administering the 10 blots to patients in the asylum. Ben-Eschenburg wanted to give the inkblots to children and another colleague, Georg Roemer, worked in the school system and was determined to use the test with students. Rorschach cataloged the kinds of patients he wanted to include as subjects in his inkblot experiment. These included two groups of normal individuals, the educated and uneducated, along with patients from the hospital who had been given a broad variety of diagnoses. Many of the subjects we diagnosed with schizophrenia and some with manic-depression. Rorschach's spirits were generally quite high, however, the stress of finding a printer and publisher for his experiment took a visible toll. He was exacting and uncompromising in his requirements. The blots had to be printed according to his specifications for size, color, and tone.

Eventually, his book, entitled *Psychodiagnostik* went to press. A small group gathered to celebrate the fruition of his project. Members of the research team assembled to toast each other but mostly to acknowledge Rorschach for his vision.

As I prepared to leave, he pulled me aside as said, "Anton, I am so glad that you were a part of this. Such a long journey from the time you arrived here five years ago. It has been my pleasure to watch you grow, my friend. To have included you in this project was not only beneficial for you and the work, but meaningful to me, as well." He grabbed my arm and pulled me closer, softly saying with a wink, "Oh, and just between us, we know there are 11 inkblots. Ten that will be published, and one that will forever remain our secret."

With this, he gave a warm hug and returned to the revelry.

Johanna Schtimhultz moved to Herisau, her research at Staatsarchiv having been completed shortly after the publication of Rorschach's inkblot experiment. In my remaining days at the hospital, I frequently saw her huddled with Rorschach, speaking in hushed, but intense, tones about the dangers she felt that the cults posed. I participated in a few of these discussions. Rorschach seemed aware that Miss Schtimhultz's interpretations went beyond the observable data. He would patiently listen to her efforts to connect things she had discovered about the Binggeli's with random occurrences at the hospital. For example, she insisted that when Rorschach received a letter without a postmark, it was an indication that the cultists were attempting to probe the Herisau, trying to discern what it was that Rorschach had discovered about their group. When two hospital staff members abruptly quit, Schtimhultz linked this to an overarching plan she believed had been made to penetrate the Rorschach group. Although many of her assertions made little sense, Rorschach listened with interest and respect. When she warned that the 90-year-old Binggeli, himself, would don a disguise and attempt to take Rorschach's life, she was finally asked to tender her resignation. She did so reluctantly but assured Rorschach that she would keep watch from afar.

I had decisions to make. Supporting a wife and eventually a family on a modest income from the hospital would be difficult enough; however, my employment as a research assistant was drawing to a close. Rorschach's work had reached a point of completion with the publication of his book.

One day he asked to speak with me about my future. He led me into his office, lit his pipe, and said, "I am aware that because our project has come to an end, you will soon be out of work, Anton. You know that Olga and I are delighted that you and Greti will be married, but I believe you might be worried about your income now that the work here is ending and you will soon have a wife to support. I imagine that Greti will continue on as our art and music teacher, but you may be feeling uncertain about what is to come next for you. Perhaps, we can find some work for you here, as well. You could become an aide, assisting the nurses and physicians, and who knows where that will lead, Anton. The point is, if you'd like, we can find work for you here."

I was grateful for all he had done over the years and for his present offer. At the same time, there was something mildly unsettling about his patronage, something distantly reminiscent of Chaim's promise to always look after me. Here, Rorschach seemed to be vowing to "find a place for me, to ensure that I would be taken care of." The security of this promise was spoiled by the discomfort I began to feel that I would forever remain in the shadow of another benefactor.

That evening I took a long walk. For the first time in many years, I thought about Shev, Nicholai Keloskovich. Whether hallucinatory mentor or spiritual guide, his words had many times illuminated a dark path of uncertainty. However, that evening, there was no Shev, but instead an idea that I should go to Zurich and find Jean Karl Vacheron. I didn't know if the old man was still alive or if he would even recall our encounter from the train station, but I knew that I must try to see him. I wasn't sure what I was looking for, only that I would visit him and bring along the gold chronograph he'd asked to see. Beyond that, I had no idea what to expect. Perhaps, it was time to change my path, which had taken me from inkblots, to mudhuts, to mainsprings, and back to inkblots. Perhaps it was time to apply my talents to earning a living making watches. I had to find out.

Rorschach asked that I return to Zurich a final time to collect the records Johanna Schtimhultz left at Staatsarchiv. Her obsessive belief in a conspiracy to kill Rorschach caused her to abandon the initial research she'd compiled. The files she left behind were in disarray. I collected what remained of her papers and notes and left the archives.

As I walked toward the train station, I was tempted to call upon Jean Karl to see if my future might lie in watch making. I decided to do this but wanted to bring Papa's valuable watches with me to see if Vacheron would offer to buy them. I vowed to make a special trip to Zurich to see if he would pay a fair price for the old timepieces and then offer me a job as an apprentice watchmaker. With these thoughts swirling through my mind, I took the train back to Herisau. By the time I arrived, I was eager to tell Greti of my decision to seek employment at Vacheron and Constantin.

When I approached her flat, I immediately sensed something was wrong. Greti was not home. The concierge informed me that she was with Olga Rorschach. I had been away for several days. Before I left, she'd learned from Olga that Rorschach was ill. They expected that this was a minor affliction that would pass. That Greti was now with Olga, concerned me that his affliction was *not* minor.

I heard Olga's wailing from the street as I walked toward their apartment. Rorschach's children sat motionless on the stoop. Inside the apartment, I found Greti, who explained through her tears that Hermann's appendix had burst and that he had died the night before. She held me tightly and sobbed on my shoulder. Several others tried to comfort Olga, now inconsolable and blaming herself for not having brought a doctor to see her dear husband earlier. The apartment was crowded with familiar faces, all showing a mixture of shock and grief. Oberholzer took charge and had two hospital aides escort Johanna Schtimhultz out of the Rorschach apartment after she made loud accusations that Hermann Rorschach had not died of a ruptured appendix but had been poisoned by Johannes Binggel's cultists.

A deadening sensation made it hard for me to move. What began as a numbness in my extremities brought a cessation of motility, as I sat unable to move or speak. Oskar Pfister stood to share Rorschach's favorite poem, written by Gottried Keller. The Pastor said that the poem was a homage to Rorschach's deep connection to the visual world. I sat motionless as Pfister read the final lines,

> And still will I roam in the evening field,
> With only the sinking star for a friend;
> Drink in, o eyes, all your lashes can hold
> Of the golden abundance of the world!

CHAPTER 16

Better Tomorrow, Stronger With Time

I didn't remember how long it had been since I'd been back. The passage of time eluded me. The cold hallways, high arched ceilings, and dark amphitheater of the Bürgholzli were as I had remembered. I was escorted to my chair on the brightly lit stage. The small chair had the same stiff back and hard seat as the one I'd occupied during my first trip to the amphitheater so long ago. Squinting my eyes toward the dark rows above me, I could make out grayish figures in their lab coats as they began to take their seats. I thought how little and how much was different – what remained the same and what had been forever changed.

As I sat in the dark silence of the amphitheater, my restless mind beckoned me to wander down long forgotten passageways. In such moments, I often thought of Shev. The oft quoted words of his favorite poet, Omar Khayyam, came to mind.

The moving finger writes and having writ moves on
Nor all thy Piety nor Wit

Shall lure it back to cancel half a Line,
Nor all thy Tears wash out a Word of it.

Shev, for that is how I shall always remember him, was trying to tell me that one must come to terms with the past, which despite the musings of mathematicians and wishful minds of sad people, cannot be changed. Rorschach tried to help me see that forgiveness and acceptance of the inevitable is the only viable path forward.

But oh, how much I tried to "lure it back to cancel half a line," to reclaim or recover what I had lost. As a boy, I'd smeared mud on my skin, wishing this would magically bring back a mother who would remain lost to me forever. After the crucible of death at Tannenberg, my madness convinced me that I could wave a wand and reverse time itself. And when Hermann Rorschach suddenly died, I was unable to walk, my faux catatonia a neurotic homage, a wishful act of desperation to bring him back. If I couldn't move, then surely Rorschach would return to heal me.

My mind wandered back to Rorschach's untimely death. His funeral, which now seems so long ago, remains a vivid scene in my mind. I recall Greti wheeling me into the cathedral for the service, much like some unknown person had once wheeled me to the gates of the Bürgholzli. We were in a long line of mourners waiting to climb the steps to view his body as it lay in state. Greti wheeled my chair up to the steps and placed her hand on the shoulder of her fiancé, who, at the news of the great man's death, had relapsed into a catatonic paralysis. As she began to climb the steps, she suddenly looked around and saw me standing behind her. Grabbing my hand, we walked to his casket together to say our final goodbyes.

Loving Greti was clearly overjoyed that I had regained my mobility, but she was even more loving for not drawing attention to my unexplained recovery. Inching forward, we stood looking down at Hermann Rorschach. Dressed in a familiar charcoal gray suit, a golden chain looped from one vest pocket to the other. I recognized the familiar stem of the watch I had given him. I hadn't been able to cry until that moment, but did so at the thought that he would be buried with this watch close to his heart.

Many spoke at the service. Rorschach's mentor Bleuler gave one of the eulogies and said that Swiss psychiatry had been dealt a terrible loss. An old colleague, Walter Morgenthaler spoke about Rorschach's immense talent as a physician and researcher, but most of all, his uncommon warmth and kindness.

My mind returned to the present. While I remained seated on the brightly lit stage of the old amphitheater, I thought back to my conversation with Greti after the funeral. We had taken a long walk that evening, and I told her that I thought it would be best to postpone our wedding. I explained that I needed time alone to think. I wasn't sure where I would go or how much time I would need, but I was certain that I needed time alone. With a warm hug and a promise that I would return, we said goodbye.

What began as a pilgrimage of a few days turned into a lengthier wandering. Counting up the weeks, I was gone for just over a month. I went without a plan, only the vague sense that I was searching for something, what I wasn't sure. I had been unsettled by Johanna Schtimhultz' mad rantings that Rorschach had been poisoned by the cultists. I knew nothing of this, but I thought perhaps I could find my way back to the Joglland forest where I had encountered the Brothers of the Woodland years before. Maybe there had been survivors of the massacre that day. Perhaps they knew of Binggeli and could shed light on Schtimhultz' theory. After roaming the forest for several days, I realized that I was still seeking my mother – that the sudden death of Rorschach was too much like the sudden disappearance of Mama when I was too small to understand. Now a grown man, I realized that I still had no understanding of why she left, where she went, and what became of her.

After my sojourn in the empty forest, my fog began to lift, and I realized three things. First, how much I missed my Noni and how desperate I was to get back to her. Second, I knew it was time to change the direction of my life, not by being the madman in a clock, but by taking hold of my life and deciding my own fate. Third, I realized that I had to accept I would never find Mama.

When I returned to Herisau, I hugged Greti as tightly as I could. I told her that I wanted to spend our lives together and grow old with her, but that I needed to make a trip to Zurich to settle some final business. I had previously told her about my encounter with old Jean Karl Vacheron in the train station and of his invitation to come and see him if I ever wanted to make timepieces again. I told her I didn't know if he would remember me or if he was still alive.

Greti said, "Go my love. Do what you must. I will be here waiting for you."

The headquarters of Vacheron and Constantin were as I had always imagined – elegant, stylish, and with an opulent air of old aristocracy. It took some time to convince the gatekeepers that I knew the elder Mr. Vacheron. Finally, after an hour or more of waiting, I was brought into his large suite of offices. Jean Karl looked older and more frail, but I could tell his mind was sharp. He eyed me quickly and broke into a grin, "Ah the Samaritan watchman from the train platform! Come in, come in."

I had brought along both of Papa's vintage watches, the Vacheron and Patck Philip. Jean Karl's eyes grew wide as he gazed at the polished pieces. He studied the crack in the crystal of the Vacheron and softly said, "Tis nothing. May I hold them, young man?"

I nodded and told him that I had brought them to sell, and that I was also interested to see if he might have work in his vast organization.

Vacheron asked if he could show the pieces to his horologists to assess their true value. He also said that he might have some ideas about work within his company. He was later summoned by one of his senior jewelers, a tall balding gentleman, who had written up an assessment of the watches' worth.

Their combined value was assessed as slightly more than I would have been able to earn in two years! I readily accepted his generous offer.

Vacheron said, "As for your interest in working for V-C, I think there is always room for young men who show potential. You could certainly work in one of our repair shops, assisting the master horologists and jewelers; but my boy, with the wealth you have acquired today, I think there is more that we might be able to plan for you."

He explained that I now had enough capital to apprentice for some of the premier horologists in Europe. However, such apprenticeships did not come cheap. Horologists accepted students who showed promise but expected payment for their tutelage. With the proper period of training, I could walk into a top position as a master horologist for Vacheron Constantin, "That is if we could keep you," Jean Karl added with a wink.

I remember thanking him for his generosity and for having given me so much to contemplate about my future. I was eager to share the news with Greti and tell her that there was no reason for us to delay our wedding any longer. We were married in a small ceremony later that week.

My mind jolted back to the dark amphitheater where I was beginning to roast under the klieg lights that illuminated the stage. But my restless thoughts took me back to the night I'd packed my belongings from Otto's back room and thanked him for his kindness.

"It was always pleasureful Arturo, or is it Anton? And I should thank you for the delightedness of you acquaintance."

How strange it was to have run into his weasel nephew Heinrich, the last night as I left Otto's shop. The weasel was startled as I came up behind him in the alley and held my finger to his back. I'm not proud that I threatened to hunt him down and kill him on the spot if he ever bothered the old man again. Bullies often turn out to be cowards when finally confronted by those who see through their charade. I heard in subsequent years that Heinrich had abruptly moved to another city and never returned to Herisau to bother his poor uncle.

My reverie about the past was suddenly interrupted by several white-coated men walking onto the stage and taking their seats. Then, Herr Bleuler himself walked to a podium and began to speak. In the quiet echoes of the chamber, he spoke of his experience as a healer, who had devoted his career to research, clinical practice, and teaching. He continued for several minutes, speaking about the suffering souls in the world and their afflictions of body, mind, and spirit. Bleuler said it was the mission of Bürgholzli to uphold the finest traditions in educating those who came to these great lecture halls to learn about these afflictions.

Suddenly the stillness and quiet in the hallowed chamber was interrupted by the high-pitched sound of a small voice, growing louder, as a dark curly-haired little girl stood at the railing in the upper balcony and shouted,

"Papa, Papa! I SEE YOU PAPA!"

As she waved her tiny hand feverishly back and forth, an embarrassed looking Greti suddenly emerged from the dark rows behind her, carrying a baby in her arms. Freeing one arm, she reached for the little girl and whispered loudly enough for all to hear, "Shhh. Come Katamarina, come. Come sit with Mama and your brother, and we watch Papa together."

Bleuler, who had paused during this unexpected interruption, glanced and smiled in my direction before continuing with his remarks.

I listened with one ear and thought how I had taken Vacheron's advice after all. I'd invested the money he paid for the vintage watches in my training to change the course of my life. But I realized that, for me, making watches had always been something that son's did to get their papas to see them. In my life, there had been those who had *always* seen me. They were the healers and seekers – Rorschach, Nadya, and of course, Mama.

At this, I shifted my full attention back to Bleuler, as he turned and faced me and the others seated in rows behind me.

"And, my students, this part of your journey has come to an end. Your hard work, training and devotion has brought you to this auspicious moment in time, when I can welcome you as fellow physicians, as new graduates into the healing profession of medicine. It is indeed a noble profession. We have taught you about the body and the mind, about medicines and treatments for the afflicted and wretched, but you must always be physicians to yourselves.

With that one thought in mind, I'll close by paraphrasing words of the young writer, Khalil Gibran, when he said, 'The teacher who is indeed wise does not bid you to enter the house of his wisdom but rather leads you to the threshold of your own mind.'"

Epilogue

How does one capture, in words, the life he has lived? I needed the courage and open-hearted honesty, compassion, gratitude, and forgiveness of self that enabled me to complete this task. Only with these companions was I able to live my life twice.

Writing was never the deterrent, for by the time I had begun to write my story, I had authored several books. Glancing up from the comfortable desk in my home study, I survey the titles that have brought me acclaim from the professional community. No, it was not the writing, but it was the sober recounting of my life, with eyes fully open, that I had so long avoided. Now the task was complete.

For over three decades since my graduation from Burghölzli, I have lived a rich and fulfilling life – as adoring husband and father, grandfather, and, sadly, as grieving father and widower. I have been a devoted psychiatrist and psychoanalyst, writer, and gardener. My years with Greti, my dear Noni, were unimaginable blessings. We raised four beautiful and strong children together. For all my training and reading, it was really Greti who instilled goodness in them. I miss her every day when I watch the bluebirds feed in our garden.

After Katamarina, we had Nicolai, and then the twins Nonyenka and Chaim. Loving children, all so different. Katamarina's spirit was untamable. Like her grandmother she was born a dancer and sacrificed much of her youth to join the Bolshoi Ballet. An injury from which she never fully recovered ended her career as a dancer and brought her back to a village near Herisau. There, she bought a small farm, where she started a family of her own. When she is able, she comes to visit, bringing fresh vegetables from her gardens.

As a boy, Nicolai had a quiet intelligence, just like his mama. He loved poetry and music. We were thrilled when he married a wonderful artist, Clara. Their interests were broader than Herisau could accommodate, so they moved to Zurich, where they opened a now famous gallery. They blessed us with three beautiful and impish grandchildren. It has become harder now to travel to Zurich, and I've missed watching them grow.

Our twins were a miracle. Greti was ill through much of this difficult pregnancy; but to our eternal gratitude, they survived a difficult labor and delivery. Nonyenka looked like her mother, but she was very quiet and kept to herself. Chaim, always big for his age, filled the room with his magnetic smile. But smiles always fade. Soon the madmen and monsters returned to Europe and led millions to death and destruction. Where is the justice that I should lose two precious Chaims, neither of whom could resist the clarion call into battle? Like his uncle, my son felt a loyalty to mother Russia. The grief was suffocating when he was killed in the Battle of Stalingrad. Greti was never the same.

She grew weaker by the year. Having Katamarina close was a comfort, but I think she felt that she had lost Chaim again when Nonyenka moved away to study in Moscow. One uncommonly cold winter, Greti succumbed to the influenza. The doctors were unable to save her.

Fortunately, there was no return of psychogenic paralysis. I stood and walked with my three children to Greti's funeral and have continued moving ever since. I am mostly retired now but see an occasional patient in my home office near the hospital. When Katamarina comes, she brings her rascally daughter Juni Roo, the light in my sky. Together we search for fairies in the garden. Katamarina and I laugh and build bird houses. She still helps edit an occasional paper or manuscript.

Rorschach attempted to write about hallucinations, but I felt his work was incomplete. Had he lived a full life, he would, no doubt, have developed his ideas on a broad range of subjects, his inkblot experiment among them. I feel a special pride for having written *Beyond Madness: Mystery and Meaning in Reflex Hallucinations.* No one could fully appreciate the reasons I chose to write about this subject. Unfortunately, unlike my other work on *Rorschach's Inkblot Experiment and the Disturbances of the Mind,* the book on hallucinations was not held in high esteem by some colleagues, who considered it to be no more than mutterings to the wind. They rejected the idea that hallucinations could be any more than shadows of madness.

My research enabled me to establish contacts with archivists in major capitals throughout Europe and in America as well. Secretly, however, I used many of my contacts to probe some of the unanswered questions not completely put to rest over the last 40 years. I hunted for names of those I knew long ago, with a burning interest in what had become of them. Of course, I began by searching for traces of what had happened to Papa and Nadya. Unfortunately, I found the Soviet Bureau of Information to be a locked box. No records were to be released to anyone outside of the Politburo.

Months of searching for answers about my father and aunt enabled me to feel at peace with Papa. I accepted that Chaim was his natural son, and I was a "foundling." But, Papa did not have to take us in. He chose, perhaps at his sister's urging, to raise me as his "son." I was also grateful that Papa's watches funded my medical education. Though taking his watches was not a noble act, if I had not appropriated them, they would have been destroyed or ransacked by other thieves long ago. More than anything, I felt compassion for Papa when I realized he had spent his life futilely chasing an admiring gaze from his own father.

I located an A. Glagolev who had served as a corporal in the 36th Infantry of the 2nd Army. He had saved my life more than once. I was happy to learn that he had survived the war and had become mayor of a small town near Kiev.

I found the address of Vasily Steponovich's parents and wrote them a long letter, extolling the virtues of their fine and courageous son, "one of the most decent men I have ever known." Sadly, six months later the letter was returned unopened.

Most of my searches were in vain. Much as I expected, I found nothing about my Romani family in Hungary.

And, of course, I could not rest until I had thoroughly searched the records at Burghölzli Hospital, looking for records of women of Romani descent admitted as patients between 1904 and 1912. I compiled a list and cross-referenced it with those who might have been assigned to Carl Jung as their physician. Eventually, I ceased this obsessive preoccupation because it led nowhere. And as for Mama's "message for Jung"? I concluded this was part of a delusional fever that had little basis in reality. Whether she had ever been at Burghölzli would remain a mystery.

Strangest of all was my search for Nicolai Keloskovich. Several years of probing deep stacks in major university archives turned up nothing, until one day, I received notice from a Danish librarian that there *had* been a 16th century priest named "Nicolai Keloskovich," who'd disappeared while on a mission in Japan. News of this discovery brought both a chill and a smile, as I reflected on what might have been Shev's last joke.

The light is fading. Cardinals approach for their dusk feeding. My wall clock ticks softly, a smaller and more contemporary Breguet. For the opposite wall, I framed the yellowed parchment of an inkblot. The familiar, misty edge of nostalgia washes over me as I think about my well-lived life. Much lost, but much discovered and gained. Blessed and grateful. I found my peace. Thank you, Vasily. I treasure these moments of solitude with my faithful shepard, "Klex," and his nemesis, "Rheshevsky," an annoying, mercurial Siamese cat.

I am settled comfortably between clock and blot. A light tapping at the door arouses me. Mrs. Straussman, my housekeeper, knows that I wish not to be disturbed.

Clearing my throat, I speak up, "Yes, Fraulein Straussman, what is it?"

"I'm so terribly sorry Herr Zellinsky but there is someone here to see you."

Feeling a mild irritation – I was not expecting patients today and prefered solitude – I instruct her to "Please, send whomever is here to the hospital clinic. The doctors on call will see them."

"Yes, Herr Doctor, I told her that. But this old white-haired woman just stands there in her long skirt with faded colors and says that she has come a long way to see… Anton. Then, she says to tell you that she brings a song for *Kicsi*…."

Acknowledgements

There are so many people without whose direct and/or indirect support this book would not have been possible. They are the relationships, personal and professional, that bind me as a person and writer.

It begins with my parents – Angela DiTolla, a kind and loving mother (ah, to have had "the good mother inside" is a true gift) and Ralph Kleiger a loving and complex father – both of whom found expression in my story. I thank my father for telling me about my great grandfather Herman Zalinsky, of Brest-Litovsk, the old watchmaker, who could "make watches from the ground up!"

To my courageous sister Margy, my "Irish twin," and brother-in-law Larry, who may live in Steamboat Springs but are always in my heart.

There are my wonderful children, Nike and Katie, who somehow mystically emerged in the telling of this story. You are my moon and stars. Nike, you're a man of enormous heart and goodness for all to see and feel. How'd I get so lucky to have you as my son? Katie, how can I thank you enough….

My grandchildren, Riley, Brooke, and Sloane, and their devoted parents, aunt, and uncle – Colleen, Nicole, Tom, Jodie and Greg – for whom I am so "blessed and grateful" for your love. Thank you for helping stir the wind beneath my wings.

I've been fortunate to be ensconced in several supportive groups of friends, bound together by shared interests, values, and love. My Topeka Men's group has provided a connection of the heart for 35 years. I love you men and thank you for "seeing me." Colleagues from the original Menninger

Clinic, dear friends from SPA, the International Rorschach Society, and R-PAS Research Development Group have been there, providing intellectual stimulation, emotional support, and fellowship for many years.

Of course, I must acknowledge Hermann Rorschach, whose experiment with "accidental forms" changed my life and gave rise to this story. Damion Searles' wonderfully comprehensive book, *The Inkblots,* was a valuable resource, as I attempted to make Rorschach come to life in this story.

Heart-felt gratitude to those who made themselves available to read portions of the book. Here, I mention Joan Most, Laura Wright, and Steve Lerner, along with Charles Peterson and Wendy Swidler. Special thanks to Marvin Acklin, who magically showed up one day with a treasure trove of old documents about the Burghölzli Clinic that contributed greatly to the narrative backdrop of the story.

I'm grateful to Sarah Taber, whose early reading and editorial input helped immeasurably with my writing and storytelling. I'd also like to thank Literary Agents, Jennifer Weltz and Emily Williamson, who devoted time to reading portions of the manuscript and provided encouragement, feedback, and insights that I took to heart. I am grateful for IPBooks for welcoming me into their family of fiction writers. Thanks especially to Tamar Schwartz and Dr. Arnie Richards for their support and assistance. Finally, Kathy Kovacic of Blackthorn Studio is credited with designing a book cover that captures the spirit and mystery of *The 11th Inkblot.*

There were three people without whose loving involvement, patience, and generous investment of time Anton's story would have remained a distant fantasy. First, to my dear friend Tom Averill, thank you. Your wise, caring mentorship from start to finish was invaluable. I've learned so much listening to you and reading your wonderful books for 35 years, and of course, enjoying a wee dram of scotch together!

Next, there is my talented daughter Katie Kleiger. Katie, you read all of this and shared your ideas and tears. Most significantly, thank you for allowing me to use lyrics from your beautiful song *Adaptations*, which I changed to *Idővel jobban leszek* for the book. Thank you for lending your boundless creativity in re-writing some of the lyrics to fit the story. No, dear Katie, it is <u>you</u> who are weightless. Such a source of inspiration!

Finally, and especially, I want to thank my wife, my muse, Nannette. I've been an ardent student in your classroom, as you've taught me what it means to live a fruitful life. This book is for you. I'm grateful for your constant patience and generous time spent listening as I told this story. Your keen editorial eye and creative insights were enormously helpful. I appreciate your loving and careful reading, critiquing, rereading, and editing – page after page, night after night, until you were absolutely exhausted. You live in this book, my dear Noni. Thank you.

Author Notes

Some of the people, events, and places depicted in *The 11ᵗʰ Inkblot*, though grounded in history and geography, were amply embellished by my imagination. Source material for watchmaking included the tome, *The Mastery of Time*, by Dominique Fléchon (2011, Paris: Flammarion). Those with rudimentary knowledge of the intricacies of watchmaking will recognize the corners I cut and liberties I took in trying to make a complex subject seem simpler than it is.

I relied on Dennis E. Showalter's *Tannenberg. Clash of Empires* (2004, Washington, D.C.: Brassey's Inc.), Barbara W. Tuchman's *Guns Of August* (1982, New York: Bonanza Books), *The American Heritage History of World War I* (1964, S. L. A. Marshall, New York: Simon & Schuster) and Béla Zombory-Moldován's *The Burning of the World. A Memoir of 1914* (2014, New York: NYRB) to learn something about the Eastern European geopolitical landscape at the outset of World War I, the military campaign that led to the Battle of Tannenberg, and the ground experience of infantry soldiers fighting in the Eastern Front. It is factually true that General Samsonov commanded the ill-fated Second Army, which was destroyed at Tannenberg. The Germans had intercepted Russian telegraph messages, which had been transmitted unencrypted; and Samsonov did, in fact, take his own life shortly after his army was routed.

My father, Pvt. Ralph Richard Kleiger, served in the 36th Infantry Division in WWII. Several of the events depicted in Chapters 5 and 6 were adapted from stories that continued to haunt him until the day he died.

Most of the towns described in *The 11th Inkblot* existed and/or still exist, although their precise location and proximity to surrounding areas is not exact. I took liberties in imagining journeys from Zastavia to larger towns and eventually travel by train to Warsaw and into Hungary. Estimating the amount of time it might have taken to make such journeys by foot or by train was admittedly inexact.

Inclusion of multiple languages was aided by Google Translator and other online resources. I took artistic license in attempting to find the right non-English words and expressions and take responsibility for errors that might be found in my translation efforts.

I relied on multiple online sources to learn about the richness of the Romani culture. I attempted to portray the Romani in a respectful manner, unencumbered by existing stereotypes. However, some may find my depiction of characters, language, and their culture as narrow and misleading. I apologize for any unknowing misrepresentations.

Hermann Rorschach, Eugen Bleuler, and Carl Gustav Jung were luminaries in European psychiatry in the early 20th century. Interactions between these figures and others at the Burghölzli Clinic were largely products of my imagination, sprinkled with some of what is written about their professional connections. Bleuler was Rorschach's advisor. Allusions to tensions in the Bleuler–Jung relationship is generally known to have existed. I relied on John Kerr's *A Most Dangerous Method* (1994, New York: Vintage) to imagine more about that tension as well as qualities of Jung's character. I acknowledge that some might take exception to my caricature of Jung, who over the course of his long career contributed mightily to the fields of psychiatry, psychoanalysis, psychology, and the broader culture of mental health. Admittedly biased towards Hermann Rorschach, my attempt to humanize this enigmatic figure was aided greatly by Searles' *The Inkblots* (2017, New York: Crown Publishing Group) and Akava's *Subjectivity in Motion*, (2013, New York: Routledge) both of which provided a great deal of information about the life and character of Hermann Rorschach and the scientific culture at the Burghölzli Clinic in the early 20ᵗʰ Century.

I obtained from Wikimedia Commons noncopyrighted images in the public domain for each of the pages that introduced a new part of the book. The image of a pocket watch in Part I is entitled "Elgin Open Faced Pocket Watch, 7 Jewels, size 3-0, Pendant Set Grade 418, Circa 1918 (16194009928).jpg." (File: Vintage Elgin Open Face Pocket Watch, 7 Jewels, Size 3-0, Pendant Set, Grade 418, Circa 1918 (16194009928).jpg).

Part II image of Russian soldier was from a WWI poster (00.2 jpg) by Leonid Pasternak to help victims of the war. (https://upload.wikimedia.org/wikipedia/commons/3/39/Russian_poster_WWI_002.jpg).

The Part III "Gypsy Woman with Mandolin" is credited to Jean Baptiste-Camille Corot, c. 1870 NGA 41578.jpg, QS:P31,Q3305213 (https://commons.wikimedia.org/wiki/File:Jean-Baptiste-Camille_Corot,_Gypsy_Woman_with_Mandolin,_c._1870,_NGA_41578.jpg).

Finally, the inkblot image introducing Part IV is one of Justinus Kerner's original Klexographien (Buchausgabe von, 1890), (https://commons.wikimedia.org/wiki/Category:Kleksographien_(Justinus_Kerner)#/media/File:Kerner_Kleksographien_12.jpg).

Lyrics sung by Kata in Chapter 9 are from Katie Kleiger's song *Adaptations*. The quote in Chapter 10 is from August Strindberg's *Tschandala* (Series B: English Translations of Works of Scandanavian Literature, Norvik Pr, 2008, originally published in 1889). The Gottfried Keller Poem, "Evening Song," quoted at the end of Chapter 15, was described as one of Rorschach's favorite poems in Damion Searles' *The Inkblots*, cited above.

Finally, the frequent use of quotes, referenced by Shev, were correctly attributed to their sources, though I did not include chapter notes with exact citations and references. I relied on several internet search tools to find popular quotations in the public domain that I felt painted a picture of what Shev was trying to express and helped embellish the character I was trying to create. As for the sources of his ribald humor, well, over a span of 67 years, one hears a lot of colorful stories. Those about Rheshevsky were adapted from a Wikipedia reference concerning Russian jokes about a cavalry officer called Poruchik Rzhevsky, (Seth Graham, 2004, "A Cultural Analysis of the Russo-Soviet Anekdot," University of Pittsburg, Unpublished Doctoral Dissertation).